Navy SEALs ... the ultim...

SEA ...

"A sexy, smoldering ... and the woman who ... his heart into ... passion... This is a must-read!"

—*RT Book Reviews*, 4 Stars

"Funny, fun, and extremely intriguing... I haven't read a book by Terry Spear that didn't keep me glued to the pages and still wanting more. If you are looking for a good mystery, a fantastic group of 'people,' plus funny, sweet, and steamy romance, then *SEAL Wolf In Too Deep* is what you need in your hands."

—*Fresh Fiction*

"Another winner...Once again the author had me captivated with her storytelling... A unique blend of romance, mystery, and adventure."

—*Night Owl Reviews*

SEAL Wolf Hunting

"Once again, Terry Spear has created a top notch paranormal romance that will captivate and thrill readers from beginning to end."

—*The Romance Reviews*, 5 Stars, Reviewer Top Pick

"A sultry nail-biter...the suspense will keep readers flipping the pages feverishly."

—*RT Book Reviews*

Also by Terry Spear

Heart of the Wolf
Heart of the Wolf
To Tempt the Wolf
Legend of the White Wolf
Seduced by the Wolf

Silver Town Wolf
Destiny of the Wolf
Wolf Fever
Dreaming of the Wolf
Silence of the Wolf
A Silver Wolf Christmas
Alpha Wolf Need Not Apply
*Between a Wolf and a
Hard Place*

Highland Wolf
Heart of the Highland Wolf
A Howl for a Highlander
*A Highland Werewolf
Wedding*
Hero of a Highland Wolf
*A Highland Wolf
Christmas*

SEAL Wolf
*A SEAL in Wolf's
Clothing*
A SEAL Wolf Christmas
SEAL Wolf Hunting
SEAL Wolf In Too Deep

Heart of the Jaguar
Savage Hunger
Jaguar Fever
Jaguar Hunt
Jaguar Pride
A Very Jaguar Christmas

Billionaire Wolf
*Billionaire in Wolf's
Clothing*

SEAL WOLF UNDERCOVER

TERRY SPEAR

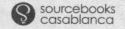

sourcebooks
casablanca

Published by Sourcebooks Casablanca, an imprint of Sourcebooks, Inc.
P.O. Box 4410, Naperville, Illinois 60567–4410
(630) 961–3900
Fax: (630) 961–2168
www.sourcebooks.com

Printed and bound in Canada.
MBP 10 9 8 7 6 5 4 3 2 1

Thanks, Kelley Granzow, for helping me to get my seats on the flight to San Diego after a nightmare of making arrangements to attend the RWA conference! And thanks for supporting the servicemen and women with all your dedication in sending them care packages that help to make life for them away from home just a little better. You're an angel.

Prologue

Six months ago — San Diego, California

FORMER SEAL AND CURRENT PI VAUGHN GREYSTOKE leaned back on his barstool in the Clawed and Dangerous Kitty Cat Club, smelling cats everywhere. He wasn't sure what to make of the packed place. His twin brother, Brock, slapped him on the back. "Drink up. You're way behind."

Douglas Wendish, a friend from their wolf pack in Colorado, was dancing again with his date. Vaughn's date was more for show, and Brock's looked too tipsy to do anything more than sit and stare into space. Around them, women in skimpy leopard-skin bikinis and men in leopard-skin loincloths were grinding on elevated platforms in the jungle-themed club.

Genuine potted palms and ferns, rock walls covered in moss, and vines crisscrossing over the ceiling made it feel like they were really in the Amazon rain forest. The chirping of crickets, the calls from macaws, and the sound of water rushing over rocks in the jungle played in the background while the music offered a riveting South American jungle beat.

Lots of gyrating females were twisting around on the floor, but only one really caught Vaughn's eye. A dark-haired beauty wearing a tight black skirt split up the side that showed off shapely legs, a pair of sparkly sandals that exposed red-hot toenails, and a low-cut leopard-print blouse that revealed a nice swell of breasts. Unfortunately, she seemed to already be taken.

Vaughn was fascinated with the way she danced with the redheaded guy—sensuously, but not like they needed a room. The way she moved her body made Vaughn feel *he* needed a room. *With her.* Observing her, he was swept up by the jungle heat, the warm bodies, the cold beer, the infectious laughter, and her hot moves. Then the redhead she was with leaned down and kissed her. She wrapped her arms around his waist, tilted her chin up, and kissed him back. In that instant, Vaughn wanted more than anything to be on the receiving and *giving* end.

"Hot," Brock said. "Wonder if she smells like she's got a ton of cats at home too."

Fine with Vaughn. As long as he had her.

"Have another beer," his brother said. "That might cool you off."

The only way Vaughn would cool off was by taking an ice-cold shower.

A woman—who smelled overwhelmingly of cats—asked him to dance, and so he did, if only to get his mind off the brunette woman. "I'm Kira. You must be new here," the blond purred next to his cheek, her body pressing closer to him than he really wanted.

"Name's Vaughn. Does it show that I'm new here?"

"Colorado license plates," she said.

He smiled. Here he'd thought she'd heard an accent, though he didn't believe he really had one. "So you live around here?" he asked out of politeness.

"Yeah, nearby. You pulled up when we did. I always notice out-of-state license plates."

She sounded like a private investigator or a cop. "Own a lot of cats?"

She smiled in a wicked way. "Love them." She didn't say that she owned any, though. "What about you? Own a lot of dogs?"

He smiled back. Wouldn't she be surprised if she knew he was all wolf? "Dogs are man's best friend."

"So I've been told. Are you going to be around for a few days? Return to the club?"

"Not sure. Do you hang out here all the time?"

"Every chance I can get." Kira glanced at his table. She must have been wondering about his date.

"She looks bored."

"She doesn't care to dance."

Then the black-haired woman Kira had been talking to came over and asked him to dance. Bethany. Three more cat women danced with him after that. He guessed they didn't mind that he smelled like a dog. He wondered if they could even tell. He could tell they were cat lovers because of his enhanced wolf's ability to smell.

Afterward, he took his seat at his table again, glad to have danced, though he wished he could have been with the brunette.

Douglas returned with his date, but Vaughn had already forgotten her name. No, wait… Wendy. If his friend mated her, she'd be Wendy Wendish. Douglas pulled out his camera and began taking pictures. *Again.* But then Kira asked Douglas to dance. She acted as though she hadn't already danced with Vaughn. He only smiled at the fickle woman, wondering if she was looking for someone to spend the night with. He clearly hadn't fit the bill.

When Douglas returned, he smiled at Vaughn. "Saw you dancing with her first. She's just dancing with everyone, I suspect, until she finds the guy she wants to hook up with."

Vaughn shook his head. Humans.

"Hey, see someone I know. Be back in a minute." Douglas took off while Vaughn watched him, expecting him to dance with another woman.

Instead, he was talking to some guy, probably about boating, as much as Douglas loved to boat. Vaughn, Brock, and Douglas were all going out on the water tomorrow. One of these times, Vaughn was going to convince Douglas to take a plunge into the water and show him how much fun swimming as a human could be.

Vaughn observed the brunette laughing at something the redhead said at their table. She turned her head in Vaughn's direction, as if she realized someone was watching her. He hadn't meant to stare, but everything about her appealed, and he just couldn't take his eyes off her.

He smiled. She smiled. In that instant, he felt they'd made a connection. As lame as that was. When she left the club tonight, she was going home with the muscular guy who had his arm wrapped around her like he was afraid he'd lose her. From what Vaughn could tell, she hadn't once shown any interest in anyone else but her date. Oh sure, when she was seated at her table and sipping from a drink, she was watching other dancers, but she wasn't focusing on any one person. Not like he was focusing on her.

Her gaze caught his again, and he couldn't help but smile. Not that her checking him out meant anything. But he sure could fantasize.

—◆◆—

Formerly an army intelligence officer and now a PI, Jillian Matthews had agreed to go out with her brother Miles's friend as a favor, but man, did the guy have octopus arms! Oh sure, he was fun, but way more interested than she was. The guy several tables over... Now *he* captured her attention. If she didn't know better, she'd say he was all wolf, though some human males showed the same wolfish interest in a woman, even if she was with someone else. She'd never think about dumping a guy on a date when he was being nice, especially when it was to pay her brother back for his help in solving one of her cases. But she'd made sure she said it was only one date, unless she changed her mind.

Everything about the club was a blast—the music, drinks, dancers, and atmosphere—yet the man at the other table truly stole her attention tonight.

"Did you want to come back tomorrow night?" Miles asked.

She smiled at her brother. She'd love to if that other guy was going to be here. He had dark hair, chiseled features, and tanned biceps. He was muscular but not overdone, and had a darkly intriguing smile that made her melt.

"Sure," she said, secretly wishing she could see Tall, Dark, and Intriguing again at the club. Maybe tomorrow he would ask her to dance or she'd ask him. The guy's own date looked bored, and Jillian hadn't seen him dance until women began asking him. As soon as a blond did, it was like a signal to other single women that he was interested and available. If Jillian had been without a date, even she would have asked him to dance. She'd help him move that gorgeous body right up close and personal. Her own date wasn't interested in dancing with anyone else, so she curbed the inclination. She could envision hanging on to the guy too, if he still piqued her interest, and not allowing any other woman to take a turn with him.

"Hey, you ready to go?" Miles asked, breaking into her fantasy. "If I'm going to help you on that next case, I need some sleep."

His date was a human woman, and Jillian knew her brother too well. Sleep wasn't what he had in mind.

"Yeah, agreed."

"I can take you back to your hotel," her date said, as if he was looking for some mattress action too.

"Oh, thanks so much, but no, that's fine. Miles is right. We have to get up before the crack of dawn."

She and Miles rose from the table, Jillian's date not making a move to leave. "See you tomorrow night then," he said.

Not if she could help it. She gathered her sweater and bag, and though she didn't want to seem too obviously interested in the other guy, she glanced back at him. He inclined his head a little to her, and her whole body flushed with heat.

He was so hot. Yeah, he was the date she wanted tomorrow night, whether he had a date with him or not.

Then suddenly a scream caught Jillian's attention. One of the corner chains holding a dancer's platform had broken loose, and the dancer on it screamed again. Thank God the dancer had reacted quickly enough to grab one of the remaining four chains holding the platform before she fell. Dangling twenty feet above the patrons, she clung precariously to the end of the chain, looking up as if she was thinking of trying to climb it. Before Jillian could do anything, the wolfish guy she had been admiring had climbed the ladder to the platform. He leaped to one of the chains still holding the platform, climbed the chain, and shimmied across the top to reach the chain the dancer was holding on to.

The music was still in heavy jungle-beat mode, most patrons unaware of the potential tragedy unfolding before them. Jillian rushed to tell a server to get help and to turn off the music so the guy rescuing the woman could concentrate.

"Hell, that's part of the show," the server said, smiling at her. "You're not from around here, are you?"

"The guy trying to rescue her is part of it too?"

The server glanced up at him. "No. Once in a blue moon we get some hero type who has to show off how macho he is. He must not be from around here either."

"He could injure himself! Kill himself even!"

"Safety nets spring up and will catch them if they fall. We've only had one case where we had to use them, and everyone, including the would-be hero, loved it."

Then the man managed to climb down the chain to the woman and had her crawl up his body. As agile as she was, she probably could have made it up the chain by herself if the heroic guy hadn't tried to rescue her. The dancer wrapped her legs around his waist and her arms around his neck as he made the treacherous climb up.

Even so, Jillian was practically holding her breath. The visitor wasn't part of the show, and any misstep on his part could mean the two of them would fall. Maybe he knew this was part of the show. Maybe the waiter just didn't realize that.

The music was still playing, but a lot more of the patrons had stopped to watch, probably because only *once in a blue moon* someone came to the dancer's rescue.

At the top edge of the platform, the guy made his way across the wooden edge until he reached the next corner chain. He paused there for the longest time. The music was still playing, the only lights the ones highlighting the dancers on their platforms. The other dancers no longer moved, riveted by their fellow dancer and the heroic guy. If he jumped to the ladder and missed, that would be the end of the show, and the dancer and the good Samaritan would fall. What if the net didn't appear in time?

Jillian wanted to do something, anything to help him. All she could do was lamely watch and pray he was successful.

He leaped for the ladder, and her heart stopped. One of his hands grabbed the ladder, the other swinging to grab hold too. Then he climbed down, the woman still clinging to him.

Jillian wanted to give him a hug and thank him for being a hero, wishing she had a guy like that in her life, when he reached the floor. The woman he'd saved gave him a big kiss, several other women crowding around him to give him hugs and kisses, and her brother said, "Show's over. Let's go."

At the hotel later that night, Miles told her he had a job the next day and would be leaving bright and early in the morning, so he couldn't help her with her case, and Jillian had to head back to Tacoma for her next PI assignment.

The hot guy would just be one of those dreams she had when she needed some fantasy in her life.

But she would always remember the handsome Samaritan who had risked his life, unless the dancer had made it clear to him that it was just part of the show and a safety net could catch them if they fell. Still, he had been there for the dancer when she had seemed to need someone to save her, and he had only meant to come to her rescue.

How could Jillian not admire such able-bodied heroism?

Chapter 1

Present day—Oregon

"MILES, WHEN YOU GET THIS MESSAGE, CALL ME. I'M working with a group of jaguar shifters on a case and don't know when I'll return to the cabin. I'll be working for the jaguars' boss, Martin Sullivan, on the case. Call me." Jillian Matthews parked at a cabin a mile from theirs, where her brother had intended to visit with his friend, Douglas Wendish. Douglas was a wolf like them, but she'd never met him before. She thought her brother might already be there. But he would have answered the phone, wouldn't he? Maybe they were running as wolves. She couldn't help but be anxious about Miles. He'd been shot only a week ago running as a wolf in these same woods.

As soon as she got out of her car in the cold, misty Oregon forest, Jillian knew something was wrong. Smoke curled from the stone chimney of the log cabin, as if welcoming a visitor inside to warm up, but chairs on the front porch were overturned, the smell of fresh blood wafted in the air, and the door was wide open.

Her heart beating triple time, she pulled out her Glock and called Leidolf, the local red pack leader who owned the cabins, to ask for backup and possibly his EMTs for medical support.

"Wait for backup," Leidolf said in a commanding, pack leader way.

"Going in. Call you when I know more." He wasn't her pack leader, and someone inside could be injured or dying.

She pocketed her phone and readied her Glock. Listening for any sounds, she approached the deck and heard someone moaning inside. She took a deep breath and smelled other scents. Humans. Wolves. A cat.

She climbed up on the deck, making it creak, but she kept moving cautiously forward in case someone might still be a threat inside. Other than the low moan, she couldn't make out any other sounds.

Barely breathing, she stole into the cabin as quietly as a wolf. When she saw a boot behind the couch, her heart thundered and she rushed around the furniture. A blond-haired man was sprawled on his back, his hand gripping his throat, blood trickling through his fingers.

"Hold on!" Jillian bolted for the kitchen nearby, grabbed a bunch of paper towels, and raced back to him. Holding the towels against his throat, she asked, "Douglas?"

The injured man stared at her, his blue eyes half lidded, and gave a little nod.

"You're going to be fine." She set her gun on the floor next to her so she could reach it if she needed to, then quickly called Leidolf back while holding the towels against Douglas's wound. "Douglas Wendish needs an ambulance ASAP. He's lost a lot of blood." Leidolf would have the records on who had rented his pack's cabins and know Douglas was a wolf.

"Everyone's on their way. ETA—ten minutes. Cause of wound?"

Jillian considered the bite wounds on Douglas's arms

and his neck. "Someone bit him on the throat and arms. He was trying to defend himself."

She took in a deep breath, trying to smell any sign that her brother had been there, worried that he could be a victim too. But he hadn't been here. So where in the world was he? "Do you know who bit you?" Jillian asked Douglas.

Barely having any strength, he shook his head.

She heard the ambulance and breathed a tentative sigh of relief. Douglas was in bad shape, but at least with the paramedics here, he might have a chance. This couldn't be a coincidence. They'd already had a case of a jaguar shifter being shot at Leidolf's ranch, the shooting of her brother, and now this. Leidolf had asked her to help the jaguars in the United Shifters Force, the USF, to figure it all out.

As soon as Leidolf's police officers arrived and the paramedics took care of Douglas, she drove back to her cabin, anxious to see if Miles had taken a wolf run and returned there. At least she could leave him a note to warn him about what had happened in case he didn't check his phone right away. She prayed he wasn't in trouble again.

When Douglas Wendish called Vaughn Greystoke, worried about not being able to reach his friend, Vaughn had told him he'd meet with him and look into it. Vaughn had resolved a missing person's case in southern Oregon and wasn't too far from Douglas's location. Douglas was one of his pack mates from Colorado and a close friend, so he knew Vaughn was nearby.

Douglas texted back forty-five minutes later: My

friend got ahold of me. No need to worry about it. Case of miscommunication. Thanks!

Vaughn was almost to the cabin, so he figured he'd just drop in, say hi, and return home to Colorado. When he tried to get ahold of Douglas to tell him that, there was no response.

While Vaughn didn't want to jump to any conclusion, he couldn't help it. That was some of the trouble with being a wolf, a SEAL, and a PI. After asking for Vaughn's help, Douglas wouldn't have ignored Vaughn's call. Perhaps he had gone running as a wolf with his friend. Vaughn would have called the local pack leader, Leidolf, to have some of his men check on Douglas, but Vaughn was so close to the cabin's location now that he would probably get there before Leidolf could send anyone.

When Vaughn arrived at the cabin, no vehicles were parked there, and two chairs and a small table had been knocked over on the deck. A light rain was falling, and a gentle breeze was blowing.

He got out of his Land Rover, gun readied, and moved quickly to the porch. He smelled Douglas's blood right away, as well as several wolves—some of them Leidolf's men's scents—and a cat's scent. His heart pounding, he rushed into the cabin, navigated around the sofa, and came face-to-face with a big, male gray wolf, his nose touching the blood on the floor before he whipped his head around.

Vaughn was startled, and the wolf looked just as shocked to see him. Before Vaughn could prepare for the wolf's reaction, he leaped at Vaughn. Huge paws slammed against Vaughn's shoulders. Unable to brace himself in time, Vaughn fell backward and hit the floor hard, losing his Glock under the damn sofa.

He grabbed the knife in his boot, but the gray wolf didn't attack him. Instead, it shot out the door.

"Damn it to hell." Vaughn shoved his hand under the sofa for the gun, pulling it from the accumulated dust bunnies. He shook it off and raced out of the cabin just in time to see the direction the wolf had run.

Vaughn holstered his gun and immediately called Leidolf and began to strip.

"This is Vaughn Greystoke. I'm at Douglas Wendish's cabin near your ranch and—"

"We've got him in surgery. A wolf named Jillian Matthews found him and called me. He's in a drug-induced coma."

"Hell."

"We're taking care of him."

"A wolf was here. I'm going after him. Get me a nearby cabin so I can investigate this, will you?"

Leidolf told Vaughn which cabin he'd give him, the same one where Vaughn had stayed last year on vacation. Leidolf would have his men park Vaughn's vehicle there. Vaughn gave him the code to unlock the car door. "Going after him."

Then Vaughn threw his clothes, cell, and gun in the car, locked it, and shifted. He tore after the wolf, hoping he'd reach him quickly. He intended to get some answers from him pronto.

Loping through the Oregon forest as a wolf, Vaughn was hot on the trail of the other one. He prayed Douglas would pull through after the vicious attack he must have suffered.

For the moment, Vaughn and the other wolf were running through the evergreen forests near the Columbia River Gorge, the sound of yet another waterfall rushing over the top of a cliff nearby. A light, icy rain continued to fall, the guard hairs of Vaughn's outer coat repelling the droplets.

For about an hour, he chased the wolf through the underbrush of the misty forest, the birds diving for cover in the Douglas fir and western hemlocks as soon as they saw him coming. Vaughn wondered where the wolf was going. He'd been looping around as if trying to reach a location, but then moving in another direction, most likely fearing Vaughn would catch up to him.

Then somewhere in the deep forest ahead, the wolf suddenly howled. Calling for help? Out there?

That meant he'd stopped long enough to howl. Vaughn raced forward to close the gap, trying to reach the wolf before he ran off again. Or before reinforcements arrived.

Why else would the wolf howl? Other members of his pack must be out there. Maybe he thought he could scare Vaughn off, making him *think* a wolf shifter pack was out there and would back him up any minute. Vaughn had used that ploy himself a time or two. He wasn't giving up on his prey no matter what. He had to learn the truth. Had the wolf standing next to the bloody mess on the cabin floor been the same wolf who had torn into Douglas? If the blood on the wolf's muzzle was any indication, and the way he had run off, Vaughn would have to say he certainly could be.

Yet how had a she-wolf, Jillian Matthews, found

Douglas, called Leidolf for help, and not been injured by this same wolf?

The chance that this wolf would have left Douglas for dead, run off, then returned after Leidolf's people had come for Douglas would be pretty slim. Unless the wolf had nearly killed Douglas in anger, then got his rage under control and came back to get rid of any evidence. Maybe he realized he hadn't made sure Douglas was dead and went back to see. What if Jillian had actually witnessed the attack, and that's how she knew a wolf had severely injured Douglas and needed Leidolf's help?

Leidolf hadn't said Jillian had seen the attack though. Not that Vaughn had given him a chance to respond much. Except for a quick mention that Leidolf would give him the cabin located closest to Douglas's on the north side while he investigated the attempted murder, Vaughn hadn't had time to do anything but agree. He was certain Leidolf had as many questions for him as Vaughn had for Jillian. Like how had Vaughn happened to be at the cabin so soon after the incident when he lived in Colorado?

And Vaughn wanted to know just who Jillian was. Douglas's girlfriend? He didn't remember Douglas dating anyone by that name.

Right now, Vaughn was so busy tracking the wolf's scent that when something hit a tree near him, and then a shot rang out, it took him a second to realize someone was shooting at him. He growled softly, irritated that anyone would be hunting out there. He continued his pursuit, another round slamming into a tree near his chest. No damn hunter was going to stop Vaughn from his mission. He had to take down the wolf and learn if he'd nearly killed Douglas.

Vaughn dodged around a hemlock, hoping the hunter would think he'd taken off in another direction. But he couldn't detour from his path for long or he'd lose the wolf. As soon as Vaughn was in the clear again, a third round clipped the shrubs in front of him. *Damn it!* He would soon be out of the shooter's range. Just a little bit farther. Then he felt the kick of the fourth round impacting with his right shoulder and heard the sound of another round firing right afterward.

Trying to dodge behind a tree to get out of the hunter's sights, Vaughn stumbled over fallen branches. He didn't have time to look for the shooter. The hunter fired another shot, and the round whizzed past Vaughn's head, sinking into the trunk of a massive maple tree with a thud. *Hell.* No matter how much he wanted to continue on the wolf's trail, he couldn't. Not with the shooter actively hunting him down.

Right before Vaughn sidetracked to the river a few feet below the rocky cliff there, he saw something golden moving so fast in the undergrowth that he could barely believe his eyes.

A big cat? Jaguar? Shifter? What in the world was going on? He'd never seen a jaguar shifter before.

Vaughn jumped into the river, the cold water enveloping him as he went under. He surfaced and let it carry him away, the whole time mentally cursing the shooter.

What of the cat he'd witnessed running through the woods? He hadn't imagined observing a jaguar. He wasn't delirious. Yet seeing one of them in an Oregon forest was like finding a unicorn. Had one gotten free from the Oregon Zoo? Or a big-cat reserve? Then again, his pack leaders had said jaguar shifters lived among them. Taking the wolf down had to be Vaughn's priority, yet he wished he'd been able to chase after the big cat too and learn what in the world it was doing there, in the same vicinity as the other trouble.

Hell, maybe the jaguar, and not a wolf, was responsible for Douglas's wound.

―᷈᷈᷈᷈―

Jillian couldn't believe that a *lupus garou* could be trying to kill her brother. The wolf chasing Miles had to be a shifter. She knew he wasn't running with Miles for fun. Not with the way her brother had howled, calling to her for help. If the other wolf had been in trouble too, he would have howled along with her brother. No, this one had been hell-bent on Miles's trail. Worse, she worried he could be the wolf who had nearly killed Douglas.

She ran through the woods to track where the wounded wolf had gone once he'd finally veered from her brother's path. Wild wolves had been sighted in Oregon, so at first she'd thought it might have claimed the territory and was chasing Miles out of the area or, worse, planned to kill him. When she couldn't scare the wolf off with the first three rounds she'd fired, she was certain he was a shifter. She found drops of blood collected on vegetation, the light rain already diluting it, and followed them to the river where the trail ended.

In the misty rain, she glanced in the direction the river was flowing and thought she saw a wolf's head bobbing up and down in the water. She couldn't be certain, considering the conditions: the water was dark, the object was far away, and the day was overcast.

She continued to watch until whatever it was disappeared beyond a bend in the river. Her heart pounding, she ran in the direction of her cabin, hoping her brother was there and could tell her what was going on. If she hadn't needed to hang on to her rifle and cell phone, she would have shifted and run as a wolf. Much faster that way.

She was glad the wolf was no longer chasing her brother, but she did hate that she'd had to shoot him. With their shifter ability to heal faster than humans, he would be fine in no time.

As soon as the cabin came into view, she hurried to the front door, unlocked it, and called out to her brother. He didn't respond, and she didn't hear him in the back bedroom. She stalked back to the room, but he wasn't there. Why wouldn't he have come here? Unless he was afraid of bringing the big, bad wolf to their doorstep.

For now, she had other business to take care of. She left a message for her brother, telling him to call her at once, that she was working with some jaguar shifters. And that Douglas was in dire straits after someone attacked him. She would be staying at the red wolf pack's ranch part of the time. She considered trying to track down her brother as a wolf, but with the other wolf wounded and leaving the area, she figured Miles would be okay for now.

Teaming up with jaguars was something totally new for Jillian. Never in a million years would she have believed she'd be working with a combined force of jaguar shifters and a wolf—and with another, if they could solicit his help. On the way to her cabin, Leidolf had informed her about a hard-core Navy SEAL, also turned PI—and from what she'd read about his profile, a loner in his investigative work—who was in the area and investigating the attack on Douglas.

From a photo Leidolf had sent to the team, the PI was one hot-looking specimen of a wolf and single, though she just happened to notice that information by chance. And he looked a hell of a lot like the guy she'd seen at the Clawed and Dangerous Kitty Cat Club in San Diego. The good Samaritan. That meant he had been a wolf all along. She should have known.

Hoping she'd hear from Miles soon, Jillian quickly packed a bag and left to join the jaguar shifters at the cabin nearby to meet up with the SEAL wolf. She also put in a call to Leidolf for an update on Douglas's condition.

Vaughn bobbed up and down in the icy water, thankful his wolf's double coat protected him from the chilling cold. He had to take care of his wound first, hoping it wasn't too bad and he would heal quickly enough. He was certain the gray wolf couldn't have suddenly armed himself with a rifle, so he was still running as a wolf, and that meant Vaughn could try to find his scent later.

What if the gray wolf had an accomplice? Maybe that's why he howled. To get help from a wolf shifter friend or pack member who would shoot Vaughn instead of coming to his aid as a wolf. The shooter wouldn't have been some random hunter then. A marksman lying in wait while Vaughn tried to take down the wolf seemed too damned convenient to be mere coincidence.

Because of the numbing effect of the cold water and the shock from the impact of the round on his shoulder, he still wasn't feeling any pain. *Thankfully*. He'd make it to shore close to where his cabin was and slip into the place, take care of this bloody mess, rest a while, eat, and take off again.

Lupus garous healed faster than humans, but they didn't heal instantaneously. He couldn't wear a bandage on his shoulder as a wolf either. He would need to rest his shoulder for a time before he could shift again. Chasing the wolf as a human, Vaughn would never be able to catch up. Not until the wolf settled somewhere.

Vaughn recognized the trees and shrubs near the water's edge, and the telltale marker—three stacked boulders, the result of an avalanche centuries ago—he'd run past before that indicated where his cabin was situated, just north of Douglas's. He fought the swift flow of the currents so he could scramble onto the rocky shore. He could tell his strength was already dwindling.

He needed to get an update from Leidolf on Douglas's condition and let his pack leaders know about it too.

He was trying to keep on his feet, stumbling over rocks and branches, and stumbling where there were none. He was just a little north of his cabin, not too much farther to go. He was sticking to the woods and avoiding the river view in front of the cabin, just in case. The next couple of cabins were about a half mile away, including the one where Vaughn had found Douglas's blood. Vaughn was nearly in view of his own cabin when he heard a woman's voice as she spoke to someone else.

"We'll just wait for him. You're so impatient, Everett."

"We should have tracked him down."

Staying low and prowling closer, to his surprise and irritation, Vaughn saw two men and a woman standing on his front deck, drinking bottled water.

What the hell. He really didn't need this aggravation right now. Why did they want to see him? He didn't know them from Adam.

The woman was a brunette, her hair tied back in a ponytail, and her eyes were dark brown. A man with shaggier dark hair and green eyes looked like he was with the woman. From the man's protective stance, Vaughn was certain they were together. Another man was occupying his own space on the other side of the deck, watching the river, his short-cropped hair black and his eyes blue, with a square jaw that looked like it could take a fist. His eyes narrowed, his expression was ominous.

All of them were dressed in jeans, rain jackets, and hiking boots. The men looked hard-core, like they could dish out some real punishment. The three were in great shape, regular hikers in the woods, Vaughn guessed. Something about their posture and appearance suggested they were former military or police. They just had that official look about them. Leidolf's people? Nah. He didn't recognize any of them.

All of them could be wearing shoulder-holstered weapons. Vaughn couldn't tell from the lay of their jackets.

Furious with them for intruding, he remained hidden in the woods, standing perfectly still. What the hell were they doing here?

He couldn't just walk up to them as a wolf. A wounded wolf. They'd shoot him for sure if they were armed. He couldn't sneak around to the back and get into his cabin that way, because Leidolf's cabin rental manager would have locked all the windows.

Then again, Vaughn's bags were still in his vehicle parked nearby, courtesy of Leidolf.

If Vaughn could have sneaked inside somehow, he would have grabbed a towel and pretended to have taken a shower—although hiding the gunshot wound would still have been problematic. If he shifted and headed for the cabin naked as could be, he would be sporting a bloody bullet hole in his shoulder, bleeding all over the place, and have no way to explain how he got shot.

Screw 'em. He didn't have time for this.

He had to stop the bleeding, and he assumed they weren't leaving. If anyone asked, he'd just tell them some damn hunter shot him accidentally. Why was he running around naked in the woods as chilly as it was? He was conducting survival training. He was sure they wouldn't believe him, but he didn't owe them an explanation anyway. He just hoped none of them called the police to report the gunshot wound. He'd heal faster than normal, and because of that, he couldn't see a human doctor.

The pain was just beginning to hit, and he growled softly with annoyance.

All three people glanced in his direction, as if they'd heard his low wolf's growl. Which would have been impossible. Unless he hadn't growled as low as he thought he had, as angry as he was. *Or* unless they were wolves. What if they were members of the pack the wolf he'd been chasing belonged to? Because of the way the breeze was blowing away from all of them, he couldn't smell them anymore than they could smell him. What if one of these people had shot him? *Terrific.*

Not having much of a choice, he shifted and headed out of the woods in the raw, the chilly air bracing. With a narrow-eyed look that meant he would shift again and take them all on, he said, "What the hell are you doing trespassing on private property?"

Chapter 2

FROM THE CABIN'S LIVING ROOM WINDOW, JILLIAN SAW the lethal-looking SEAL wolf totally in the raw, sporting a bloodied wound on his right shoulder. Vaughn Greystoke. In the flesh. Unless she was completely mistaken and he had a twin brother who had been the hot guy she saw in the Kitty Cat Club six months ago, this was the guy who had risked his neck for the dancer for no reason. Jillian couldn't believe it was really him. She had always wondered if anyone at the club told him the dancer hadn't needed his rescue.

The injury he was sporting looked suspiciously like a gunshot wound. He seemed ready to kick some ass despite that, or maybe because someone had wounded him.

Who would have been out in the woods shooting a wolf? The same man who had shot her brother? She wanted to tear into the man who would do such a...

Her jaw dropped. *She* had wounded a wolf. Had she hit *this* one? How many wolves would be running around this area, besides her brother? The one who had injured Douglas, of course. Vaughn Greystoke must have been the wolf chasing Miles. No wonder her brother had been terrified.

How could she have known the guy hunting her brother was the same *lupus garou* the jaguars wanted to solicit help from? After Leidolf had received the call from Vaughn, he'd told the team of jaguars and one wolf—her—that Vaughn would be a great addition to their group in helping to learn what was going on. Plus, Vaughn had a personal stake in it.

Jillian grabbed a kitchen towel, rushed to the cabin's door, and jerked it open, realizing at the same time that the wolf would probably be pissed she was in his cabin. Not to mention that she had probably shot him.

But Leidolf's men had brought the key to the cabin, and she had obtained fresh towels from the staff. She had left the towels in the bathroom for when the PI arrived. He hadn't moved in yet, so it shouldn't matter to him. The growly wolf turned his attention from the jaguar shifters standing on his deck to her, his brown eyes narrowing even more, if that was possible. A light amount of dark hair trailed down to his groin. Completely naked, his muscles well-sculpted as if he worked out a lot, he was even hotter than the photo she had of him when he was fully clothed, *if* she hadn't wanted to kill him for going after her brother. She was used to more intellectual types who weren't that built, she had to admit. *He* was total eye candy.

Quickly explaining the situation, Everett Anderson rushed off the porch to give Vaughn a hand, his wife helping, too, as Howard bolted from the deck to join them. "What the hell happened to you? We came to ask you to join us. You look like you have a serious problem of your own. We'll get you to Leidolf's doctor. Who did this to you?"

"A hunter, or the wolf I was chasing had an accomplice." Vaughn's growly, dark voice sent shivers up her spine. Interested shivers, not scared shivers. Though she could just imagine how alarmed her brother had to have been if this was the angry wolf who had been chasing him.

What was the chance someone else had been in the woods shooting at Vaughn? Miniscule. It was much more likely that *Jillian* had shot the wolf. She hadn't heard anyone else firing shots in the woods.

"You're jaguar shifters?" Vaughn's expression indicated his surprise.

"Yes. We're with the United Shifter Force, the USF. We're a joint group that is soliciting help from wolves to work with us on cases like this, involving wolves and jaguars in conflict. I'm Everett Anderson, JAG agent; my wife, Demetria, Guardian agent; and Howard Sternum, Enforcer agent, all jaguar shifters. Though I guess technically we're now USF agents. Your pack leaders, Devlyn and Bella Greystoke, know about us. We formed the group after finding the pack that an Arctic wolf shifter cub belonged to. Did they mention anything about us to you when we were trying to locate the boy's parents?"

"Yes, they did. It was a real shock to all of us. By the way, I saw a jaguar running through the woods after I was shot and before I leaped into the river." Vaughn arched a brow as if he thought maybe one of these was the one he had seen.

Jillian didn't believe any of them would have had time to run around in the woods as a jaguar and then return here to join them. Though she hadn't been with the three of them for some time.

"Not one of us. What did he look like?" Everett asked, sounding concerned.

Vaughn gave him a sideways glance. "Like a jaguar."

The jaguars chuckled.

"Too bad you couldn't have gotten a picture of him," Everett said.

As a wolf? Vaughn just shook his head.

"Was it male? Or female?" Demetria asked.

"Big balls. I'd say male." Vaughn continued to walk toward the deck, his gaze again shifting to Jillian as Everett slid his arm around Vaughn's back to help stabilize him. Vaughn opened his mouth as if to say he didn't need any help, but he stumbled a bit and was looking so pale that he must have thought better of it. A guy could act all macho as much as he wanted, but if he did a face-plant in the dirt, how would that look? Not tough at all.

"That's Jillian—" Everett began to say, glancing her way as she moved off the deck to join them.

"Matthews." She barely refrained from throwing the kitchen towel at Vaughn, as irritated as she was with him now that she assumed he'd been chasing her brother. Getting her annoyance under control, she pressed the towel against Vaughn's wound and applied pressure, taking a deep breath of his scent. Animals took in other animals' scents. It was a natural thing to do: smelling sex—he was definitely *all* male; emotions—hotly annoyed; interest in another wolf—yep, just like he was breathing in her scent and cataloging it. They also did it so they'd recognize one another in their wolf forms.

This was the wolf she'd shot who had ended up in the river. No doubt about it.

His eyes widened, nearly black now as he stared at her in disbelief. "You're a wolf. Not a jaguar shifter. And we've…seen each other before."

Ohmigod, it was him. "Yeah. At the Clawed and

Dangerous Kitty Cat Club in San Diego?" Darned if the way he intrigued her wasn't causing her to react in a purely wolfish and very interested way. She couldn't disguise the way her own scent would tell him how much so. She could be as angry with him as she wanted, but she couldn't deny the physical attraction. Just like she'd been hot and bothered by him when she'd seen him at the club months earlier. This close up, he overwhelmed her senses. "And it appears I shot you."

The jaguars' jaws all dropped. She swore Vaughn almost smiled at her. Was he thinking of a way to pay her back? Or something else? Keep your friends close, but your enemies closer?

She cast him the same kind of dark almost-smile. She hoped the jaguars didn't think she was a loose cannon.

She didn't feel an ounce of remorse. Well, maybe a little. She hadn't wanted to shoot him, but her brother's howl had told her he was terrified, desperate, and he'd needed her help in the worst way. She'd had to do something about the wolf because he wouldn't stop chasing Miles.

The jaguars on the newly formed force had asked her to join them because she was already involved in the investigation of the jaguar shooting at Leidolf's ranch, at his request as a favor to him. She knew the area. Neither she nor the jaguars had had any clue that Vaughn was chasing after her brother. Did he think Miles had tried to kill Douglas? She wouldn't allow anyone to hurt her brother, no matter how much Vaughn might believe her brother was guilty of a crime. Leidolf hadn't told them Vaughn had been in hot pursuit of a wolf while wearing his wolf coat.

"We believe you're out here looking for the same man we are." Demetria hurried to get a first aid kit from their Jeep.

Like hell Vaughn was, if he thought Miles had torn into Douglas.

A flash of lightning struck the ground in the woods about a mile away. A few seconds later, a loud clap of thunder shook the ground, and a deluge of rain poured down on them. With Howard and Everett helping him, Vaughn unsteadily climbed the steps to his deck, made it to the open door, and then inside.

"Hell, if you're looking for the same man I was when *she* shot me"—Vaughn looked pointedly at Jillian—"I missed my opportunity to take him down. I'm fine. Or will be after a couple of hours. If the *she-wolf* hadn't been creating issues, I would have had my man." He gave Jillian a caustic look and settled on a leather bar-stool. "*And* I work alone."

"How well is that working out for you?" Jillian was still holding the towel in place over his bloody wound, unable to quit breathing in his maddeningly tantalizing scent—a mixture of male, testosterone, fresh water, and the woods. She furrowed her brow at him. "Obviously, we've been after the wrong man."

Vaughn stared her right down. "Like hell we have. *You* let him get away."

Jillian shook her head. "No. I mean *you*. *You* were after the wrong man, so *we* were wrong in wanting you on the team. You'd be useless to us if you can't do a better job of figuring out who the real criminal is."

"What makes you think Miles is involved in this?" Demetria asked Vaughn, throwing a supersize black bath towel on his lap, then pulling a container of perox-ide and bandages out of the first aid kit.

Vaughn jerked the towel up with his left hand and mopped the raindrops rolling off his hair and down his face and chest. "Miles? That's his name?"

"Miles Matthews," Jillian clarified, watching to see the SEAL's reaction.

Vaughn's brows lifted. "Is Miles a relative of yours?"

Jillian swore he looked like he believed she was in cahoots with her brother, and they had been involved together in the fiendishly horrible attack. "He's my brother. Like Demetria asked, what makes you suspect he's done anything wrong?"

"As a wolf, he was standing over the bloody area where Douglas had obviously been viciously attacked." Vaughn's harsh look bored into Jillian, as if waiting for her to prove he was wrong.

Shocked to the core that her brother had been there after the fact and Vaughn had caught him there, she quickly focused on the evidence Vaughn thought he had. For one thing, her brother's scent hadn't been in the cabin when she had discovered Douglas. "So you questioned him like any reasonable investigator would." Jillian knew he couldn't have if her brother had been a wolf. That would have been a one-sided conversation. "Standing next to where Douglas had fallen from his injuries doesn't automatically say he's guilty."

"Miles was a wolf. Douglas's blood was all over the floor. Then Miles took off. He didn't leave me any choice but to try to take him down."

"Kill him?" She glowered at Vaughn.

"Hell...take him down."

"We don't believe he's involved." Everett brought in more towels from Vaughn's linen closet for everyone to use to dry off.

"Why not? Last word I had from Douglas was there was some miscommunication with his friend and then he'd heard from him. Next thing I know, I'm staring at a wolf and a puddle of Douglas's blood. And since his own sister is trying to kill me, I'd say it was a good bet." Vaughn's gaze still bored into Jillian's, an attempt at intimidation.

"Miles hadn't been there before I arrived." She wasn't easily intimidated and scowled right back at Vaughn.

"If she was trying to kill you, you'd be dead." Howard smiled. "She's a former army officer, you know."

"I doubt she was only trying to wound me," Vaughn said, challenging her. "The fifth round nearly hit me in the head. The first three, I don't know what that was all about. Lousy shots, I guess."

"Howard's right. If I'd wanted to kill you, I would have with the first round. I fired the other rounds as a warning, to scare you off." Lousy shots, her foot. He was just trying to rile her because she'd wounded him. "No matter what, you were relentlessly going after my brother. I needed to wound you so I could stop you from hurting him. If I could have, I would have questioned you." At gunpoint.

"Question me?" Vaughn gave a sarcastic laugh. "You're a little confused as to who was in the wrong here, unless that's your intention. Get the heat off your brother for a bit? Blame me instead?" Vaughn winced as Demetria poured peroxide on his wound.

"I'm sure she'll forgive you if you agree to work for

the team." Demetria cleaned off the blood and finished bandaging his wound.

"She'll forgive *me*?" Vaughn's dark brows lifted again.

"For going after her brother." Demetria smiled.

Jillian loved working with the jaguars. They trusted her instincts as much as their own. She hadn't expected Demetria to say what she had though. She loved her for it.

"You've got to be bullshitting me."

Jillian almost laughed at his growly words. She wondered if he always got his way. This had to be a rude awakening for the SEAL.

"Nope. Now, do you want to join the team?" Demetria asked, as if Jillian shooting him was of no consequence.

Jillian sure hoped he would work with them now, so she could keep an eye on him.

Studying Vaughn, Howard folded his arms. "I don't think he's a team player."

Demetria and Everett looked at Howard and grinned.

"What? I play well with the rest of you." Howard's blue eyes were smiling, but he appeared as lethal as they come.

Jillian had heard he hadn't been a team player either, until he began to work with Everett and Demetria.

"Come on, let's go. This is a waste of our time." Jillian motioned to the naked man still seated on the barstool, the black towel spread over his lap, his legs bare, his shoulder bandaged.

"For now, we'll move you to Leidolf's ranch. We're staying at one of the guest houses," Demetria said, as if Vaughn didn't have any choice. "Leidolf's physician, Dr. Camden Wilders, can take care of your injury. While we're searching for the man who injured Douglas, you can recuperate. If the guy who attacked Douglas thinks you're after him, and you're hurt and staying alone in a cabin out in the wilderness, you could be in real trouble."

"All of you are staying at the guest house?" Vaughn was looking straight at Jillian.

What? Did he now think *she* was the one who had torn into his pack member? Or just that she was in collusion with her brother? If Vaughn was staying at the same place she was, did he believe he could learn for sure if she was or not?

"Yeah. Demetria and her mate have the master bedroom suite. Howard and I have our own rooms. You will too. We share the same bathroom. That means you have to put the toilet seat down after you've used it. *If* you join us." Jillian would never have said that to any guy, and certainly hadn't to Howard, but Vaughn just pushed her buttons.

Vaughn gave her another almost-smile, as if her words challenged him to see just what she would do if he *didn't* put the toilet seat down.

He looked pale though, and for an instant, she felt guilty again about having shot him. Then she reminded herself he was trying to take down her brother when she knew Miles was perfectly innocent of injuring anyone.

"So what were members of the USF doing here if I'd just learned Douglas had been attacked?"

"A jaguar was shot at Leidolf's ranch," Everett said.

"Shifter?" Vaughn asked.

"Yes, but we don't know who it is. One of Leidolf's men heard shots fired when he was clearing brush. Trent thought it was a hunter illegally hunting on the pack's forested land. Then he saw the jaguar, and the cat went down as another shot went off. By the time Trent reached the woods, the cat was gone, but he left drops of blood. The jaguar must have been stunned at first, or pretended it had been mortally wounded.

"Trent hurried back to the ranch house, cognizant that the shooter could still be out there and there was a slight chance the jaguar wasn't a shifter, but a wounded cat. Trent's cell battery had died, so by the time he could send word to Leidolf and get men out to search, both the cat and the shooter were gone," Everett said. "Leidolf's men continued to look for an injured man or jaguar, but neither the hunter nor the man left a scent trail."

"Hunter's spray. A jaguar wouldn't have used the concealing spray. Had to be a shifter then," Vaughn said. "And they had to be up to no good."

"Right. Some of Leidolf's men tried to track the wounded jaguar, both his blood and pugmarks in the damp soil, but lost him at one of the streams. No jaguars are missing from reserves or the zoo, but like you said, it had to be a shifter because he left no scent. The one you saw... Did it seem injured in any way?"

"No. He was moving fast. Maybe he was afraid the hunter in the woods would come after him next." Vaughn looked at Jillian.

"As long as the jaguar wasn't going after my brother, no. Though if I'd realized the cat might have injured Douglas, I would have."

"We better get you to Leidolf's ranch, whether you want to join us or not," Demetria suddenly said. "You can decide later, but I think you're going to need some blood."

"Make it hers, and we have a deal." Vaughn inclined

his head toward Jillian. "*And* she has to give me a kiss to say she's sorry for shooting me. Maybe even a dance later like I know she wanted to have with me at the Kitty Cat Club."

Jillian had opened her mouth to tell him off when Vaughn's eyes rolled into the back of his head. She gasped and grabbed his naked, muscular torso in one big body hug to stop him from falling off the barstool.

In a dead faint, he began tumbling off the stool while everyone else tried to stop him from hitting the hardwood floor.

Chapter 3

"THE DOCTOR SAID SOMEONE WITH THE SAME BLOOD type needs to volunteer to give blood because he doesn't have any on hand. Dr. Wilders is leaving the bullet where it is because it will do less damage than if he digs it out. Eventually, Vaughn's body will repel it, though it might take a while," Demetria said to Jillian as they stood near Vaughn's hospital bed after Leidolf's doctor had taken care of him in the clinic on the south side of the ranch. "You have to give him blood. That was his provision for going along with this."

Sally, one of the nurses, was waiting for a decision nearby.

Jillian frowned at Vaughn as he lay in the bed, wearing a hospital gown decorated with a moon and stars. His eyes were still closed, and his breathing was shallow. Jillian folded her arms. "Vaughn is going along with *what*? Looking for the *real* bad guy? Being on the team with us? Or just allowing Dr. Wilders to take care of him? Vaughn didn't really say for sure. Not before he fell off the barstool in a dead faint." She imagined he would hate that he'd fainted in front of all of them. So much for him successfully working alone.

Demetria motioned to Vaughn. "Your blood type just happens to be B positive. Just like his is."

"Isn't yours too?" Jillian knew it was because they had to know everyone's blood type in case anyone on the team was injured, and so they could donate blood to each other in an emergency.

Demetria only smiled.

"All right. I'll do it. Through coercion. It would serve him right if I was some other blood type." Then Jillian frowned. "Unless he already knew what it was." Had he somehow learned all there was about her brother and her? Now that really torqued her off.

Jillian lay down on the bed next to Vaughn's and waited for the nurse to take blood from her. "Are you certain he even needs it? I imagine he could just eat lots of bloody steaks and be raring to go, as ornery as he is."

The redheaded nurse smiled.

"Afraid of giving a little blood?" Vaughn asked.

Jillian whipped her head around to see him looking at her, his eyes barely open. He still appeared a bit wan. She thought she'd been having a private conversation with Demetria and the nurse. She should have known the hulking SEAL wolf brute had been conscious the whole time. "Aren't you afraid I'll taint your blood with mine?"

"As feisty as you are, no. I think it'll add a little zest to my life. I'll have the bloody steak too though." He closed his eyes and smiled just a hint. "If you cook it."

Jillian snapped her gaping mouth shut.

"I'll buy the steaks," Demetria said.

"I'll bring the beer," Howard said.

Jillian turned to see Howard leaning against the wall, smiling. She hadn't realized he had returned to the clinic after helping wheel Vaughn into the room and then parking the Jeep. "Hell, from what I can see, the jaguars play together much better than the wolves," Howard said.

Vaughn's eyes closed again, and he grunted.

"I play well with others. But some wolves, and probably some jaguars, are incorrigible loners," Jillian said.

Vaughn smiled. "*And*...you owe me that kiss to say you're sorry. Unless you're still with that muscle-bound guy from the club." Then he frowned. "How's Douglas?" As if he suddenly remembered his friend had been injured. Which meant he had to still be really out of it.

"In a drug-induced coma for now," Demetria said. "He lost a lot of blood before Jillian and others came to help him."

"And?"

"It will take time to know if he's going to make it. Dr. Wilders says it's touch and go for now. But the staff is doing everything they can for him."

Vaughn closed his eyes, and Jillian wished she had reached the cabin earlier and gotten help for Douglas that much sooner. She had done everything she could to stem the bleeding and had called Leidolf for help at once. But if she had arrived at the cabin earlier, she might have come face-to-face with the animal who had nearly killed him.

Vaughn couldn't believe he was laid up in a red-wolf-pack clinic. Any more than he could believe he'd passed out in front of the jaguars and the wolf at his cabin. Or that his pack member was clinging to life. And to meet the woman he'd fantasized about when he'd seen her dancing at the Kitty Cat Club six months ago? He smiled to himself. He'd thought of a lot of ways of meeting her, but this hadn't been one of them.

"Okay, so what do we do next?" Jillian asked Demetria.

Vaughn didn't care what the rest of them did while looking into this matter. He had one real lead—Jillian's brother. He wasn't going to stop going after Miles until he caught him and discovered what he had to do with any of this. Vaughn just wished he didn't feel so out of it. He guessed he'd lost more blood than he thought as he opened his eyes again and watched Jillian.

"I'm chasing down your brother." Vaughn hated sounding so weak when he wanted to firmly emphasize that what *he* planned to do was nonnegotiable. "I want to know why he was wearing a wolf coat and standing over the bloody area where Douglas had been brutally attacked earlier."

Jillian glowered at Vaughn from the other bed, eyes narrowed and dark-brown hair spread out on the pillow as if she was ready for him to come join her. He didn't know why he had the hots for her. He hadn't wanted any particular woman in a long time. He wouldn't have thought he'd feel that way about a woman who had just shot him. Her mouth curved down just a bit, so appealing that he really did want to kiss her. Which was insane.

"And of course my brother had the victim's blood on him, right?" she asked hotly.

"Yeah. As a matter of fact, he did. On his muzzle." Vaughn waited for that to sink in.

She looked a little surprised.

"Maybe you ought to come with me so once I catch up to him, I'll know if you're going to try to shoot me again. I'll be more prepared to defend myself that way." He was serious about it, as protective as she was of her brother.

Demetria offered Jillian a cup of orange juice as she finished giving Vaughn blood.

Ready to get back to work, Vaughn began to sit up, but his vision blurred, his mind blackening, and he fell back against the pillow hard before he passed out again. *Hell.* When his mind and vision cleared, he saw Jillian reaching for him. As quickly as she'd reached his bed, she must have jumped to come to his aid. Their gazes met, her cheeks blossoming in color, her eyes wide. Amused that she had been putting on such a tough act with him, he smiled.

Then she grabbed hold of his bed rail, her face ashen. Dizzy from giving him blood? Before he could comment on her own well-being or grab for her arm to assist her, she quickly turned to Demetria. "I've got stuff to do. I'll meet up with you at dinner."

Vaughn felt like he'd aged a hundred years. "Don't let her go after her brother and warn him off." He knew that's just what she would do as soon as she had a chance. "One of you needs to stick to her like glue."

Jillian let her breath out in a huff and stalked out of the room.

"I'm serious," Vaughn said to Demetria, wishing he could climb right out of this bed and take off after the vixen.

Neither Howard nor Demetria made any move to follow Jillian.

"We believe Jillian is right about her brother, unless we learn differently. Take it easy. Get your rest. The staff will feed you here tonight, and we'll check on you first thing in the morning," Demetria said. "If you're going to work with the team, you need to be in good shape, not ready to keel over again."

Howard nodded. "Get some rest, man. But I'll warn you now, if you think you're going to take the she-wolf on, this jaguar is on *her* side. So watch what you do or say."

Vaughn shook his head. He couldn't see how everyone would think he was wrong in his assumptions. Everyone with any kind of investigative background should feel the same way as he did, and not let their obvious friendship with Jillian color their perspective. Yeah, sure, her brother was innocent until proven guilty, but the way Miles had run off proved he couldn't be trusted.

"Sleep," Demetria said, and she and Howard left the room.

Vaughn lay there for a while with every intention of hauling himself right out of the bed, heading back to the cabin, and picking up Miles's trail. He thought if he just moved slowly enough, he wouldn't be so dizzy. He closed his eyes, trying to keep his head from spinning.

If he'd had a hangover from partying way too much—which he rarely did—that would have been one thing. The hell of it was, no one had ever managed to shoot him on *any* mission he'd gone on. Shot at, yes. Wolf fights, yes. Hand-to-hand combat when he'd lost his weapon during a fight, yes. A former army officer shooting him and putting him temporarily out of commission was completely irksome.

Then he smelled the scent of a female red wolf, the nurse. He opened his eyes to see the redhead—Sally, he thought her name was—walking over to the bed. He noticed the clock said it was an hour later than the last time he had looked, right before he had closed his eyes. He couldn't believe he'd slept for a whole hour. She smiled at him and inserted something into his IV.

"What's that for?" He was trying not to growl, but he wasn't about to let the medical staff fill his veins with anything that would slow him down even further.

"Antibiotics." She smiled again.

He swore she was lying. Or he was just being paranoid. He took a deep breath and let it out. Okay, he could live with antibiotics. That should help get him on his feet faster. The liquid dripped into his veins, burning on the way in, and he felt his head beginning to swim. He glowered at the nurse. At least he tried to. He wasn't certain he was doing much more than looking at her, the way he was growing so groggy.

"Get some rest," the nurse said.

"You gave me something to knock me out," he accused, so annoyed that he couldn't think straight. He was going to jerk the IV out, but the nurse had already strapped down his left arm and was working on his right when he realized what she had done. He understood then how out of it he really was.

If Jillian had anything to do with him being drugged, he'd put *her* under lock and key!

—∿—

"He is so pigheaded!" Jillian put out the silverware while Everett placed the platter of grilled chicken in the center of the table at the guest house at Leidolf's ranch. Four hours had passed since they'd left Vaughn alone at the clinic to recuperate, but she couldn't get her mind off that annoyingly stubborn wolf.

"I take it you're talking about Vaughn." Everett pulled Demetria into his arms and kissed her.

Newlyweds.

"Yes, who else?" Jillian sighed and set the bowl of potato salad on the table. She couldn't quit thinking about him. About his obsession over her brother. About the way he had acted as though she was guilty for protecting Miles. Vaughn's expression had shown real concern when she had rushed to help him and nearly passed out herself. She'd moved way too quickly after giving him blood.

She couldn't stop thinking about her brother either, and hoping he was okay. Or that Douglas would recover fully. She wished they could question him about who had bitten him and why.

"Vaughn will change his mind about your brother when he realizes someone else is responsible for his pack member's attack. You can imagine how it must have looked to him... Well, to anyone who might have seen your brother as a wolf standing over the bloody scene. He said Miles had blood on his muzzle. Then Miles ran. Not that I blame your brother. If I'd been a wolf under those circumstances and saw a very lethal man who smelled like a wolf catch me in a situation like that, I would have run too." Demetria sat at the table opposite Jillian.

"But when there was no body even there?" Jillian asked.

"Vaughn probably assumed Miles had dragged the body off. Then he returned to clean up."

Everett took the seat next to his mate. "Yeah, besides, if he thinks your brother did it, I believe the best avenue is if at least one of us pairs up with him until we learn the truth."

"I'll do it." Howard sat next to Jillian. "He needs

someone to watch over him who's just as hardheaded as he is."

"I'll go too. As soon as we catch up to my brother, I'll reassure Miles that no one's going to terminate him. If Vaughn tries to hurt him, I'll just shoot him again." Jillian smiled.

Howard shook his head. "Tell me if I make you mad, will you? I don't want to ever get on your bad side."

The Enforcer branch called on its agents, like Howard, to terminate rogue jaguars when there was no other choice. So coming from him, the comment was funny. Jillian still had a hard time believing jaguar shifters existed and that they had such an organized way of dealing with rogues or people who mistreated their kind and full jaguars. The wolf packs took care of their own, so it was different working with more of a police force like this.

The jaguar agents dealt with situations all over, though U.S. jaguars mostly lived in the southern states, predominantly the ones that bordered Mexico. So none of the three jaguars had even been to Oregon. That made sense because if anyone caught them running as jaguars there, it would incite a manhunt for the big cats and be all over the news. Which made Jillian wonder why a jaguar *had* been running around in his cat coat out here.

"We're curious about this chance meeting you had with Vaughn at the Clawed and Dangerous Kitty Cat Club. How long ago was that?" Demetria spooned some potato salad onto her plate.

"Six months ago." Jillian knew what was coming next. None of them had realized the other shifters existed back then.

Demetria smiled. "That must have seemed strange to you. Not about seeing a fellow wolf, but that so many of the patrons smelled like cats."

"Yeah. I figured because the place was jungle-cat themed, it was a cat lover's paradise. We had a blast. I didn't know Vaughn was a wolf. I never actually met him."

"Aww. But you must have connected in some way."

"Like we did," Everett said to Demetria.

"So you were on a date and he was too, and that ended things before they could get started," Demetria said.

"Yeah. Miles was with me, and he had a date. Our dates were human. Vaughn's date might have been human too."

"Seems like fate that you met at that earlier time," Demetria said.

"And shot him this time."

Everyone chuckled.

Howard grabbed the bowl of potato salad and scooped up several spoonfuls. "You make the best potato salad, Demetria."

"You do." Jillian had already gotten the recipe that Demetria's grandmother had passed down. "I want to leave tomorrow to find my brother first thing, no matter what shape Vaughn is in. In any event, he will probably need a couple more days to recuperate." If she had her way, she'd just dope him up for several days to ensure he stayed put. Wouldn't that be better for him anyway? So he could get some much-needed rest and heal faster?

"I doubt he'll stay in that bed much longer than tomorrow. You saw the way he's already tried to get out of it." Demetria grabbed a chicken leg and took a bite.

"The doctor can help him stay put." Jillian spooned up some potato salad.

Howard laughed. "If he thought you put the doctor up to drugging him, you'll be in even deeper trouble with him."

"Maybe if you kiss him like he wants you to, he'll settle down." Demetria smiled.

"Not happening. Giving him blood was one thing. Kissing him? That's definitely not part of the mission. Besides, he's just giving me a hard time. He's not being serious."

"That's the way to stick to your guns," Howard said. "I wouldn't kiss him either."

Everyone smiled.

Howard's ears tinged a little red. "I mean, if I were you."

Jillian thought she heard someone's footfalls crunching on the gravel drive out front. She suspected Leidolf had some news for them and wanted to talk to them personally. As the alpha leader of the red wolf pack, he was ready to make someone pay for injuring a jaguar shifter and a wolf on his property.

When a knock sounded, Jillian said, "I'll see who it is." She hurried to answer the door, but when she pulled it open, she was shocked to see Vaughn standing on the porch looking red-faced, sweating and weaving unsteadily on his feet, wearing jeans, boots, and an open shirt. At least the rain had stopped so he wasn't soaking wet. He had to be damn cold wearing no jacket or sweater, his shirt wide open to the elements. She guessed he'd had trouble buttoning his shirt because of being all bandaged up.

"Are you gonna let me in?" Vaughn reached out to grab hold of the doorjamb.

Jillian's first thought was he was in her space, and she needed to take a step back and let him into the warm house. Her second thought was he was getting ready to collapse on her. She lunged forward and wrapped her arms around him, though she wouldn't be able to stop him if he went down. He was all hot, hard muscles and sexy as sin. He took his hand off the doorjamb and wrapped his good arm around her, but not in a way that said he was ready to collapse. More in a way that said he really liked the way she was holding him close to her breast.

Afraid to let go of him in case he did collapse, she still held on to him, but as soon as she opened her mouth to tell him he should be right back in his bed at the clinic if he was feeling this shaky, he leaned down and kissed her!

She should have socked him! Or pushed him away! So why in the world was she leaning into the kiss, pursuing his lips even when he began to pull away? She wanted to taste the sweetness and firmness, tangle tongues with the brute, and run her hands up the back of his shirt to feel the way his taut muscles responded to her touch.

Maybe because she hadn't returned from answering the door, or because they'd heard Vaughn's gruff voice, Everett and Howard hurried to the front door. They hesitated to help, as if they'd seen Jillian and Vaughn kissing and thought they shouldn't interfere.

Her whole body was already way too hot, and now she felt as if she would erupt into flames!

"Help me before this annoying wolf crashes onto the

porch," Jillian warned. Yet until the men grabbed hold of him, she wasn't releasing her death hold on the aggravatingly hot SEAL wolf, even though she was conflicted about whether he really needed anyone's assistance.

Chapter 4

EVERETT AND HOWARD RUSHED TO HELP VAUGHN inside the guest house as Jillian quickly released her hold on him. She wanted to order them to take the wolf straight back to the clinic. Chain him to the bed even.

"The she-wolf was doing all right on her own." Vaughn looked amused. "She could have handled me. Further."

"Hell, you're supposed to be sleeping so your body has time to heal." Everett sounded surprised, amused, and impressed, though he glanced at Jillian. She couldn't believe how embarrassed she was, that she had fallen for the wolf's charms, despite still being angry with him over her brother.

But Everett's being impressed about Vaughn leaving the hospital so soon after he'd been shot? Had to be a macho guy thing. If someone had shot her, she'd be taking it easy for as long as the doctor said she needed to.

"Have you ever had a prolonged stay in a clinic or hospital?" Vaughn asked Everett.

"A time or two," Everett said.

"Well, then you know that sleep isn't part of the medical regimen."

Now Vaughn sounded like her brother when *he* wouldn't stay at the clinic longer than he had to.

As soon as they reached the dining room, Vaughn's gaze latched on to the chicken. He took a seat at the head of the table as if that was his place and he expected someone to feed him.

Jillian knew the man was going to be impossible to work with. "Do you need to be hand-fed?"

She swore Vaughn gave her a glimmer of a smile, his lips curving up so slightly that she wasn't sure if she'd imagined it or he really had smiled.

"Howard can do the job," she said, in case Vaughn thought *she* was going to spoon-feed him. After what had just happened between them, she wasn't about to give him the idea that she was interested in taking any of this further.

Demetria got a plate and served him potato salad and a couple of chicken legs. "Everett's right. You can't be running around like this."

Jillian frowned. "You shouldn't be running around half naked either."

Vaughn gave her a dark smile.

She swore she was blushing to the roots of her hair.

"I couldn't find my jacket among the clothes someone left for me at the clinic. Besides, I couldn't button my shirt."

Jillian poured him a glass of water, then refilled everyone else's glasses too so she didn't seem to be catering to Mr. Macho Wolf. She gave herself extra ice so she could cool down. "You mean no one on the hospital staff would give you a hand?"

"I didn't want to bother anyone. Besides, I'm not going anywhere else...*tonight*. I thought you said you were saving a room here for me." Vaughn began to eat a chicken leg. "You can't grill chicken outside and then expect me to smell it and ignore it." Then he frowned. "Why would you be grilling chicken outside?"

"Covered patio. Howard and I felt like grilling it," Everett said.

"You were supposed to be sleeping soundly," Jillian said. Irritated with Vaughn, she suspected he'd know now if she left on her own tomorrow to look for her brother.

"Was that *your* idea?" Vaughn lifted a dark brow. "The sleepy-time drugs, I mean. You're probably disappointed they only worked for a couple of hours."

"I imagine it was Dr. Wilders's idea, but I whole-heartedly agree with him. If he had thought to ask me, I would have told him it would be a good idea to knock you out for the rest of the week." Jillian grabbed another chicken leg. "So you could heal up properly," she clarified.

The jaguars were all smiling.

"So what have you learned?" Vaughn asked Everett.

"Demetria, Howard, and I have been trying to locate the jaguar who was shot. As a shifter, he would heal faster, and if he hadn't been hit anywhere too vital, he could have made it to somewhere safe and holed up until he was fine. Once he hit the creek, we couldn't locate any sign of him. No scent, no tracks left behind. He must have allowed the stream to carry him for a couple miles or more. We did find pugmarks leading to the creek. We didn't smell his scent anywhere, which means he was using hunter's spray."

"So then he was up to no good. No one saw a wounded jaguar or a wounded, naked man, I take it," Vaughn said.

"No. We canvased the area south of there, asking if anyone had witnessed someone who had been injured, gunshot wound. No one had seen anything," Demetria said. "But we did find shell casings."

"Good. So if we can find the gun that fired them and the cat that was wounded, we'll get somewhere," Vaughn said. "What was the time frame for this? A long time before Douglas was attacked?"

"Four days ago," Demetria said.

"So unless he was wounded too badly, the jaguar could be moving around like he'd never been injured. Meaning, he could have been the one I saw in the woods."

Jillian was eating another piece of chicken when Vaughn suddenly leaned back in his chair and studied her. "So…what have you been doing all this time while the jaguars have been off questioning everyone? Searching for the injured jaguar like you should have been doing?"

She should have guessed he'd ask. "Well, you'll probably be surprised to hear it, but I've been searching for my brother after you terrorized him half to death."

"*And?* Did you locate him? Then again, you probably wouldn't tell me if you had."

"Nope, I didn't locate him. I'd tell you if I had so you'd get off his back once you heard his explanation for why he ran when he saw you at Douglas's cabin. He was supposed to meet Douglas, his friend, so him being there after Douglas was injured isn't a surprise."

Vaughn watched her for a moment longer, then nodded. "I need to return to my cabin and get my bags and my Land Rover." He grabbed another chicken leg.

"It's already done." Demetria lifted her glass of water. "The Land Rover's parked out back. Your bags were put in your room, in case you agreed to work with us. If you hadn't wanted to, your vehicle would be here and you could just pack up and return to your cabin."

"Now why would I want to do that? When I think my best chance at getting to Miles is through his sister." Vaughn leveled a dark look in Jillian's direction.

She had been afraid of that. "How did you know about my blood type?" If Jillian was going to work with Vaughn, she wanted to know if he'd been investigating her and her brother all along for some reason.

"B positive? Lucky guess." Vaughn scooped up some more potato salad. "This is really good. Did you make it?"

Jillian said, "The recipe is Demetria's."

"But she and I made it," Demetria said. "And thanks."

"So you didn't really know my blood type?" Jillian pushed.

"How would I know something like that?" Then Vaughn smiled. "What? You think I've been investigating you? Well, I'll put your concern to rest. No, I haven't. I didn't know the name of the wolf I was chasing. I guess I should be grateful for our fortuitous meeting this time— when my shoulder doesn't hurt so much. Where would your brother have gone? To your place? Your parents'? That's usually where a wolf on the run ends up. Hiding out with family. Or in his sister's case, using her to protect him from the good guy—that's me—by shooting him."

"Ha!" Jillian got a call on her cell and saw it was Leidolf. She quickly answered her phone. "Yes, Leidolf?" She thought maybe he had some breaking news.

"If Vaughn isn't there…"

She immediately turned her attention to Vaughn. She couldn't believe he had left the clinic without permission. She didn't know why his action surprised her. No wonder no one had helped him to button his shirt!

"...we have a runaway patient on our hands," Leidolf said. "The nurse had unstrapped him so he could use the bathroom. When she returned later to check on him, he was gone."

Then again, Jillian could believe it, as hardheaded and strong-willed as Vaughn seemed to be. Now that she thought about it, she hadn't heard any vehicle dropping him off, even though it was a half-mile hike from the clinic. For an uninjured shifter, no problem. But in his condition?

She frowned at Vaughn. "He's here. I thought he had gotten permission from the doctor. We should have figured he hadn't." She wondered how Vaughn had known to come there if he had sneaked out of the clinic and hadn't asked anyone where the guest house was. Unless he'd asked someone earlier.

"No harm done as long as he's feeling all right," Leidolf said. "And it's understandable."

She eyed Vaughn and the stack of chicken bones on his plate. "By the way he's chowing down, I'd say he's feeling okay."

"Good. If you need Dr. Wilders, just give him a call."

"Will do. Thanks and good night."

"'Night."

Jillian pocketed her phone and leaned back in her chair, eyeing Vaughn with annoyance. She was still wondering if she could slip away really early tomorrow morning to try to find her brother. She assumed that by tomorrow, Miles would return to their cabin, if for nothing more than to get his bags and car and take off. She hoped he didn't.

When she'd left Vaughn at the clinic and the jaguars

had gone to speak to Douglas if he regained consciousness, she'd returned to their cabin to see if her brother
was there. He hadn't been for some hours. His phone
was still in his bedroom, his car still parked out front—
though she wasn't telling Vaughn that—so she assumed
Miles was still running as a wolf. "You walked clear
across the ranch from the clinic to the guest house, and
you didn't get permission to leave there?"

"I left about an hour ago, and nobody's even missed
me until now. Right?" Vaughn shrugged with his good
shoulder.

"How did you even know to come to the ranch
house?" Jillian asked. Maybe he really *was* good at
tracking people.

"I smelled the chicken."

Everett and Howard laughed. Demetria smiled. Jillian
rolled her eyes.

"I opened the clinic window to smell the breeze, and
a blast of the aroma of grilling chicken hit me. What was
I supposed to do? Eat that lame hospital food?"

"What in the world were you doing opening a window
in the first place?" Jillian asked.

"I don't like the antiseptic smell of a hospital. Do you?"

No, she didn't, but she wouldn't have left the bed
if she'd been wounded. "So you didn't even know we
were the ones cooking the chicken?" Jillian couldn't
believe he'd barge in on someone else in the wolf pack.

"Not at first. I figured no one would mind if I joined
a wolf family for dinner after what I've been through...
shot by another wolf for no good reason."

"You were shot for a very good reason," Jillian said.

The jaguars smiled.

"I smelled everyone's scents on the front porch, so I knew I was at the right house. And I had an open invite to stay here."

Demetria and Howard started clearing away the dishes. "You sure you don't want to stick with Everett and me when we do our investigation, Howard?" Demetria asked.

Howard chuckled darkly. "I like to go where the conflict is."

Chapter 5

After dinner, Jillian and Howard cleaned up the kitchen, while Demetria fixed them all cups of decaf coffee. "We have the evidence Leidolf's police officers took from the cabin. You can go through the boxes over there." She motioned to the living room.

Vaughn appeared ready to leave his chair to check it out.

Jillian still thought he should be in bed under the doctor's care. She did admire him for wanting to investigate what was going on right away. But the rest of them would continue to look into it until he could recuperate a bit.

"Did you find anything that might help?" Vaughn asked, settling back down to drink his coffee.

"Clothes belonging to Douglas, toiletries, food he'd purchased from a grocery store about half an hour from the cabin. His phone. We checked the tons of photos he had, but we'll need you to look at them to identify those with your pack members. We didn't see a whole lot of texting, and nothing really suspicious. There were a few photos of Miles and some of you, Vaughn, with friends."

Instantly, Jillian was interested in Douglas's phone. What if the texts led to whoever had attacked Douglas? What if the person who shot her brother was in one of the pictures? Then, of course, she was curious about pictures of Vaughn with friends.

"There were also brochures on hiking, a book on shipwrecks, and trash...mostly wrappers from food, used paper towels, and so on."

"Receipts?" Vaughn asked.

"For the groceries and gas," Demetria said. "We're going to retire for the night and get an early start on it tomorrow morning."

"Sounds like a plan to me. 'Night, all." Everett took Demetria's hand, kissed her, and headed down the hall with her to the master bedroom.

Jillian handed Vaughn some gloves to wear while searching through the evidence. He put them on and moved to the living room to begin going through the boxes of stuff.

"Are you okay? You probably need to rest more." Jillian brought her laptop into the room.

"Yeah. But if I don't do this tonight, I'll keep thinking about it and won't get any sleep. You don't have to stay with me."

Howard was still in the kitchen rummaging around like he hadn't gotten enough to eat.

"You're right. I don't. But you might see something we missed, and I want to know about it." In truth, she wanted to be there in case Vaughn started to feel poorly or wanted to bounce any ideas off her. She'd noticed that after eating dinner, he had more color in his cheeks. She hoped he'd be all right staying with them when she still thought he should be in bed at the clinic.

They took a seat on the couch, and Vaughn began sifting through the stuff that Leidolf's men had recovered from Douglas's cabin.

Glad Vaughn hadn't grabbed Douglas's phone yet, Jillian set her laptop on the coffee table, then lifted the cell phone off the table and flipped through the text messages. Demetria was right. Douglas hadn't texted a lot. A few times to the pack leaders, a couple to Miles recently about getting together, but what caught her eye were a few to Vaughn about Vaughn's girlfriend.

"So how hot and heavy were things with your girl-friend?" Jillian only asked because Vaughn had kissed her like there wasn't anyone else in his life.

Vaughn looked up from examining Douglas's jacket and pants pockets and frowned. "What? Let me see."

She wasn't going to give up the phone for anything. Instead, she read out loud, "'How are things going with Cindy? Can you handle a woman who's also going to be a SEAL?'"

Jillian looked up at Vaughn. He wasn't smiling. "A SEAL? Really?" She knew the U.S. Navy was begin-ning to train women SEALs, but a female wolf who was a SEAL? Besides, Vaughn wasn't in the service any longer.

"When was that dated?" Vaughn went back to sorting things as if the message wasn't the least bit important. "And how is that relevant to the case we're looking into?"

"You know that in this business, we can't ever dis-count anything. This could be completely relevant to the case." She glanced at the date. "It's dated a month ago."

"Okay, so see? A month ago, and no more mention of Cindy. The fact he had to ask meant nothing came of it."

"Why not?"

Vaughn looked up at her again and gave her a glim-mer of a smile.

She shrugged. "She was looking for more of a commitment, but you weren't?"

"She is one of the first SEAL women in training, so that's all she's concentrating on. We're friends, but not even close friends. She's a pack member, heard me talking about SEAL missions, ones I could mention, and she got interested in the program once they opened it to women. And for your information, she has taken an interest in some guy in her class. Now how can that possibly relate to this case?"

Satisfied, Jillian smiled and continued to look at text messages. "The last one he got was from you. The last one he sent was to you."

"Right. He was concerned when a friend hadn't gotten ahold of him. He knows I look into missing person cases and had just finished one in southern Oregon. So I wasn't all that far away. I texted him back to tell him I was coming and learn more about what was going on. He didn't respond. I was headed up there anyway, so I kept driving, then got another text about forty-five minutes later saying that his friend had gotten in touch with him and it was a case of miscommunication. By then, I was so close that I figured I'd just drop by and visit for a bit. But when I texted to tell him I was coming anyway, no response again."

"Was Miles the friend he was looking to see? Since he didn't say in the text?"

"Did he text Miles? Is that how he got ahold of him?" Vaughn asked.

"No. There was no text in between the one he sent you and then the one in which he said he'd talked to the friend. Either he reached him by phone, or the friend arrived to see him."

"Hell, then the so-called friend could have been the person who tore into him."

"And my brother, another friend, showed up later."

"Could be. Before I arrived, I wondered if I should let Douglas know I was almost there."

"Or slip in like a wolf in case there was trouble brewing," Jillian said. "So which approach did you use? *Forget it*. I already know. You didn't let him know you were coming. You're a SEAL wolf after all."

"Exactly. When I arrived, I didn't see any vehicles. So had Douglas run out? The front door was standing wide open, and I immediately grew alarmed. Nothing felt right. I smelled Douglas's blood. I had my gun out, but I hadn't expected to see a bloodied wolf standing next to the bloodied floor."

"The door was closed when we left. Miles would have used the wolf door. Wait, you had your gun out and you didn't just shoot Miles?"

"Someone must have opened the door." Vaughn hadn't planned to tell anyone the next part of the story. "As for shooting Miles, do you think I'd shoot a person for just standing there? Despite what it looked like?"

Appearing as though she didn't believe him, she narrowed her eyes at him.

"Okay, he jumped on me." Vaughn really hadn't wanted to tell her that her brother had actually knocked him down and taken off. So startled to see a wolf there in the first place, he hadn't been prepared for the wolf's lunge. The wolf was heavy and tall while standing on his hind legs, so his front paws had slammed against Vaughn's shoulders, and he'd gone down, losing his gun and cursing at the same time.

Jillian's lips parted. Then she frowned again. "And you didn't shoot him?"

Vaughn took a drink of his coffee. He wasn't going to tell her he'd lost his blasted gun under the couch and had to retrieve it! But also, when Miles didn't bite him, Vaughn figured he'd had issues with Douglas, not with him.

She smiled. "He knocked you down! Well, not that I'm glad about it, except that you couldn't shoot him."

"Yeah, you are." Vaughn smiled. He really liked her. "Can you get ahold of your brother?"

"Most likely, he's still running as a wolf." She gave Vaughn an annoyed look, as if he should know that already.

"Where would he be headed? How would you know where to find him?"

"We were staying at a cabin, and that's where some of his stuff is. His car too. I've been looking into…" Jillian paused.

Vaughn knew that look on her face. She hadn't meant to tell him whatever she had been about to say.

"Looking into Miles's business here?"

"Okay, listen. My brother was shot a week ago. He'd been staying at the cabin, but was out on a run. He made it back to the cabin and called me. I was already on my way down to visit with him and would have been there earlier, but I was still wrapping up a couple of cases. I called Leidolf and asked him to get some people out to the cabin to take Miles to the ranch. Dr. Wilders took care of him.

"After a couple days of recuperating, and against my better judgment, Miles wanted to stay at the cabin again, like he'd planned. He said a friend had texted him that he was coming to the area and wanted to get together with him. That Douglas had rented the same cabin he usually did when they came out here."

"Douglas Wendish."

"Yes."

"So you're looking for the person who shot Miles too."

"Yes."

"Do you think that's connected with Douglas's attack?" Vaughn leaned against the couch, feeling weary, but he wanted to discuss this tonight so he could begin to process it.

"Maybe not. But what if it is? Right after the shooting, I asked Miles what he'd been doing...job-wise, girlfriend-wise, if he'd run into anyone who had a vendetta against him. Nothing seemed to be relevant. He thought it was just a random hunter. Not anyone out to get him. I didn't know about Douglas's injury until after Miles left our cabin, or I would have questioned him more."

Vaughn couldn't see the connection considering the methods used to attempt to kill people—shooting, biting. But the fact that both Miles and Douglas had been targeted still made him suspicious. "Okay, so we have one animal attack. And the shooting of a jaguar and then a wolf, your brother. Did you find the shell casings for when Miles was shot?"

"No. I spent hours going over the area. So did Leidolf's men. Either we missed the right area, or whoever did it was extra careful and picked them up. But Dr. Wilders did remove the round."

"In the other case, Leidolf's men have the shell

casings. Which could mean a number of things. He's not the same shooter. He's the same shooter and was too busy trying to avoid getting caught on Leidolf's land, so he left the casings behind. In Miles's case, he didn't have to worry, because no one was looking for him, so he had more time to grab any evidence."

"True."

Vaughn hadn't found anything in the rest of the box. He glanced over to see what Jillian was doing. She was looking meticulously through the tons of photos.

His shoulder hurting again, Vaughn settled back against the couch. "How did you end up at Douglas's cabin and find him like that?"

"Miles said he was going to meet Douglas at the cabin near us. He told me they usually share a cabin when they get together, but Douglas couldn't get away from work, so Miles asked if I was free, and invited me to take off and visit with him instead. Then Douglas managed to get away and rented his own cabin. I hadn't planned to stay so the guys could visit, but with all the attacks, I decided to help investigate. I didn't know Miles was planning on going over to Douglas's place as a wolf. I couldn't get ahold of him, and I needed to tell him I was going to be working with the jaguar shifter team so he wouldn't worry about me not being at the cabin with any regularity. When I discovered Douglas had been attacked and was bleeding badly, I asked if he knew who attacked him, but he was pretty out of it. He shook his head. I wasn't able to get a description of what the shifter looked like, if he could have even offered one, before the EMTs arrived and sedated him.

"My brother hadn't been to Douglas's cabin yet. I

would have smelled his scent. I went to the clinic again to see if Douglas could tell us anything about who had bitten him, but the doctor had given him drugs to induce a coma. While Leidolf's police officers were gathering evidence at the cabin, I returned to Miles's and my cabin to look for him. He must have ended up at Douglas's place right before you arrived."

"But you'd actually met up with the jaguar agents beforehand?"

"Yeah. I was staying with Miles and investigating what had happened to him when Leidolf asked me to help some jaguar shifters on a case they were working as a favor to him. He said he'd never had this much trouble in the area, and he hoped I could help. When I arrived there, I had lunch with the jaguar shifters, and we talked about what was going on with their kind, and I told them what had happened with Miles.

"At the time, none of us believed the jaguar case and Miles's case were connected. Except that they were both shootings. And the locations are only about a half hour apart, both on Leidolf's property. I wanted to learn if Miles thought there might be a connection we couldn't see. When I was at our cabin, I heard Miles howl for help. Immediately, I worried that the person who shot him was after him again. Instead, I saw a wolf chasing him."

"The rest I know."

She scooted over closer to Vaughn, and he raised his brows. She wasn't getting friendly. She touched his forehead, checking to make sure he wasn't running a fever. He looked tired, and as much as she'd love to continue this discussion, she knew he should be in bed.

"You were chasing my brother with a hunter's need to take down his prey. I'm sure if the roles were reversed, you would have reacted in the same way."

"If I had seen a female wolf chasing a bigger male?" He smiled.

Thankfully, he had no fever. She pulled her hand away. "A wolf chasing your brother, if you had one."

"A she-wolf chasing my brother, Brock? He's a Navy SEAL wolf like me, but a total pain in the butt. I would have laughed and encouraged you."

"Okay, so it's not the same with you and your brother. My brother *isn't* a SEAL. He's always getting himself into..." She abruptly stopped speaking and began looking through Douglas's huge photo album on his cell again.

"Trouble?"

She didn't say, not when it could put her brother in a bad light. Even the fact he had been shot could have, if Vaughn thought her brother was up to no good and someone shot him for it.

"Bad trouble, or just stupid kinds of stuff?" Vaughn asked.

"He's a good guy, all right? He just..." She couldn't help thinking of all the dumb things he'd pulled over the years.

—⁓—

Vaughn reached over, lifted Jillian's chin, turned her head gently so he could see her eyes, and released her. Her soft-green eyes were misty with tears, and he felt like she'd sucker punched him. He hoped that her reaction didn't mean her brother was really up to bad stuff.

He went for a little lighthearted humor. "Why do you think my brother and I went into the navy? So they'd knock some sense into us."

She smiled a little at that, and he was glad he seemed to have cheered her up a bit.

"Not anything really bad, though enough to be a problem for our kind," she admitted.

"Okay, so like *what*, for instance?"

"Riding a snowmobile when the rental place was closed for the night."

"So breaking and entering, and stealing a snowmobile."

"He returned it filled with gas, and the owner never knew about it."

"But he told you about it?"

"Not exactly. I needed to find him and discovered him returning the snowmobile."

"Okay, been there, done that."

Jillian raised her brows at him.

"I told you why my brother and I joined the navy. What else has he done?"

She let out her breath and set the phone on the coffee table. "He borrowed a friend's sled, with his permission this time, to run in a race…with his friends pulling the sled as wolves. He pretended they were part husky."

Vaughn laughed. He could just imagine doing something that dumb.

"Thankfully, my father caught up with him and stopped him before he showed up at the race to participate. Can you imagine what would have happened? The judge and others might have suspected they were all wolves, and then how could Miles have explained that?"

"True." Vaughn was still smiling.

Jillian looked furious with him. "What if he'd been caught?"

"He wasn't."

"Right. But he could have been."

"Anything worse than that?" Vaughn asked, getting serious again.

"What's worse than that? What if they had taken the wolves away from him and put them in a wolf reserve?"

"Okay, agreed."

"Nothing worse than that. Just the same old stuff. One time, he and some of his friends were painting wolves on a freight boxcar. A train employee tried to arrest them, but they got away. I mean, painting graffiti on private property is illegal! It doesn't matter that some people get away with it."

"Were the wolves well-painted?" Vaughn thought anything that pictured wolves was a good thing. However, from the look of disbelief on Jillian's face, she didn't agree.

"It doesn't matter!"

It did to Vaughn. If they couldn't paint wolves well, they had no business doing it.

"Okay, then he and his friends taped wolf doors shut one year. Talk about a lot of pissed-off wolves."

Vaughn tried to hide a smile on that one. "Anything more recent?"

"He just never stays with a job very long."

"All right. I'll give your brother a chance to explain himself. We just need to get in touch with him."

"Okay."

He didn't think Jillian believed he felt her brother was blameless, as far as the attack went. To Vaughn's thinking, he wasn't. Anything could lead a man to fight someone, if he was pushed hard enough.

"I'm calling it a night." Howard was finishing up an apple in the kitchen. Vaughn had forgotten he was in there. Howard had his phone in hand, and Vaughn wondered if he'd been catching up on emails.

Looking exhausted herself, Jillian sighed, closed her laptop, and set Douglas's phone on the table. "Come on, Vaughn. Let's get some sleep. We can start this again tomorrow."

"All right. Are you worried about me?" Vaughn pulled off the gloves and set them on the coffee table, then stood up from the couch, took her hand, and pulled her up.

"No. I figure you're too cantankerous to die on us tonight. Though if you'd like some more of that sleepy-time juice to help you rest, I'll drive you back to the clinic."

"Having no one disturb my sleep all evening will be the best thing for me. If *you* want to stay with me for the night to ensure I don't run a fever or anything, I wouldn't object. *Too* strenuously."

Howard chuckled.

"I bet not. Howard can stay with you if *you're* worried." Jillian headed for the hallway to the bedrooms.

Vaughn laughed. "It wouldn't be the same."

"Your room is next to mine and across the hall from Howard's." Jillian walked down the hall toward the three bedrooms. "If anyone needs to use the bathroom, go ahead. I want to take a shower after that."

"Does putting the toilet seat down go for him too?" Vaughn jerked his thumb in Howard's direction.

"I wasn't born in no barn." Howard smirked.

"Just checking, because I wouldn't want Jillian to accuse the wrong man if the seat is left up."

She smiled and walked into her bedroom and closed the door.

"Hey, for what it's worth, welcome to the team," Howard said. "I never thought I'd be saying that to a couple of wolves."

"I usually work alone in my PI business, though on the SEAL team, I was one hundred percent there for the guys. I've definitely never worked with jaguars before. As long as we get our man, or men, or"—Vaughn paused—"woman, we're good."

"Works for me."

Vaughn checked out his room. His bags were sitting neatly on the floor next to the wall. A queen-size bed, a dresser, two end tables, a small writing desk, and a chair furnished the room. Huge chess pieces sat on shelves on one wall, and the decor was all black and white with touches of red. A picture of a black wolf and a white wolf standing in a field of red poppies took center stage on one of the walls.

He appreciated that they'd moved him in as if he was already part of the team, and he was glad to be working with them too.

Howard closed his bedroom door, and Vaughn grabbed his toiletry bag to brush his teeth and take care of any other business he needed to. He wondered how working with the she-wolf would turn out when he finally caught up with her brother. If the guy hadn't been involved in the attack on Douglas, why had he run?

Vaughn had to quit thinking about it and go to bed

and get some rest. Tomorrow, after they checked on Douglas, he was planning to get on the road again and head to Jillian's cabin. He retired to his room and took off all his clothes, then climbed into bed. He closed his eyes, but listened to Howard use the bathroom next, then shut his door across the hall. Then Vaughn heard the shower running, and the thought of Jillian washing up ran through his mind.

Hell, in no way did he want to think of her naked in the shower, the water running down every inch of her toned skin. He still couldn't believe she'd grabbed him in the front doorway. He'd just leaned his hand against the doorjamb, feeling a little unsteady on his feet but nowhere near ready to collapse at any moment.

When she'd thrown her arms around him, he'd thought for a second she meant to tell him how sorry she was that she had wounded him, and was giving him a big hug for it. She was all soft curves and sweet-scented female wolf. Then he realized she had been worried he was going to drop to the floor in a dead faint. As if the petite wolf could have kept him off the floor!

He loved her sexy fragrance—she-wolf and the soft scent of jasmine—still clinging to his chest. He thought again about the Kitty Cat Club, and about how much he had wished she'd been there the second night he, Douglas, and his brother had gone. He hadn't even taken a date, hoping he could ask the dark-haired beauty to dance, even if the muscled guy had brought her there again. Though she'd reminded him of a wolf—wishful thinking probably on his part—he hadn't believed she truly was one. Just another big-time, cat-loving human.

Trying to get his mind off her, again, Vaughn turned on his side. A dull ache throbbed in his shoulder. He rolled over again onto his back. He always slept on his stomach. At this rate, he'd never get to sleep. After some time, he heard Jillian leave the bathroom, enter her bedroom, and shut the door.

He let out his breath and stared at the ceiling. Maybe they had some chocolate in the kitchen. That would make him feel better. He got up, nearly killed his shoulder trying to pull on a pair of black boxer briefs—which he wouldn't have bothered with if there wasn't a houseful of people—and left the bedroom. The place was quiet except for the ticking of a grandfather clock in the living room and the hum of the refrigerator in the kitchen.

Vaughn didn't want to disturb anyone, so he made his way down the hall as quietly as he could. When he reached the kitchen, he looked in all the pantries. No chocolate. What was the chance that they would have ice cream in the freezer on a chilly Oregon night like this?

He opened the freezer and saw a box of his favorite toffee chocolate ice-cream bars, as if they knew what he liked and had gotten them for him. He pulled the box out and felt how empty it was, but smiled to see there was still one left. The night was looking up. He shut the freezer door, pulled out the ice-cream bar, and tossed the box into the trash. In seventh heaven, he tore off the wrapper and began to eat the ice cream. He was surprised anyone else ate ice cream in the winter like he did. No one else in his family would.

"What are you doing?" a very irate she-wolf asked, hands on her hips and frowning furiously at him.

He dropped his jaw in surprise, not having heard

Jillian walk into the kitchen. He wasn't easily startled like that. He guessed he'd been so busy enjoying the ice-cream bar that he hadn't heard her. Then he considered her bedroom attire. Fitted fleece yoga pants and a top, purple with pink teddy bears. Somehow, he couldn't see her—after she'd shot him—as a pink-and-purple teddy bear person.

She was still scowling, and he didn't think it was because he woke her.

"Don't tell me you were saving this one for yourself." He offered the half-eaten ice-cream bar to her.

"Those were *all* mine."

"I only ate half of this one. I don't mind sharing. I figured any of the food here was for all of us." He had no problem with buying groceries for the team as soon as he had a chance.

"All of it is, except for the toffee bars."

"They're your favorite too, huh? I knew you couldn't be all bad. Next box is on me. I still want that steak though."

She turned around and headed back down the hall. He followed after her, finishing the ice-cream bar. "I couldn't sleep. What can I say? I figured a little chocolate would help."

She cast Vaughn a concerned look. "Are you in pain?"

"Yeah."

"Then you should have stayed at the clinic."

"And miss out on all that grilled chicken, potato salad, and the last of the ice-cream bars?"

"I thought I was the only one who ate ice cream in the winter. Until I brought them out at lunchtime when I ate with the jaguars."

"Hell, any time is a good time for ice cream. Sorry for eating your last one," he said seriously.

She let out her breath. "You owe me a box. And…I'll share."

"And the steak?"

"Demetria's buying them. As much as Everett likes to cook on the grill, I imagine he'll be doing them right."

"Okay, you're off the hook."

"You're not, as far as my brother goes."

"We'll see what he says about the whole situation." Vaughn still didn't trust that her brother wasn't in on any of this. As far as he was concerned, if she tried to stop him from learning the truth, she was Miles's accomplice. "Hey, the hug you gave me in greeting when I first arrived here was first rate. What about a good-night kiss?"

That got one furious look from the sexy she-wolf before she closed the door to her bedroom.

Not that he should kiss her, or want to kiss her a second time, but he figured it would take the edge off the way his shoulder was beginning to hurt like a son-of-a-gun again—like kissing her had the first time. He sure didn't know why he was attracted to the woman when he knew she would rather kill him than give up her brother for questioning.

She was a challenge. That was it. He loved a woman who challenged him. Not too many could.

Chapter 6

EARLY THE NEXT AFTERNOON, VAUGHN HEARD SOME-one clanking around in the kitchen, and he hurried to get dressed, astounded it was so late. He wouldn't admit to anyone that he must have needed the sleep though.

When he walked into the kitchen, he was surprised to see only Jillian. "Where are the others?" He couldn't believe everyone else was still sleeping.

She looked refreshed, wearing blue jeans, a blue sweater, and hiking boots, her dark hair twisted high on her head. She tossed some butter into a frying pan, then brought out some eggs. "Demetria, Everett, and Howard already left to follow up on some leads. I'm fixing omelets for brunch."

"Looks like we slept in a bit. Were we the only ones?" He was normally such a light sleeper that any-thing would wake him. He never slept in, no matter how late he went to bed. He guessed after the trauma to his shoulder, he'd slept like the dead once he'd settled down.

"Not me. I've been up for hours. Are omelets okay?"

"Yeah, sure, thanks." He drew close and looked at the ingredients she'd diced up: ham, cheese, bell peppers— red, green, and yellow. He breathed in the freshly brewed coffee and the food, but mostly the she-wolf. "All of it looks good to me." He didn't mean just the food. "Want some toast?"

"Yeah, that would be great. Bread is over there. Toaster is in the pantry over there."

"Did you go looking for your brother?" He pulled out the toaster and plugged it in, then added four slices of bread and started it.

"Yes, but I didn't find him."

"Why didn't you wake me so I could come along for the ride?"

"Are you serious? You needed the extra sleep after raiding the freezer so late last night."

"And you needed to see your brother alone." Amused she didn't touch on his need for sleep because of his injury, Vaughn poured himself a cup of coffee. "While I was still sacked out, why didn't you go with the others to do more investigating after you returned from looking for Miles?"

"It's better if we look into this as a team." After she finished cooking the omelets, she served them while Vaughn pulled the toast out of the toaster.

"You mean you didn't want to leave me alone in case I had it in mind to go after your brother again."

"The thought did occur to me. Actually, the doctor said since you'd left the clinic earlier than he'd planned, someone had to stay with you to ensure you didn't start to run a fever. Demetria remained here while I looked for Miles. Howard and Everett went out to look for any more clues about the injured jaguar. When I returned, Demetria and I drew straws to see who would stay with you. You can see I lost."

He laughed. "I bet you planned it that way." He set out the plate of toast and returned for butter and peach jelly from the fridge. "Why would your brother have been in Douglas's cabin? As a wolf?"

"I told you. Douglas was a friend, and Miles went to visit him. I take it that they planned to run as wolves. Do you know for certain that the blood on my brother was Douglas's?"

Vaughn buttered his toast and slathered on the peach jelly. "No, I don't know for sure. It seemed obvious at the time. No one else was there. And he ran." Though the more Vaughn got to know Jillian, the more he wished her brother wasn't in the middle of this.

She buttered her toast. "You're forgetting one very important point. My brother didn't even arrive until after Douglas was hurt and Leidolf's men had moved him to the clinic."

"So why did Miles run?"

Jillian narrowed her eyes at him. "Are you joking? One look at you—all growly—and he probably presumed you'd think the worst of him and kill him without asking questions. Maybe he even thought you were Douglas's attacker because you showed up so unexpectedly."

Finished with brunch, she grabbed her plate and took it into the kitchen.

Vaughn finished his eggs in a hurry and joined her. "So what about the gap between the time Miles was supposed to see Douglas and when he actually arrived at the cabin and I found him there?"

She rinsed off their dishes and stuck them in the dishwasher. "I have no idea."

"Girlfriend?"

Jillian shook her head. "I wouldn't think so. I'm sure he would have told me if he was seeing someone so I'd stay away from the cabin while he was *busy*. He's not courting a she-wolf right now, so he might have met a human while he was here. But if he was supposed to be seeing Douglas, I wouldn't think he would forget his mission. He may have done some dumb things in the past, but he's always prompt about appointments. Early even.

"And he's completely loyal to his friends, almost to a fault. Even when they don't deserve it. Which is to say he's had some friends who used him because of his agreeable nature. That doesn't mean he doesn't get mad." She paused, wishing she hadn't made the comment. As soon as she did, Vaughn appeared a little too interested in the information. "Are you ready to check on Douglas? And then we can go to my cabin?"

"Yeah, sure."

They grabbed their jackets and headed over to the clinic.

"What does your brother do, besides get himself into trouble?"

"He's done everything from lawn service to helping me find people I need to talk to. He likes that the best."

"Is he good at it?"

"Yeah, he's really good at it. I keep telling him he needs to work with me on a regular basis, but he says he needs more freedom to do what he wants to do."

"What about your parents?"

"They own a rock-climbing gym in Portland, Oregon. Miles doesn't work well with Dad. After they had the place built, Miles worked with him for a couple of years, but then he said Dad micromanaged too much, and Miles took off."

"Do you get along with your dad?"

"No. You know the micromanaging thing? Same thing for me. For example, he's so bad about it that when

I'd clean a frying pan after fixing dinner, he would come over and ensure I made certain it was spotless. Handing the frying pan over to him to clean, I would tell him if I couldn't do a good enough job, he was welcome to clean it. My work, my way. He didn't fall for it. I joined the army, and after my obligation was up, I began working as a PI. Pays well sometimes. Sometimes not. I get some interesting cases. What about you?"

"Same here. If we have any spare time, we'll have to swap stories." Vaughn added, "Did you see anything important in the photos Douglas took?"

"He had taken tons of them."

"And…?" The expression on her face said she was halfway amused about something, in a catty way. He wondered if they were pictures Douglas had caught of him up close and personal with other women. "Maybe I should ask if you saw anything relevant to the case."

She laughed. "You look good in swim trunks. The woman you were with didn't look half bad in her bikini, either. Was it Cindy?" She pulled up the picture on Douglas's phone and showed it to Vaughn as they walked into the clinic.

"He's in room three," said Sally, the redheaded nurse, who smiled brightly at them. "The jaguar agents are in there visiting with him."

"Good. Thanks." Vaughn looked at the photo of him wearing his blue board shorts, standing next to Brandy in her hot-pink bikini and super tan. They'd gone boating with Douglas on Folsom Lake, and the woman had actually been dating Douglas. He'd kept motioning to Vaughn to get closer to her so he could get them both in the picture, but see more of the boat too. When

Vaughn had offered to take a picture of the two of them, Douglas had declined, saying he wanted to capture his friends instead.

"Douglas's girlfriend. For a while."

Jillian looked skeptically at Vaughn when they reached Douglas's room and paused.

"Really. I think Douglas wanted to get more of the boat in the picture than the people."

"And the other?"

"What other?" He wasn't about to speculate, because he realized Douglas liked to take lots of pictures, and no telling what *other* one Jillian might have seen and was curious about. When a girl got interested in stuff like that, she was interested in the guy. Then he frowned. Would someone have pictures of her like that with lots of guy friends?

"The one with some big-haired girl that's smooching with you? You do look a little startled. Not sure if it was because she was kissing you, or because Douglas caught the two of you on camera."

Vaughn hadn't remembered that one. "Let me see which one you're talking about." When he saw Brock with the rodeo girl, he smiled with relief. "That's my brother."

Jillian eyed it closer, then Vaughn. "Okay, can't tell from the lighting in the bar. Could be a twin."

"It is a twin. My twin. He's darker haired, and you can't tell from the picture because of the darkness in the bar, but he's blue-eyed. Any other photos of interest?" He really hoped she hadn't found any others of him with women. "Relevant to the case?"

"Probably there are others." She smiled and walked into the room. "Not sure about being relevant to the case."

Everett greeted them. "Hope you got some good sleep."

"I did. Thanks."

"We've been talking away to Douglas about you and Jillian," Demetria said, smiling. "Something to cheer him up."

Great. What in the world had they said?

"Have you got Douglas's phone with you?" Howard asked. "I'd like to see some of those interesting shots."

Vaughn liked the jaguars. Doing something like this with them on a full-time basis hadn't been in his plans, but he'd rethink that notion if he had a wolf teammate like Jillian on the force.

Chapter 7

DOUGLAS WAS STILL IN A DRUG-INDUCED COMA. JILLIAN hated to see him that way and hoped they would take him off the drugs soon, but the doctor knew best, and if this helped Douglas to recover more quickly, they would have to be patient. She watched as Vaughn took his friend's hand and squeezed. "We need you back home. A lot of people are worried about you." He paused. "Including Miles Matthews." Vaughn's lips parted.

"What?" she whispered.

"I swore Douglas squeezed my hand slightly. But I could be mistaken."

She so hoped Douglas would be all right when they weaned him off the drugs. "I'm Miles's sister, Jillian Matthews," she said to Douglas. She hoped she could add another personal touch. "I'm the person who found you injured. I'm glad to meet you and hope we can talk soon. We need to know who did this to you." She squeezed his hand and kissed his forehead.

"We've told him who we are and why we're here." Demetria caressed Douglas's shoulder in a gentle way. "How we can't wait for him to join the conversation."

They talked about the beauty of the Oregon coastline and how they could see why he'd come here on vacation, and repeated how eager they were to really visit with him.

But then Vaughn recalled how Jillian had been at the

same club as them and wanted to mention it and the fact
that these jaguar agents were the first of their kind to
find out about wolf shifters. "Remember when our pack
leaders told us about three jaguar agents trying to return
an Arctic wolf pup to his family, and we learned jaguar
shifters exist? Well, these are the three jaguar agents
who made that happen. Remember when we went to the
rocking Clawed and Dangerous Kitty Cat Club in San
Diego? When we finally learned about the jaguar shifters, we all realized some of those cat-lover patrons had
to be genuine jaguar shifters. Well, Jillian was there that
night too…a wolf like us and just as confused."

"Wait, Douglas was there?" Jillian asked.

"Yeah. My twin brother, Brock, too."

"And dates," Jillian said. "Miles and I were there
together."

"And dates," Vaughn said.

She smiled. Then frowned. "Would Douglas have
taken photos? I didn't see any of you at the club."

"It was pretty dark. I remember him taking pictures.
They might not have turned out and he deleted them."

"Or they're so dark that I couldn't see anyone well in
the pictures and just bypassed them. I can upload them
to my laptop and check them out. I'll just use a program
to brighten the exposure on them."

"Sounds good," Vaughn said.

Though she swore he didn't sound like he was really
glad about it. Why not? Because of what else she might
see of him in photos? She smiled.

Then they left Douglas to rest with promises they'd
return.

Despite Vaughn's shoulder wound, he seemed to be

doing fine. Jillian was glad for that. She wasn't certain how Vaughn would feel if he had to run as a wolf and use his shoulder more though. He'd been favoring his right arm whenever he ate or did anything. He appeared to be left-handed, which was a good thing. Unless he had the notion to shoot her brother. She believed he still thought her brother could have attacked Douglas.

She thought she knew her brother better than that. But what if something had happened, and it had led to violence? What if her brother had been defending himself? Then again, an unarmed shifter in his human form was no match for a shifter in his wolf form. She was certain he hadn't been there before she got there though. He would have had to have worn hunter's spray, removed it, and returned. Then she realized she must have gotten there soon after the attack happened. The shifter had to have run off into the woods. There was only one gravel road to the cabin, and if anyone had been driving on it, he would have passed her.

"Were there any photos of Miles on Douglas's phone?" Vaughn asked Jillian as they left the clinic.

"Yeah, one of him with a curvaceous blond. Really snuggled up close. But maybe Douglas just wanted to get more of the boat in the picture and had them move closer together." She cocked a brow as she waited for Vaughn's response.

He just smiled.

"She danced with you too, as I recall."

Vaughn frowned at that. "I danced with several women that night."

"I know."

"I'm surprised you noticed."

"I doubt you really are."

He chuckled.

"Hey, what you did that night was really remarkable. Saving that dancer? I tried to get them to turn up the lights and turn off the music so you could concentrate better and see what you were doing."

"Thanks." He frowned. "I'm surprised they weren't sued. Maybe they compensated her for it."

"And you?" Jillian asked.

"Free drinks and food whenever I visit."

She shook her head. "That wouldn't have been enough."

"I did what anyone would have done, had they been trained for it."

"Still, that was amazing. I just couldn't believe it." She figured that he didn't know the truth, so she wasn't going to burst his heroic bubble.

"Thanks. I was just glad it had a good outcome. Any photos of Douglas?"

"No selfies. Just a couple of group shots that he was in. Maybe you can look at them and see if you recognize anyone who might be with your pack."

"I'll take a look at them," Howard said, eager to help.

She just bet he would.

"So what do you plan to do next?" Vaughn asked Everett and Demetria.

"We're going to take the receipts Douglas had for the grocery store and gas station, and learn if anyone remembers having seen him. We'll check if he was with anyone at the time," Demetria said. "What about you? Are you still going to look for Miles?"

"Yes, we're going to my cabin to see if my brother has returned." If he hadn't, Jillian figured she could at least check Miles's cell phone and see if he had any photos that might help them solve this whole business. But she sure hoped he was there, safe and sound.

"Yeah. We'll keep in touch. Miles might know something about what went down," Vaughn said.

Jillian couldn't believe Vaughn wasn't still saying her brother did it. What a change in attitude! She so appreciated him for it.

"Are you sure a wolf tore into Douglas?" Everett asked as they headed for their vehicles.

"You mean you think a jaguar shifter could possibly have done this?" Jillian was surprised that one of the jaguar shifters would suggest it. "Did Leidolf's doctor examine his wounds and determine the cause of the bite?"

"He'll be doing a further exam today," Demetria said. "Between taking care of ranching injuries, Vaughn's bullet wounds, and Douglas's condition, and delivering a couple of sets of twins, Dr. Wilders has been busy. The DNA samples from the bite wound should be available soon. He'll let all of us know his findings once he has them."

"Good," Vaughn said. "We'll have the attacker's DNA then."

"Agreed. Are you going with us or with them, Howard?" Everett asked.

"I'm going with them. I'm a badass Enforcer agent, if you didn't know that," Howard said to the wolves. "So if we've got to take someone down, I can come in real handy."

"You're not taking down my brother," Jillian warned.

Howard smiled at her.

"My Jeep or your Land Rover?" she asked, though

she glanced at Howard to see if he had a vehicle and wanted to drive.

"I don't have a vehicle here. I flew in and met up with Leidolf at the airport and have been investigating matters with Demetria and Everett since then. They picked up a rental Jeep."

"We can take my Land Rover, if you don't mind driving." Vaughn climbed into the passenger seat and handed her the keys. "I'd just filled the gas tank. If you'll give me Douglas's phone, I'll check out the pictures."

Since Vaughn didn't offer to drive, Jillian wondered if he must still be hurting. "Yeah, sure." She handed him the phone. "Oh, and I liked the shot of you where you were giving mouth-to-mouth resuscitation to another bathing beauty. I didn't know folks wore bikinis so much in Colorado. Unless that was your brother."

Howard chuckled.

"It gets hot in the summer," Vaughn said as he rolled through the photos.

Looking for that particular one? "Blue bikini, a blond, and you were in board shorts." She noted he didn't say the photo had to be his brother's this time. Maybe he didn't know that Douglas had taken it while Vaughn was kissing a woman on a beach towel poolside. "Miles probably won't be at the cabin now. I just wanted you to know that. If he's worried about you following him there, he'll grab his things and take off. He'll get in touch with me later, once he feels safe."

"No problem, but we might find a clue about his friendship with Douglas. Or something else. Did your brother have a vehicle at the cabin too?" Vaughn asked.

"We both did. He came in from California. I was up

in Tacoma working a case. He was in between jobs, so he asked if I could get away and join him at the cabin where we used to go for vacations a few years ago when Douglas couldn't make it. I said sure and made time on my schedule. We do our own thing most of the time, but normally we run a little together and have meals at night with each other. Then someone shot him while I was on my way to join him here. He was so out of it that he called me instead of Leidolf, who was so close and had the medical support he needed. I hadn't planned on conducting any investigations during my vacation."

"He had no idea who hit him? How badly was he injured?"

"He didn't see anything. Just felt the impact when it hit his rump and heard the report. He figured it was just some hunter out shooting for sport. He headed straight for the cabin, shifted, got a towel to stem the bleeding, then called me."

"Did you tell everyone investigating the case what the make, model, and license plate of Miles's vehicle is?" Vaughn asked.

"No. Because he's *not* a suspect." She'd thought Vaughn had finally quit thinking of her brother as a suspect.

"Standing over a crime scene with blood on his muzzle doesn't sound good." Howard finally buckled up in the backseat.

"Do you want to go with your jaguar friends?" Jillian slowed the Land Rover down and fully intended to let him out right here. He could hitch a ride with Demetria and Everett, who were following them to the main road off the ranch.

"Nope. I'm right where I belong."

Jillian's cell phone rang, and Vaughn fished it out of her pack.

"What are you doing?" she asked him, her voice hot with annoyance. It was her bag, and if she wanted to speak to the caller, she would.

"I'm answering your phone in case it's important," Vaughn said.

Her skin perspired lightly with the notion the call could be from her brother. She wanted to grab the phone away from Vaughn, but how would that look? Like she believed her brother was guilty.

"Hey, Demetria," Vaughn said over Jillian's phone. "I'll sync Jillian's phone to the Land Rover. Howard's too, so that we can get calls back and forth if we need to. I'll put you on speaker for now."

Jillian was relieved the call wasn't from her brother, but she fought saying no to Vaughn syncing her phone to his car. If her brother called, then everyone could hear what they were speaking about. She'd have to accept the call, or again, she'd seem afraid that Miles would incriminate himself.

"Well, I was calling Jillian, but since you answered, I just wanted to make sure that you get your rest. No sense in killing yourself before we learn the truth about all of this," Demetria said.

Jillian smiled at Vaughn. Teach him to answer her phone for her and then put it on speaker. "Uh, yeah, will do."

"Talk later when we have more information," Demetria said.

"Same with us. Out here." Vaughn slipped the phone back into Jillian's pack.

Jillian asked him, "How well do you know Douglas?"

"He works at the leather-goods factory our pack owns and is at all of the pack gatherings. I'm not there a lot of the time because of work commitments, but Douglas is a real pack participant. He never had a mate and is in his midthirties, and he loves to boat. Brock and I have gone out with him several times, and he's the kind of friend everyone should have. He has no mortgages or other financial obligations, as far as I know. He isn't into gambling. And he gets along with everyone."

"Was anyone else 'on vacation' from the pack at about the same time?" Jillian asked. "I'm wondering if he came alone."

"As soon as I let my pack leaders know what had happened to him, I asked what they knew about his vacation plans. Leidolf contacted them right away while I was chasing your brother, and he also told them what had happened to me. Douglas was alone. He's come here a few times over the years, but gone to several other places too. He seemed to love the water, despite not liking to swim, so he always takes vacations someplace that has a body of water...the ocean or large lakes."

"And from the pictures we saw on his phone, the boats were all different," Jillian said.

"Yeah, he always rented them, didn't own one of his own. He said they didn't get used enough to make it worthwhile to have one. He liked to go to lots of different locales, so it was easier just to rent a boat wherever he ended up."

"Did you take some vacations with him? From the pictures on his phone, it looks like you did."

"If I was free and he asked me, sure. I haven't since the trip to San Diego though."

"This picture was recent. Four months ago."

"That was local. A group of us went out on a party boat on one of the lakes, so it wasn't really a vacation, just an outing."

"Hey, sounds like something I'd love to do. Jaguars love the water," Howard said. "You can pass back the phone as soon as you're done with it."

"Can you think of anyone who would want to injure your brother?" Vaughn asked, handing the phone to Howard.

"No. And he wouldn't think of anyone either. He never gets into fights. He's more likely to walk away from an argument than try to win it. That has to do with my dad and not liking confrontation." She didn't see her brother's car as they pulled up. "We're here."

As soon as they reached the cabin, she parked. In a way, she wished Miles would have been there so they could talk to him about what had happened and clear him in Vaughn's eyes. Now she couldn't even look at the pictures on his phone to see if she might recognize someone. She also had a niggling fear that Miles could be in danger.

Her phone rang again, and she tensed. When she saw Miles's number, she practically held her breath.

"Answer it," Vaughn said, glowering at her as if he knew just what she was thinking.

She was certain *Vaughn* would answer the phone, if she didn't accept the call. She gave him a scathing look and answered, quickly saying, "I've got company."

Her brother immediately ended the call.

Chapter 8

"LET ME GET THIS STRAIGHT," VAUGHN GROWLED AT Jillian. "We are working *together* on solving the crimes committed here, right?"

Howard laughed. "I'm sure glad I'm with the two of you. I don't know when we'll ever solve the case, but it's sure entertaining to see how we're going to do it."

Jillian's jaw was set as she opened her car door. "Sure. We'll start with examining the cabin for any evidence of foul play. *Together*."

"You said you didn't think your brother was guilty of any crime. So why not talk to him?" Vaughn couldn't help how furious he was. If her brother wasn't guilty of anything, they needed to clear this up pronto. If Miles knew something, even if he didn't think he did, they needed to learn about it and see if it led them in the right direction.

"Listen," Jillian said, getting out of the car and placing her hands on her hips, "he's my brother. He might have talked about anything, thinking he was having a private conversation with family…me, his sister. I had to let him know I wasn't alone. That if he needed to tell me something, he also needed to know others were listening to the conversation. It was up to him to decide if he wanted to talk in front of anyone else. Apparently, he didn't."

"Which means he could be damn guilty." Vaughn pinned her with a glower.

She took off for the cabin. "I'm not the bad guy. Neither is my brother."

"If he is, you're covering for him, whether you believe he's guilty or not. Hell, maybe *you* were the one who did it."

Jillian whipped around, her mouth hanging agape. "You think *I* tore into Douglas?"

"Maybe you got there before your brother did. It's only your word that you arrived at Douglas's cabin after someone attacked him. Maybe your brother shows up and discovers what you did. Being a protective brother, he warns you to call Leidolf to take care of Douglas so you're not accused of attempted murder. You do.

"Miles leaves, but returns—well after Leidolf's men have taken injured Douglas and the evidence away—to see if anything else was left behind. Before he could leave some evidence that muddied the waters, I caught your brother standing in front of the blood left behind. Maybe you're right. Miles had nothing to do with it. Maybe he's helping *you* cover up that *you* did it."

Her eyes were wide in disbelief. "What about *you*!"

Vaughn nearly laughed. He hadn't expected her to accuse *him*. He didn't believe she had injured Douglas either. But he wanted her to realize that by covering for her brother, *she* could be a suspect.

"Yeah, you! Who says you didn't wound him? What if you did it in the heat of an argument over some old pack feud, hadn't planned it, and then took off to get cleaning supplies to take care of the mess? I arrive, find Douglas in bad shape, and call Leidolf for help. After we left, Miles arrives to see his friend and finds the blood on the floor. Miles ends up getting some blood on him, if that really happened. Who says he really did end up with blood on his muzzle? We only have your word that he did.

"So after you injure Douglas, you return to the scene of the crime and unexpectedly come face-to-face with Miles at the cabin. He smells your scent and realizes you're the one who injured his friend. Miles takes off, certain you're going to kill him if you can catch him. He'd be the perfect patsy all tied up in one neat little package. Now you can't dispose of the body, most likely believing Douglas was dead, because I've already gotten help and removed him from the cabin. And you can't hide the evidence like you'd planned because Leidolf's men have already gathered it and taken it away. You have to silence the witness though. And you'd have to take care of Douglas before he comes out of his coma. You call Leidolf to tell him you're going after a suspect. Then you go after my brother to take care of loose ends."

Standing on the deck, Howard was smirking, waiting to see how this all played out.

Vaughn smiled at Jillian. She appeared a little taken aback that he would be amused at her accusation. She didn't look amused. He liked how gutsy she was and how she didn't take his comment about her actually attacking his pack member to heart. He liked how quick she was to turn the tables on him, but at the same time make some valid points.

"Should we...check out the cabin now?" Howard asked.

"For what it's worth, Douglas owes you his life," Vaughn said to Jillian. "And I can't thank you enough for that."

She looked up at him, appearing a little surprised that he hadn't been serious about accusing her of the crime. "If he's all right when he comes out of the coma."

"Agreed, but you've given him a chance to live, and for that I'm thankful."

They headed inside the cabin, and Vaughn asked, "Which room is Miles's?" He could have just smelled for Miles's scent, but he wanted Jillian's cooperation, even if she didn't want to give it. He still couldn't believe she had warned Miles.

"Down the hall, second room on the right."

For her sake, Vaughn truly hoped he didn't find anything that would indicate her brother had been involved in the attack.

When they reached the bedroom, he saw the bed was unmade, and drawers were open and empty. The closet door was open; nothing in there either. He looked under the bed, but didn't find anything. He yanked back the covers of the bed. Then he spied a tiny bit of red silk and lace and pulled the covers back further. A pair of feminine lace panties were lying crumpled on the sheets. He glanced over his shoulder at Jillian to see her response. Her cheeks were flaming red, and her mouth was parted in a way that said she was as surprised to see them there as he was, her gaze quickly shifting to his. Vaughn lifted the panties off the mattress and realized they belonged to someone who smelled of cat. Yet he hadn't smelled anyone other than Jillian and her brother who had been in the cabin recently.

"Cat, but she had to have worn hunter's spray or we would smell her scent in the cabin."

Howard checked out the scent. "Don't recognize her, but jaguar for sure."

Jillian closed her gaping mouth.

Vaughn wasn't shocked her brother had been with someone, but he was bowled over with the notion that canines and felines could be mixing it up together. Talk about an odd pairing. But now that they knew jaguar shifters existed, they did have that in common with the cats. They were all shifters. Would they even be able to have shifter kids?

"Looks like he packed up in a hurry and took off." Vaughn still felt that Miles's every action said he was guilty—of something.

Howard tucked the panties in a baggie. "Evidence," he clarified when both Vaughn and Jillian watched him.

They left the bedroom, and Vaughn glanced in Jillian's room. Her bed was neatly made, and it appeared as though she could still be staying there.

"My stuff is still here," she confirmed, sounding irritated with him. "I do have a couple of bags at Leidolf's guest house, but I'm staying in this area too in case my brother needs to get in touch with me."

"Like he did earlier, when you warned him away from talking to you in the car."

She gave Vaughn a caustic look, but didn't comment.

Vaughn walked into the kitchen and checked out all the cabinets.

"Any ice-cream bars in the freezer?" he asked, teasing her now, trying to lighten the mood a bit.

Howard looked puzzled. "Is that some kind of clue?"

Jillian rolled her eyes.

While Vaughn and Howard looked through the fridge and the rest of the cabinets, she went outside to make a call to her brother. He didn't pick up. When she got his message machine, she said, "What the hell is going on? I've teamed up with the wolf who went after you. I shot him even. He's investigating—" The voice mail cut her off.

She hoped her brother didn't think she'd killed Vaughn. She tried again. "He's investigating the attack on his pack member. We're working together. So call me and we can talk. He's sure you—" The message ended again. "Damn it."

Vaughn exited the cabin and saw the phone in her hand. "Did you get ahold of him?"

"No. If I had, you would be the first to know."

From his expression, he clearly thought she was being sarcastic.

"I left him a message though. I told him I shot you for chasing after him." She smiled at Vaughn.

His mouth curving just a hint, he lifted his brows.

"But that you were still investigating him." Jillian had tried several times to get ahold of her brother last night, but hadn't had any success. When she saw his car still parked at the cabin this morning, she presumed he had still been running as a wolf. But he had apparently come back since, and packed up and left in a hurry. Now she wasn't sure what was going on.

She couldn't get the image of the red panties out of her thoughts either. She could just imagine what Vaughn had been thinking. That she obviously didn't know as much about her brother as she thought she did. When had Miles brought some woman there? Probably when Jillian had run into town for groceries earlier in the day and had been gone for a couple of hours.

She couldn't believe she hadn't smelled the woman's

scent. He must have had her wear hunter's spray so Jillian wouldn't know about it. If that was the case, she wondered how he would have convinced the woman to wear it. Unless she'd done so herself. But why? Worried how Jillian would feel about her brother hooking up with a cat? She could imagine her brother not wanting her to know, afraid she might let it slip to their parents.

But if they both really cared about each other, or even if they were just having a fling, who was she to say that anything was wrong with it? The bag with the red panties swayed in Howard's hand as he walked out to the car, and she wished he would shove the bag in his jacket pocket or something.

The woman could have at least made sure she took her panties with her! Unless she meant to leave them for Miles as a memento of their time together. Ugh.

Jillian locked up the cabin again.

"Okay, do you want to go to Douglas's cabin next? See what we can learn from there?" Vaughn asked.

"Yeah, though Leidolf's men probably cleaned up any evidence we might have gotten from the scene," Jillian said.

"I take it you didn't know about your brother seeing some woman."

"No, I didn't."

Howard shook his head. "Happens to the best of us. We just lose our heads and…"

"Attempted murder doesn't fall under that category." Jillian wished she could get in touch with her brother and iron this out with him *alone*.

When they arrived at Douglas's rental cabin, she parked, and they all left the Land Rover. Immediately,

Vaughn pulled out his gun and began hand signaling to them, silently telling them which direction to go while he went to the front door.

What had he seen?

Already frowning, Vaughn shook his head at her. What did that mean?

She and Howard moved quickly around to the back and side of the cabin so whomever Vaughn thought he'd heard wouldn't escape. Jillian wished she had heard or seen what he had. She felt like she was working blind. Howard looked as clueless as she felt. He shrugged and then disappeared around the side of the log building.

At the back of the cabin, two windows were open, although they shouldn't have been, and Jillian thought she heard a rustling movement in the trees. She knew she should pay attention to the windows in case anyone jumped out of one, but she couldn't help feeling like someone was moving around in the woods.

The front door banged open, and Vaughn hollered, "Come out with your hands up, and I won't have to shoot you."

Her heart beating spasmodically, Jillian was half watching the windows, half watching the woods when something big and golden, his fur decorated in rings of black, leaped out of the window onto her. Her gun went off as her head hit the packed soil hard. For a moment, she didn't hear anything.

Then Vaughn hollered from inside the cabin, sounding alarmed. "Jillian!"

Howard also called out to her, just as concerned.

She opened her eyes and wondered where she was for a moment. Feeling disoriented, she recalled that the jaguar had knocked her down. She twisted around to see him bound off into the woods. As she got to her feet, she thought she saw another jaguar, smaller, female, north of where the big cat had raced off, but only for a split second. Then the cat blurred into two and disappeared. Jillian rubbed her eyes, then stumbled after the bigger cat, her head pounding, and her vision swimming. The big cat was running away, or…two of them mixed together, their tails whipping back and forth. Then they were gone.

Running from the side of the house, Howard had nearly reached her. He began stripping off his clothes. "Take my things back to the cabin, will you? I'm going after the cat. This is the best way to catch him."

She hated to have to stay behind, but she heard Vaughn running to catch up to them, and she knew she and Vaughn needed to learn what they could at the cabin while Howard tried to chase down the other jaguar. Wolves wouldn't be a match for a jaguar if he decided to stand his ground and fight them.

Then Howard was completely naked, and he shifted. She had never seen a jaguar shifter shift into his animal skin, so it was a few seconds before she realized she was staring and not being proactive. She began grabbing his clothes off the ground.

"Are you all right?" Vaughn came up from behind her, gently taking hold of her arm.

Not having heard him get that close, she swallowed a startled scream.

"Sorry. I saw him take you down." Vaughn wrapped his arm around her waist, offering his support. "You appeared to be out for a few seconds while I was climbing through the window. I worried—"

"Thanks. I'll be all right." She realized then that in all the excitement, she hadn't noticed how much her head was pounding. She clutched Howard's clothes and gun in her arms. "He didn't try to kill me. He just knocked me down so I couldn't shoot him."

"Could you have shot him?"

She shook her head, and Vaughn tucked a curl behind her ear, his other arm still steady around her waist, his gaze dark. She liked his protective, caring nature.

"Because he was a jaguar?"

Like she'd only shot Vaughn because he was a wolf and jaguars were more exotic, rarer, or something. "Because he *wasn't* trying to kill me. He didn't really hurt me." If he'd wanted to hurt her, he could have taken a bite out of her or clawed at her. "Was it... Oh, I was going to say the same scent as the woman who had been with Miles, but this was a male."

"I didn't smell his scent at all. Which means he's wearing that damn hunter's spray. I saw a blond-haired man looking out the window just as we drew close to the house. Then he moved quickly away from the window."

"Did he look like any pictures that Douglas had on his phone?" she asked.

"I couldn't tell. He moved so fast that I didn't see enough except that he was fair-haired. I'll look at the photos again, but I doubt I'd be able to successfully identify him."

Jillian sighed. "I have to admit that him being a jaguar made it difficult to even think about shooting him, if I'd had time to aim."

"I understand. It's easier to shoot wolves."

She frowned up at Vaughn, not sure if he was teasing

her. "You were chasing down my brother. If a jaguar had been, I would have shot *him*."

Vaughn smiled, then shook his head. "Are you sure you're all right?"

"I'm fine. Just a little dizzy, nauseous."

"You lost consciousness. I knew it. Damn it." Now he sounded really worried again.

She shifted Howard's clothes to one arm, then rubbed her forehead and closed her eyes. When she opened them again, her vision was clearer, and she knew she really was fine. "Were there two of them?"

Chapter 9

As soon as Jillian asked Vaughn if he'd seen two jaguars, he knew she was worse off than he'd first suspected. "Hell, Jillian. You've suffered a concussion." Vaughn spoke softly, concerned.

"No, I'm fine." She let out her breath. "You only saw one?"

"Yeah, I only saw one." Vaughn knew she wasn't fine. "You hit your head really hard when you went down."

"I'll sit down in the cabin for a moment to clear my head. Then I'll be all right."

He scooped her up in his arms, and she let out a gasp. "This isn't necessary."

"Like hell it isn't. I need you working this case with me to clear your brother. You're not going to take a vacation on this one."

She snorted.

He smiled down at her, but he was still worried about her. He carried her back into the cabin and set her on the blue plaid couch in the living room. "I'll be right back," he said as he left the cabin to get his medical kit from the vehicle. When he returned to the living room, she'd closed her eyes and was leaning against the seat back, Howard's clothes still on her lap.

Vaughn really knew she wasn't all right then. "I'll get some water for you. I've got some pain reliever for the headache."

"Thanks. I really believe I saw a smaller one. A female. Maybe two—a male and a female."

"Hell."

"Well, did I?"

"I was too busy coming to your aid. But there wasn't a second person, or cat, in the cabin." He brought a glass of water and a couple of pills to her, then helped her to hold the glass. She was still a little shaky, and he wanted to make sure she wouldn't drop the glass when he released it.

"Yeah, but the smaller one was in the woods, not the cabin. Maybe she was the lookout. Only she didn't do a good job because the one in the cabin didn't know about us arriving until nearly too late."

"Okay, no, I didn't see another in the woods." Vaughn returned to the kitchen, couldn't find a washcloth, and went to the bathroom. He rummaged in the drawers and found one. He got it wet, then wrung out the cloth until it was just damp. Turning to leave the bathroom, he saw a spot of blue on the floor near the toilet, he thought from one of those toilet cleaners set inside the tank.

Immediately, one of the PI cases he'd worked came to mind. He'd found drugs in a gallon freezer bag inside a toilet tank. Not that Douglas would have drugs, but why would a blue spot be on the floor? Wouldn't maid service have cleaned it up if one of the housekeepers had dripped some of the cleaner?

Vaughn set the washcloth on the bathroom counter, then lifted the tank lid. And found two gallon bags floating in the water. Filled with cash.

Holy hell. What had Douglas been into?

"You're not going to believe this," Vaughn called out to Jillian.

"Don't tell me you found a body."

"Nope. A whole hell of a lot of money."

He rinsed the blue toilet bowl cleaner off the plastic, money-filled sacks in the sink. He was still furious with the cat for taking Jillian down and injuring her. "Are you still feeling dizzy?" he asked.

"A little. How much money is a lot?"

"Don't know offhand, but it's a lot. We'll have to count it." He patted the bags of money dry, then carried them and the damp washcloth into the living room.

"Why would he have so much cash on hand?" Jillian asked as Vaughn handed her the bags of money and applied a cold compress to her forehead.

He really didn't know the answer to her question. All he could think of was drug money, but he didn't believe his friend could be involved in anything so insidious. "Not sure. What if a jaguar injured Douglas, not a wolf as I thought? We're not used to thinking in terms of jaguar shifters causing trouble, and who would ever have thought jaguars would exist in this area?"

"True. And knew about the money and was trying to find it?"

"Possibly. He was in his human form. When he saw me, he must not have been armed and figured his best avenue of escape was shift into the jaguar and jump out the window. His clothes were lying on the floor beside the bed. I can think of only one reason for a jaguar shifter coming here. He was involved in the crime, and he's looking to get rid of any evidence we hadn't found and possibly searching again for the money."

"Had Douglas been flashing money around, buying contraband? Or maybe he was being blackmailed. What did his financial situation look like?" Jillian asked.

"I don't know about blackmail or anything. But as far as I know, he isn't in debt. He hasn't bought anything expensive except a new car about two years ago. I need to check further into his financial background though."

"And you already said he isn't into gambling."

"Nope. House has been paid off for years. No loans out that I know about. He likes to travel a lot, which is where he spends some of his money."

"What would he need that much money for here?"

Vaughn just didn't know. "Really don't have a clue."

"Did you smell another big cat, or just the one?"

Vaughn frowned at her, worried when she didn't seem to recall what he'd said about the cat. "I didn't smell either of them." He gave her the cold compress. "Just hold it against your head. I'll be right back. I want to search through his clothes."

"I'm coming with you."

"You should stay put." And he should be with her at all times until Doc checked her out and gave the green light.

"I have to help investigate this for myself. I might see something you don't."

"How many fingers am I holding up?"

"Oh, come on."

"All right." As much as he didn't believe she was okay, he would do as she asked.

She looked so pale that he was afraid she'd pass out on him if he jostled her around too much. He lifted her in his arms again, though his shoulder was killing him.

"What are you doing? I can walk."

"Humor me. I have no intention of letting you walk and then having to pick you up off the floor if you pass out. My shoulder hurts too much for that." He hadn't meant to reveal the way his darned shoulder was paining him.

Her worried frown deepened. "Your shoulder has to be killing you with carrying me. Put me down."

"When we get to the room." He was carrying her down the hall when he heard something moving around in the bedroom.

Before Vaughn could set Jillian on her feet and pull out his gun, a jaguar came bounding out of the room. For a minute, both Vaughn and Jillian stared at the jaguar. The cat raised his brows. Vaughn had seen Howard shift, but he hadn't seen the other big cat long enough to be able to differentiate between the two of them. Though when he took a deep breath, a breeze came through the bedroom window carrying the cat's scent to him, and he knew it was Howard.

The jaguar quickly shifted, and Howard stood before them naked. "Just me, in case you didn't know which jaguar I was and were thinking of shooting me. Though it looks to me like you have your hands full." He smiled. "Here I am working the case, attempting to chase a jaguar down, and the two of you are making up to each other? Wolves sure do things differently than us big cats."

Vaughn shook his head. "Jillian has a mild concussion from the jaguar knocking her down. She insisted she investigate the cat's clothes at the same time I did."

Howard's expression darkened. "Damn, I sure wish

I'd been able to get ahold of him. No one messes with a member of my team and gets away with it."

"Jaguars play rough." Jillian sounded irritable.

"They can. As powerful as a jaguar is, with just the swipe of his paw, he could have killed you. But he didn't, which says something." Howard looked down at the clear bags of money in Jillian's hands. "What the hell is that?"

"Money, and lots of it." Vaughn needed to call his pack leaders and see if they knew anything about it.

Howard whistled. "I take it that it's not Jillian's. Where are my clothes?"

"On the couch in the living room," she said. "Did you smell a female cat around where the male jaguar was? Or maybe she was farther northeast from his location."

"I'll check in a few minutes."

"Did you recognize the jaguar?" Vaughn asked.

"No," Howard admitted. "It was a male, but I didn't recognize him. He's not with the Enforcer Branch in any case."

"But you would have a better idea than we would from the rosette pattern he was wearing, wouldn't you, if you saw a picture of him?"

"No. I couldn't confirm whether it was someone I've seen unless I knew the person really well. Like an Enforcer I've seen in jaguar form. Or Demetria and Everett, since I've worked a lot with them. I never saw his face, only his tail end before he disappeared for good. It's like seeing the back of someone's human head if you haven't been around him much. Our official photos show faces—jaguars, humans, not the agents' tails." Howard walked off down the hall to get his clothes.

Vaughn wondered if the jaguar that had jumped out the window was the same one he'd seen racing through the woods when he'd been chasing Miles. He wouldn't have any idea without having a picture of both and comparing rosettes. Then again, how many jaguar shifters could be in the area? He gently set Jillian down on the bed.

"I'll search in the drawers to see if there might be some evidence he was looking for. Unless he knew about the money and was searching in here. You can look through his clothes." He picked them up and left them on the bed for her. Then he hollered down the hall to Howard. "I take it you couldn't catch up to him." Vaughn opened drawers and found nothing.

Howard entered the bedroom. He headed for the closet door and opened it. "I couldn't catch up with him. Not when he got into a car and it drove off."

"*It* drove off?" Jillian dumped the money out of the bags and onto the bed.

"Yeah. As in someone else was driving it."

"Like a female jaguar shifter?" Vaughn eyed the bundles of money.

"Yeah. Maybe. Car windows were highly tinted. I couldn't make out the driver before the vehicle drove off."

"I told you I saw two cats."

"She was seeing double?" Howard asked Vaughn. "I only saw the one running way ahead of me, by the time I stripped and shifted."

"She saw a male and a female. Was there anything in his clothes that would give us a clue as to what's going on?" Vaughn asked Jillian, then turned to see what she had found. She was lying on the bed, her eyes closed.

Hell. "Jillian." He hurried over to the bed and placed his hand on her arm. "Jillian."

"I'm fine." She looked up at him with half-lidded eyes.

"Good. But we're going to have the doctor check you out anyway." Vaughn took her hand and squeezed. "We can ask him if he has any news about the DNA from the bite Douglas suffered."

"Okay."

"How many of me are there?"

"One. And that's more than enough," she said, annoyed.

Vaughn and Howard laughed.

"I think maybe she loves you. Not sure. Wolf behavior sure can be confusing. Do you want me to carry her out to the Land Rover on account of your shoulder wound?" Howard asked.

"I've got her. If you could grab all the stuff the guy left behind, we can examine it closer at the ranch house."

"I'll take the cash so I can safeguard it. I saw a small-ish jaguar too. Female, I think," Jillian said, reminding them of it.

"You got it. I'll take a moment and run out back to see if I can smell a she-cat too," Howard said.

"The money is Douglas's. Lots of people have touched it, naturally, as it's all been in circulation, but the person who handled it most recently was Douglas," Jillian said.

Vaughn placed the money back in the bags. "I need to see if Leidolf can put this in a safe." Then Vaughn lifted Jillian again and tried unsuccessfully not to groan while she carried the bags of money. His shoulder was killing him, but no way was he going to let on in front of either of them. Once he had settled Jillian in the car, he called the doctor. "Hey, Doc. Jillian hit her head hard on the ground near the cabin we're investigating. A jaguar knocked her down. I need to have you take a look at her."

"No, he doesn't," Jillian said from the backseat of the car where she was lying down.

"Yeah, I'll take a look at her. Symptoms?" Dr. Wilders asked.

"Headache, dizziness, blurry vision. And she passed out again."

"I was just closing my eyes and fell asleep. Someone kept me up too late last night."

Vaughn imagined she never dozed on the job like that. "I gave her something for her headache and a cool compress."

"Okay. I'll check her out, but if she doesn't stay at the clinic for the next twenty-four hours, she'll need someone to wake her every two to three hours to make sure she's all right. She shouldn't do any physical activity either."

"We'll take care of her. Be there in about a half hour."

"See you then."

Howard came out with the cat's clothes and threw them in the back of the Land Rover. "Jillian was right. I saw pugmarks left in the damp soil. They must have been from a female jaguar northeast of where the male was running. Like the male, she left no scent."

"Two she-cats, or just one?" Vaughn asked.

"One. Did you see two, Jillian?"

"I think one, and she was just blurring a bit," Jillian said.

Howard cast Vaughn a worried look. Vaughn inclined his head to Howard, acknowledging he was concerned about her too.

"We're returning to the ranch to see the doctor, right?" Howard asked.

"Yeah, but before we go to the ranch, I want to make one stop on the way over there. I'm going to run in and check out the other bedroom real quick. Watch over her, will you?"

"Sure will."

Vaughn hurried inside and checked out the other bedroom, but he didn't smell anyone or see anything that had been left behind. He left the cabin and locked up, then looked in on Jillian.

She frowned at him, but he was glad to see she wasn't sleeping. "I'm awake, okay? I'm just fine. Howard's been talking my ear off, making sure I didn't go to sleep."

"Good." Vaughn nodded at Howard for doing a great job.

"Do you want me to drive?" Howard asked.

"Sure."

"Where do we need to stop?" Howard climbed into the driver's seat.

"The grocery store. You can stay with Jillian. I'll just run in. We'd better call Demetria and Everett to let them know two jaguars were at Douglas's cabin."

Howard called it in, and they all filled in the details as far as they knew them.

"Thanks," Demetria said. "We haven't had much luck with our search on the injured jaguar. Of course, we didn't ask if anyone saw a jaguar. If someone had, that

would have been on the news. We'll return and canvass
the area. But the found money might give us a clue to
the motivation in Douglas's attack."

"Right. Do you want to pick me up at the ranch
house?" Howard asked. "Vaughn's going to stay with
Jillian. Unless she'd rather I stay with her."

"I don't need to remain behind, or have anyone watch
over me," Jillian said.

"Doctor's orders," Vaughn said. "Besides, as much
as my shoulder is hurting, it wouldn't be a bad idea for
me to rest up another day too."

"Jeez, I told you not to carry me!"

He swore she looked a little relieved that he wanted
to stay with her to rest up a bit too. Maybe so she felt she
wasn't holding him back from investigating the crimes.

"Okay, if it means you'll have more time to heal, I'll
remain at the ranch house," she said.

"Agreed." Vaughn had never thought he'd tell someone on a mission how he needed to rest up more after
being injured so he could complete the job. He'd really
intended to push through the pain. If his declaration
made Jillian feel better, he didn't mind.

When they finally arrived at the store, she was sitting
up, belted in, and looking annoyed. "I thought we were
going to work more on the case."

Vaughn exchanged glances with Howard. Jillian's
comment made it sound as though she was having short-
term memory loss.

"Later. When you're feeling better. We'll talk about
it when I get back." Vaughn left the Land Rover and
hurried into the store. He hoped Howard would fill her
in on the plan...again. More than anything, he hoped

Jillian recalled the earlier plan and was just confused by waking up in the car and not from the head injury.

As soon as he found the ice-cream bars she liked, Vaughn picked up two boxes and an adult coloring book and colorful pencils for Jillian. He didn't know why he did, but they looked like they'd be fun if she didn't want to sleep but needed to rest. He thought it could give her something relaxing to do until they could investigate the cases further.

They dropped by the clinic after that, and while the doctor was checking out Jillian, Vaughn gave Howard the ice-cream bars to take back to the ranch house and put in the freezer. After that, Howard would drop the Land Rover off at the clinic and Demetria and Everett would pick him up. Hopefully they could find the jaguar's trail and catch up to him.

"Don't eat any of the ice-cream bars," Vaughn warned Howard outside while Doc was seeing to Jillian.

Howard laughed. "She offered them to us before."

"Well, these are hers. She needs them after what she went through."

"Two whole boxes?"

"One's to replace the other. And she has one to spare."

"I saw you bring out two sacks from the grocery store. Did you need me to take the other to the ranch too?"

"No. Thanks. There's nothing perishable in that one." Vaughn didn't want anyone to know he was giving the coloring book to Jillian, in case she didn't appreciate it or didn't want anyone else to know she was coloring in a book.

"Did you want me to take the money to Leidolf?"

"No, I'm going to count it while the doc is seeing to Jillian."

"Okay, I'll keep you posted on what's going on with us."

"Same here."

While Vaughn waited for the doctor to finish examining Jillian, he kept her phone in his pocket in case her brother tried to call her again. If nothing else, Vaughn wanted to tell Miles that she'd been hurt. The nurse let him take the money into the doc's office to count it. He began stacking the money in piles of a hundred on the doc's coffee table, then restacking them into five-hundred-dollar bundles.

The nurse returned to ask if he could use a second person to verify the count.

"Thanks, Sally. That would be great." While she did that, Vaughn called Leidolf and asked if he had a safe.

"I do."

Vaughn told him how much he thought he had, and Sally nodded that she'd counted the same amount. Twenty bundles. Ten thousand dollars.

"Do you want me to have my accountant pick it up from the clinic? I'll have him write you out a receipt for it."

"Thanks, Leidolf. That would be great." Vaughn didn't want to make any more stops if he could help it. He wanted to take Jillian straight back to the guest house.

Hoping the doctor didn't find anything really wrong with Jillian, Vaughn checked on Douglas in his hospital room. To Vaughn's regret, there was no change in his condition. Wishing Douglas would come out of it, Vaughn paced across the room, the bags of money sitting on the table until Leidolf's accountant showed up.

Hell, Vaughn was totally stressed out concerning Douglas's condition. And now with Jillian hurt too? He sat beside Douglas's bed and took hold of his hand and squeezed. "Hey, Douglas, you texted me about a friend who was not getting ahold of you. Was it Miles?" He waited, but Douglas didn't respond to his question. "Or someone else? Do you know a couple of jaguars? A male and female?"

When Douglas didn't respond, Vaughn took a deep breath, released Douglas's hand, and stood. "We need to know who bit you so we can catch the SOB." He hated to mention the money if Douglas was dealing in criminal transactions, but if he wasn't, Vaughn wanted him to know the money was safe. "Oh, and we found some money that belonged to you. Ten thousand in cash. Leidolf is putting it in his safe to secure it." Vaughn waited for a response, but there was none.

Leidolf arrived with his accountant and said, "With that much cash on hand, I wanted to be sure you met my accountant first and knew that he was legitimate."

"Thanks," Vaughn said, really appreciating Leidolf's help.

Leidolf and his accountant counted the money, verifying it was ten thousand. Then the man wrote out a receipt for it.

"We'll have it for you when you need it."

Vaughn again thanked Leidolf and they left. Jillian's phone suddenly rang in Vaughn's pocket. He fished the phone out and smiled when he saw it was Miles. "Got to take this call. I'll be back, Douglas. We need you to get well." He didn't expect a response from Douglas, but even if Douglas couldn't hear him, Vaughn wasn't taking any chances and hoped talking to Douglas would help him know Vaughn and others were concerned for him.

He headed to the waiting area and answered it pronto, hoping Miles wouldn't just hang up on him. "I'm Vaughn Greystoke. Jillian's been injured. The doctor at Leidolf's ranch is checking her over now for a head injury. She's been passing out and has had short-term memory loss." Vaughn knew he was rattling on, but he wanted to let her brother know she'd been hurt, in case he cared and wanted to see her. Vaughn was afraid that if he stopped talking, Miles would hang up on him.

"This is a setup, isn't it?" Miles sounded wary.

Vaughn didn't blame him. "No, it isn't. For what it's worth, from everything your sister has told me about you, I don't believe you wounded Douglas. I'm the lead investigator, since he's my pack member, so my word counts for a whole hell of a lot."

"You're the one who came after me."

"Hell yeah. For some answers. Were you a witness to the attack?"

"I got there after he was already gone. So no, I didn't witness anything."

"Why did you run?"

"Are you kidding me? It looked bad. I was standing next to all this blood on the floor and knew something had torn Douglas up. Hell, you had a gun in your hand, and I was certain you were going to shoot me. Then what did you do? You turned all wolf on me and chased me all over the place. I even thought you might have attacked Douglas, killed him, and disposed of the body. You had just come back to get rid of the blood and any other evidence you might have left behind. I believed a wolf might have killed him. You're a wolf. I didn't know who you were.

"The door was open when I arrived. For an instant, I even thought that a cougar might have killed him and hauled the body off. Until you showed up." Miles let out his breath. "My sister told me to call you. She didn't tell me she'd been injured. She wanted me to clear this up with both of you, but she didn't give me your cell number. Anyway, Douglas is from Colorado. How did you end up at the cabin if he's a member of your pack and you live in Colorado too? He didn't say anything about a pack member coming to see him."

"He texted me saying he was worried about a friend not showing up. Then before I arrived to see him, he said the friend got in touch with him. Was he talking about you?"

"No. I hadn't seen Douglas yet. I was planning to when I found all the blood. I don't know anything about another friend seeing him. How did my sister get hurt?"

"A jaguar at Douglas's cabin knocked her down, and she hit her head. I don't believe he meant to hurt her. He was just trying to stop her from shooting him."

"Why weren't you protecting her better than that?"

"The jaguar was damn fast. Do you know anything about him?"

"No. I just went to see Douglas. We…we were friends. I-I can't believe he's dead." Miles sounded choked up. "Can I talk with my sister?"

"Wait, you don't know? Douglas is alive. He was badly wounded and for now is in a drug-induced coma, but he's not dead. Hopefully, he will come out of it just fine."

"No. Hell, I just assumed…when I saw all that blood…" Miles paused. "Thank God he's okay. Can I see him?"

"He's not responding to anyone. But I'm sure you can. I think it's good for anyone he knows to talk to him. Just check in at the clinic. As to your sister, Doc's running tests on her now. She can call you back as soon as she's done. She's staying at the guest house on Leidolf's ranch, if you want to drop by and see her."

"So you can arrest me."

"We can talk to each other civilly about what we both know and clear this whole matter up. We just started to investigate it, but we could use a hell of a lot more information to go on. Like what you know about the person who shot you. And about the female jaguar you hooked up with."

There was a big moment of silence. "I'll think about it." Then Miles hung up on him.

Vaughn swore under his breath. He still had a million questions to ask him. At least Miles had talked to him a bit. He thought Jillian might be right, that her brother hadn't had anything to do with the attack, but they needed to speak with him further. He might recall something that would help them with the case. And he wondered if Miles thought the owner of the red panties had anything to do with any of this.

A nurse called Vaughn back to speak with the doctor, and Vaughn was worried about Jillian all over again. When he reached the exam room, she was sitting on an exam table looking grouchy, arms folded across her chest, brows furrowed.

"I'll release you, but you need to have some-one look out for you. She's fine to go, but I want her checked every two to three hours if she falls asleep," Dr. Wilders said.

"Will do."

"I didn't see any problems with the scan. But just in case…" the doctor said.

"No problem, Doc. I'm on it."

"I also wanted to tell you about the DNA findings for Douglas."

Vaughn gave Jillian a hand down from the exam table. They both waited to hear what the doctor had to say, but Vaughn wasn't really surprised to hear his findings.

"The animal that bit Douglas wasn't a wolf. A jaguar assaulted him."

Vaughn thought that's where this was headed. Especially after seeing the jaguar looking for something at the cabin. Jillian appeared relieved as she leaned against him, and he sat her down on the chair in the exam room before she collapsed.

"Are you sure?" Vaughn asked, glad for Jillian's sake that her brother hadn't actually hurt Douglas. Vaughn gently rubbed her back.

"Yeah, completely. The saliva from the wound proves it. No wolf saliva was anywhere near the teeth marks. Jaguars' teeth usually press deeper, crushing, their bite per square inch much stronger than a wolf's. I believe the jaguar was trying to hide the kind of bite and didn't chomp down as hard. Still, the teeth impressions are consistent with what a jaguar's bite would look like."

Vaughn nodded. "You are absolutely positive that a jaguar bit him and a wolf had nothing to do with it?"

"Positive."

"Good." Not that Vaughn was glad a jaguar had done it. But he was relieved Jillian's brother had been cleared.

Jillian gave Vaughn a stern look that said she'd told him so. He didn't mind admitting he'd been wrong. Given the appearance of the incriminating circumstances, he'd made an honest mistake.

"So now you can concentrate on catching the *real* bad guy," Jillian said.

"Yeah, but we still need to talk further with your brother. He might have heard or seen something that could help us solve the case. For one thing, we need to learn about the woman he'd been with to see if she is a jaguar. We have to learn what we can about her. Can you walk out on your own, or do you need a wheelchair?"

"I can walk just fine. Thanks."

"Check in with me if you have any trouble at all. Either of you," the doctor said.

"Thanks, Doc." Vaughn helped Jillian out to the Land Rover, his hand on her arm in case she got dizzy. He assumed she wouldn't like that he'd talked to her brother first either.

When they reached his vehicle, he helped her into the passenger seat. "How are you feeling?"

"I'm fine. Really."

"Good." He leaned into the car, lifted her chin, and looked into her eyes. Green with a bluish tint, beautiful, mesmerizing. Her cheeks colored a bit. That's what he wanted to see. His gaze drifted to her parted lips. Before he could stop himself, he kissed her tempting mouth, soft and malleable. He heard her slight intake of breath and her heartbeat ratcheting up a couple of notches. He was glad when she kissed him back, tentatively, but he didn't press for more, afraid her head might still be hurting. He just caressed her neck with his thumb and kissed her forehead, then backed out of the car.

"Why?" She frowned a little, and he was grateful she sounded surprised, not angry.

"For not protecting you better. For thinking your brother was guilty of attempted murder when I hadn't observed enough of the scene to know the truth. For wanting to do that when the muscled dude was kissing you at the Kitty Cat Club instead."

"I'm sorry I shot you."

He smiled. "No you're not. It's okay. Given the circumstances, I understand completely. We're wolves. You were protecting your brother."

He closed the door and then got into the driver's side, hoping his next words wouldn't rile her. "Your brother called." Even though she'd told her brother to get in touch with Vaughn, he hadn't. He'd called Jillian's number instead. So she might be perturbed that Vaughn had taken the call on her phone.

She fastened her seat belt and frowned at Vaughn. "What?"

Vaughn handed her phone to her. "He called. I talked to him." He drove them over to the guest house.

"I can't believe you talked to my brother. On *my* phone!"

"Well, you didn't give him my phone number, so he wouldn't have called me on mine, now, would he?"

"Oh." She didn't say anything for a moment. "I can't

believe he talked to you at all," she said, her voice quieter now.

"I invited him to come to the ranch and discuss what happened."

"Okay."

"I just want to talk to him. I won't arrest him."

"Unless you still think he's involved somehow in the attack. We know he didn't bite Douglas, but…"

"I think he knows more than he's saying. I mentioned the woman he'd hooked up with. I don't think there's any way it could be a coincidence that a female jaguar was at Douglas's cabin at the same time a male was inside looking for something. What would the chances be that any more jaguar shifters are in the area? Maybe Miles likes her, *a lot*. And he doesn't want to think badly of her. Hopefully, he'll realize she might know something, even if she didn't have anything to do with biting Douglas."

"I agree."

"I think your brother was worried about your injury too, which was why he was willing to hear me out."

"Oh great. What did you tell him? I was dying, and he needed to speak to me before it was too late?"

"No. But I did want him to know you had been hurt in case he wants to see you."

"Not *just* because he would want to see me, but because you would want to see *him*."

"True. And I told him Douglas was still alive. He'd thought he was dead."

"Oh no. I thought… Well, how could he have known? Oh…" Jillian stared out the window, appearing like she had a revelation.

"What?"

"He must have smelled my scent at the cabin when he discovered the blood and didn't know what to think. I didn't know Douglas, so why would I have been there?" Her cell phone rang, and she went to answer it when the car sync asked if Vaughn would accept the call from her brother.

"Go ahead." She sounded annoyed all over again.

Maybe with his sister talking this time, they could get somewhere with Miles. Vaughn could only hope.

Chapter 10

WHEN VAUGHN HAD ACCEPTED THE CALL FROM Jillian's brother, she immediately said, "Miles, we've got you on the car phone. It's just me and Vaughn—the SEAL who was chasing after you yesterday." She hoped Miles would talk more now that she was here. She couldn't believe she'd forgotten to give him Vaughn's phone number.

"The guy you shot. Yeah, we already spoke," Miles said. "I didn't bite his friend. Douglas was my friend too. I got there just a few minutes before Vaughn arrived, and I had poked at the floor with my nose to see if I could recognize whose blood it was. I know what it must have looked like. As soon as Vaughn walked in the door, gun in hand, I panicked and knocked him down. As soon as he lost his gun under the couch, I thought I had a chance to escape and ran off."

"He lost his gun under the couch?" She smiled at Vaughn.

His ears tinged a little red, but his mouth curved up a hint. So why was she not surprised Vaughn hadn't told her all that had happened between him and her brother?

"Then Vaughn was chasing after me as a wolf. How could I know that he wasn't the guy who attacked Douglas? And he had to get rid of me now too because I was an eyewitness? All this time, I thought Douglas was dead. Vaughn just told me he wasn't."

"Oh, Miles, I'm so sorry. I thought you knew. We just learned a jaguar attacked him." She wanted him to know that right away so he could relax on that count.

"A jaguar did it." Miles was quiet for a bit. "Hell."

"How did you meet Douglas? Was it at the Clawed and Dangerous Kitty Cat Club in San Diego the night we went there?" she asked. Maybe if they knew how Miles had met him, they'd be able to see more of a connection.

"Yeah, I saw him there, but we knew each other before that. We met hiking out here as wolves about ten years ago. The first time, we both were at a standoff. He didn't know I was a shifter, and I didn't know he was one. Finally, I shifted, figuring if he was all wolf, he'd run off. He shifted to let me know he was one of us. After we shifted back and ran together for a while, I met up with him later at his cabin, and we continued to get together after that whenever he had vacation time and I was free. He liked to hike and rock climb and boat. He had a friend who used to go with him, but then the friend got a mate and didn't want to leave her alone with the kids to go on vacations with Douglas.

"I was shocked to learn that someone had bitten him. Which was part of the reason I was just standing there like a dopey wolf, poking at the blood on the floor. There was so much blood that I thought Douglas was dead. He'd cut himself before, and I had to bandage his hand. So I knew the scent of his blood. I didn't even hear Vaughn drive up to the cabin and park. That's how upset I was."

"So you said you met up with Douglas at the Kitty Cat Club."

"Yeah, we were getting drinks for our dates, and we

ran into each other there. We remarked what a small world it was. We were surprised there were so many cat lovers in the place. We got to talking about boating and why he was there and why I was there... I didn't give any details about the case we were working though."

"Did Douglas mention any trouble he'd had with anyone before you met up with him?" Jillian asked.

Vaughn pulled up to the guest house and parked the vehicle.

"He wasn't there when I got there," Miles said.

"No, when you were making arrangements to meet with him. Did he say anything or act nervous about anything?" Jillian asked.

"He said we had to talk. He sounded perturbed about something. But I wasn't sure what it was all about. Usually, he's the nicest guy."

"He didn't say what," Jillian said.

"No. I wish he had."

"We ran into jaguar shifters tonight at Douglas's cabin. Did Douglas mention anything about knowing any jaguars?" she asked.

"No."

"A male and female."

Miles didn't say anything.

"Miles, we know about the woman you were seeing, a female jaguar shifter? One was at Douglas's cabin. Maybe she didn't have anything to do with his injury, but what if she was with the male we caught inside the cabin before he escaped us? The one who injured me. When Vaughn was looking for any indication of where you'd been at our cabin, he found red silk-and-lace panties between the sheets."

"Aw, hell. We wondered where they'd gone to. I don't believe she had anything to do with what happened to Douglas. I didn't even know a jaguar had injured him. But yeah, she's a jaguar."

"What is the likelihood that another female jaguar would be in this area? That any of them would be, as hard as it would be to blend in as jaguars? Why would one of them target Douglas? Maybe it all had to do with your friendship with Douglas."

Miles was quiet.

"Okay, listen, what exactly do you know about her? Name, where you met her, how long you've known her, anything that would help us to get a better picture of her."

"A photo! If Douglas didn't delete it, he's got a picture of her and her brother and me in front of a…well, a boat we took out in Belize. It was a group thing, but we became friends. On the boat. You know."

"How long ago?" Vaughn asked.

"Six months."

"And you've been seeing her for six months?" Jillian asked, surprised he'd never once told her about this woman.

"No. I mean, we were just friends on the boat. There were so few of us, it was hard not to become friends. I've only seen her a couple of times. Her name is Kira Wells. She's widowed. Her brother is Brutus Watson. I know it sounds like he's a brute, but he's the nicest guy you'd ever want to meet."

"He's here too?"

"She and her brother were in the area. I didn't even know she was going to be here. I was picking up gas for the car, and she rolls up right behind mine. You were going to be away for a few hours at the grocery store and running some other errands. I figured Kira would be long gone before you returned. I wasn't sure what you'd think of her. So we got together. And she left."

"You know how much of a coincidence that sounds like? More like it was planned. A male and female jaguar? They used hunter's spray. She used hunter's spray to see you. Did you see her at the Kitty Cat Club?" Jillian asked.

"No. I'd never met her before Belize."

"Kira?" Vaughn finally said. "I danced with a woman named Kira that night. Blond, shapely, blue-green eyes."

"Yeah," Miles said, sounding a little disappointed.

"Were you planning another date?" Jillian asked her brother.

"We were leaving it open-ended. I had to see Douglas, and I was visiting with you, so we were going to play it by ear. She and her brother were off doing some sight-seeing in the area."

"Why was she wearing hunter's spray?"

"I told her you were staying with me at the cabin. She said she'd camouflage her scent so you wouldn't know she'd ever been there. She said her brother would flip out too, if he found out about us."

"Are you getting serious?"

"Me? Nah. Really, I've only seen her twice now. I enjoy being with her. She's wild and crazy and really different from wolves, which is why I think she appeals to me. But for wolves, we have that instinctual need for procreation, for family, and I just don't feel that way with her. We're just having fun. Even wolf couples can have issues. A cat and a wolf? I'm not sure I want to deal with that right now. Especially when I don't even have a steady job."

"Are you sure you didn't meet her at the Kitty Cat Club?"

"I didn't. Not that I remember anyway. It was noisy and crowded. I bumped into a lot of people. Maybe I even bumped into her, but I don't remember. See, if she'd been a wolf, and I'd been intrigued with her, that would have been a different story."

Yeah, like Jillian had felt about Vaughn, and she hadn't even known he was a wolf at the time.

"Where is she from?" Vaughn asked.

"San Diego."

"Now that's way too much of a coincidence, Miles," Jillian said. "You realize you could be in danger if you know who injured Douglas and they know it. What if Kira was supposed to keep you from seeing Douglas while someone she knows attacked him? Her brother even?"

"That wouldn't have happened. She wasn't involved in hurting Douglas. I would have sensed something was going on."

Sure he would have, when he was thinking with his other head.

Vaughn said, "Your sister's right. What if the attacker did plan to return to take care of matters? And he saw you—and me—there? What if he decides to come after you? I hope he comes after me. I'll take care of him in a heartbeat. Maybe he thinks you know more about what happened than would be safe for him."

"You can't scare me."

"A healthy dose of fear can keep you alive. Get complacent, and you *could* be dead. You should be

aware you might not be completely safe until we catch
Douglas's attacker."

"He's right," Jillian said.

"Hey, you know me. I can look out for myself."

"Do you want me to remind you of the times I had to
rescue you over something you pulled that you thought
you could handle on your own?" Jillian wanted to knock
some sense into her brother.

Silence.

"Oh, and another thing. A gap exists between the
time I found Douglas unconscious and when you arrived
at the cabin. I thought you were going right over to his
cabin, which is why I was there...looking for you. What
were you doing all that time?"

Miles didn't say anything, and she was afraid he was
trying to come up with a reasonable explanation.

"Miles?"

"I was with Kira."

"Twice that day?"

"Yeah. You were gone again. She and her brother had
split up for a while. I was over at her place for a time.
Why were you looking for me?"

"To tell you I was working on a case with the jaguar
shifters." She explained about the shooting of the jaguar
on Leidolf's property. "So you saw Kira instead of going
to see Douglas?" She couldn't imagine her brother doing
that to Douglas. Then again, maybe the woman made
Miles forget all about the time.

"I hadn't said I was going over there that instant.
Just that I was planning to go there. We were getting
together a little later. I am on vacation. I was doing what
I usually do."

"What about the other jaguar you said was on the boat in Belize…if he was a jaguar?" Jillian asked.

"Wayne Grunsky. He was kind of quiet. While Brutus and Kira were wild and fun to be around, he was more like what I'd expect a jaguar to be like."

"Mysterious, unseen," Vaughn said.

"Yeah, like that. He was always there, listening, but in the background."

"Come see us." Jillian hoped he'd listen to reason. "You know Leidolf and several of his wolf pack members. You can stay at the ranch until we learn who did this and apprehend him. Douglas probably got a picture of him that you could identify for us."

"Maybe. Hope you're all right, Jillian."

"Mild concussion."

Her brother wasn't good at nursing duties, so he wasn't about to offer to check on her for that reason. "Is Vaughn going to watch after you?"

"Yeah, somebody has to for the next twenty-four hours. Doctor's orders. We need you to identify Kira and her brother and friend."

"Okay, yeah. I'll…I'll let you know when I'm coming over. Talk later." Then Miles ended the call.

They sat in the car for a moment more, then Vaughn got out and came to her door. He helped her out, grabbed a grocery sack, and shut her door. "Will he come over?"

"Yeah, he will. I think he's fighting with himself over this. The fact the people he calls friends could have injured me and Douglas… Well, I'm afraid he's thinking of trying to get ahold of Kira first and learn what's been going on. Now I'm worried about my brother. I hadn't thought he'd have any trouble over this latest incident, but you're right. If Kira is involved in this, Miles could be in real danger. Especially if he confronts her with what we've told him."

"He's a grown man. If he wants to come in, he will."

"Yeah, I know, but it doesn't make me stress about it any less." She eyed the sack in Vaughn's hand as he held her arm and walked her to the cabin. "What did you get?"

"Something for you. For that stress you're talking about."

What in the world had he gotten her at the grocery store that she would like? He didn't know anything about her interests. And yet, she thought he was sweet for making the effort. Then she felt bad that she hadn't gotten him anything after *she* shot him!

"Well, you might not like it."

What had he gotten her? Something *he'd* prefer reading?

"A magazine?"

"Not quite."

She couldn't imagine anything that size and shape that wasn't a magazine. She really wasn't very patient, she realized, and her curiosity was getting the best of her.

He chuckled and got the door, then escorted her to the couch. "Okay, promise you won't be irritated with me if it's something you don't want."

She folded her arms. "I haven't a clue what it could be."

He handed her the sack. She swore he looked half worried she wouldn't like it. Even if she didn't, she would try not to hurt his feelings. She didn't want to say she loved it if she didn't though. If she got hurt again, she could imagine him getting more of the same for her.

She put her hand in the sack and actually felt a slim box of something that rattled a bit and a magazine. Or a paperback—oh, graphic novel. Had to be. She pulled both items out and stared at the adult coloring book featuring a wolf on the cover in vibrant colors.

"Oh wow." She smiled up at him. "I've seen these at the grocery store and bookstores and kept thinking how much I'd like to try one, but then I thought I'd never have the time. I love it."

"I was afraid you might think it was silly. I figured if you felt stressed and wanted to get out of here to do some more investigating, but had to rest up, maybe that could help relax you."

"What about you?"

He smiled.

"Okay, which page do you want?" She thought he might love to do it too.

"It's your coloring book. You choose first. I'll make us something to eat for a late lunch, and we can color for a while and then rest." He looked through the cabinets and found a can of tuna fish. "How does a tuna-fish sandwich sound?"

"Good to me." She pulled a coloring page from the book—a peacock—set it on the table, then went into the kitchen and poured glasses of milk.

"Mayonnaise? Anything else?" he asked.

"No, that's it." She pulled out a jar of baby dill pickles and set it on the table.

Then he brought the sandwiches over, and she added a pickle to her plate.

"So what do you think about your brother?" he asked.

"That he was really lucky to have gotten there after

the attacker left, instead of arriving right before or during the crime. And I think Kira is involved and he doesn't want her to be. He's either in denial, thinking she's really not involved, or he wants to learn the truth from her before he tells us anything more."

"Which could be dangerous."

"You're right. But we don't even know where he is. Do you still think he's guilty of anything?"

"No. I just need to talk with him. To clarify more. If he knows anything further that could help with the case, we need to know it. Like you, I think Kira could be involved in every bit of this. The fact she's from San Diego makes me wonder if her brother and their friend Wayne were in the club the night we all were there. If Kira is involved and realizes Miles suspects she's involved, I believe he could be in real danger."

"I can't make him come here to stay with us unless he wants to."

"I know. Other than one of Leidolf's police officers catching up to him and arresting him for his own protection, that's about the only other option we have. Unless we find Miles first." Vaughn finished eating his sandwich and looked at the book. He found the wolf page and tore it out.

"Somehow I knew you'd want the wolf. You're not just going to color him all tan, black, and gray, are you?"

He smiled at her.

Jillian shrugged. "It's fantasy. Think of the wolf being different colors of the rainbow in a fantasy world. It's just for fun."

He was still smiling when he began flipping through the other pages.

"Or not. It's your picture. Your creation."

When she finished eating, he took the dishes into the kitchen and cleaned up, then joined her again. She pulled out all the colored pencils, and he eyed them for the longest time.

"Oh, go ahead, make it all wolflike."

"I like a wolf's color." Then he studied her for a moment. "I haven't seen you as a wolf yet."

"If I shifted now, my head would split in two."

"Still have a headache?" He was up from the table, getting her something for the pain in a flash.

She appreciated how thoughtful he was. "Thanks."

"So if this is fantasy, you're going to color your peacock in something other than blues and greens, right?"

She laughed. "I like the peacock's feathers in the brilliant colors they are naturally."

"My point exactly."

She sighed. "Point taken."

They began to color—his in gray and brown, a little gold, beige, and white. Hers was blue and green and orange, but she did add purple for some fun. She couldn't believe she was sitting at a table coloring pictures with a hot alpha SEAL wolf. He was frowning and concentrating really hard to color the tiny spaces without getting over the lines. She agreed this took her concentration, and she no longer was stressing about other matters. She enjoyed watching him while he colored too.

Jillian paused, then yawned. She needed to sleep for a while.

"Hey, let's go lie down. I think we both need the rest." Vaughn left the table and got some water and pain medicine for his shoulder.

"Are you still hurting?"

"Yeah, some. By tomorrow, I should be good."

They walked toward the bedrooms. She couldn't quit thinking about her brother. "Maybe I can still convince Miles to come here and stay at the ranch."

"Is he a twin?"

"No. Three years younger." She paused at her room, knowing this was such a bad idea, yet she couldn't help but want to suggest it anyway. "Maybe you should stay with me while we rest."

Smiling a bit, Vaughn waited expectantly.

His words and actions had helped her to change how she felt about him—from ready to strangle him for going after her brother to wanting to make it up to him for being so nice to her when she was injured. "Doc says you're to keep an eye on me. Your mission. Are you going to be the one who tells him you didn't do your job?"

Vaughn laughed a little. "I thought I was the enemy." He didn't have to be asked twice though, and took hold of her hand and led her into her room.

She liked that he didn't seem to hold a grudge. "I think me shooting you changed your mind about my brother."

He chuckled. "Learning the attacker had to be a jaguar did."

"Nah. You were already changing your mind about him way before that. You even got me a coloring book and coloring pencils."

"And ice-cream bars."

She paused at the bed. "Really?"

"For after our nap. Or maybe after dinner."

She smiled up at him.

"Or maybe now." He laughed and led her back to

the kitchen. "I can see we aren't a good influence on each other."

"What's wrong with having an ice-cream bar? The chocolate will take all our aches and pains away. It did for you last night, didn't it?"

"Getting a good-night kiss would have been even better."

"Yeah, well, it's a little early for any more of that."

His smile said he didn't believe she really meant it, and then he got them each an ice-cream bar. They carried them into the living room and took a seat to look at Douglas's stuff again.

She considered the book on sunken treasures next to one of the boxes. "They didn't have books at my cabin for anyone's reading pleasure." Jillian opened the book. "I didn't see any at your cabin either."

"I wouldn't know. I hadn't exactly moved in yet."

"True. Why would this book have been there?" She lifted the book and smelled it. "It has Douglas's scent on it. And…my brother's." She frowned. "He's not much of a reader. I can't imagine why anything like this would interest him. Or when he would have gotten his scent on it if he hadn't seen Douglas yet." She flipped through the table of contents and ran her finger down until she came to shipwrecks off the Oregon coast.

Vaughn leaned forward and took a closer look at the book. "What are the chances your brother and Douglas were interested in more than running, rock climbing, and boating?"

Chapter 11

JILLIAN COULDN'T BELIEVE MILES MIGHT BE INTO treasure hunting. Sure, he'd had a metal detector and had searched for treasure for eons whenever they had family vacations. But she didn't see him as a real, honest-to-God treasure hunter. "Would they be searching for treasure in the ocean? My brother swims, but he doesn't scuba dive. Does Douglas?" Jillian asked Vaughn as they looked over the book on sunken treasures.

Vaughn turned to the pages that listed various shipwrecks off the Oregon coast. "Not that I know of. He's afraid of the water. As a wolf, if he's forced to swim, he can. As a human, he'll boat on it, but he won't get in."

Jillian ate another bite of her ice-cream bar and got up from the couch. "I'll be right back." She went to her bedroom, grabbed her laptop, and returned to the living room.

"What are you going to look for?" Vaughn asked.

"Something. Anything. Why did Douglas come here every year? And my brother too? Had they been getting together to search for treasure off the Oregon coast?" Jillian finished her ice-cream bar and tossed the wrapper and stick in the trash.

"I take it you didn't know that your brother was doing this."

"Only when we were younger. He used a metal detector to find treasure...which meant all kinds of trash. But

I didn't think he'd ever done anything else like that. Certainly not searching for undersea treasures."

She typed in a search for Douglas Wendish on the internet. When she was investigating human cases, she always did internet searches. No telling what she might learn. Wolves were more careful about being in the public eye, so she hadn't expected to find anything about him. When she got a few hits, she assumed they were for some other Douglas Wendish. But when she saw a news article about him, she recognized him right away.

"Did you know he was a real treasure hunter?" She didn't think Vaughn could look any more surprised than he did. She brought the laptop over to him. "That's him, isn't it?" The sandy-haired man was grinning, holding up what looked like a Confederate coin. "There are several articles about him finding treasure. He says he always had dive partners, but they were camera shy."

"Wolves, most likely." Vaughn read through the article. "Well, I'll be damned."

"I'm surprised he wouldn't have asked you to accompany him since you're a diver, aren't you?" Jillian asked.

"Yeah, but I'm sure he must have already had a crew. Besides, I stay busy."

She pointed to a story on her laptop. "Here's an article about a family who found three hundred thousand dollars in gold coins and gold chains from a ship that sank off the coast of Fort Pierce, Florida, on its way from Havana to Spain. And here's an article about Douglas finding some gold at a different time."

"Good work on the internet search." Vaughn finished his ice-cream bar and put his wrapper in the trash.

"Thank you."

Vaughn flipped through the treasure book. "Here's an article on the treasures off the coast of Fort Pierce. He went there last year, I remember. Looks like he has a gold mine, pardon the pun, of treasure maps in here."

"You said he came here in the past. What if it wasn't just for a vacation all those times, but to search for some elusive treasure? If this was something that he loved doing, I can see that he might have always taken vacations where he could also do a bit of treasure hunting."

"If your brother was involved, Douglas never said anything to us."

"True. In one of the articles, the reporter mentioned Douglas had been searching for five years for the Confederate gold coins. It's not like going to the grocery store, and there they are on the shelf. It would take a lot of dedication, trial and error, luck even, and time." She looked back at the laptop. "Lots of ships have sunk off the Oregon coast. Some ran aground on sand bars and were refloated, and others were scrapped." She moved closer to where Vaughn was sitting on the couch so she could show him the article that really got her attention.

She got a little closer to him than she'd planned, though she wanted to be near enough so he could see the screen. But her leg was touching his, and as if he couldn't see the monitor well enough, he leaned into her space even more.

Trying to get her mind on the article and off the hot wolf sitting next to her, she pointed to the screen. "This is the one I'd go after. The ship was carrying wealthy Spanish passengers and might have sunk off the Oregon coast. The ship was also carrying beeswax in its cargo hold. People keep finding beeswax on the shore. Now, it also states that several ships traveling that same route carried beeswax, but if it was the same ship, the Spanish passengers were fleeing their homeland due to strife, and they would have taken all their valuables with them. How much do you want to bet Douglas has been looking for that treasure for some time?"

"Could be. Or just got interested in it after he'd been coming here for a while. So what would the deal be with your brother? He didn't know Douglas was going to be in the area until the last minute. He was already here."

"Yes, and Miles had already contacted me to have me join him. We usually do our separate things during the day, so the guys could have gone diving and I wouldn't have known about it."

"I'd like to know just who his camera-shy divers were. You didn't see Miles with any scuba gear, did you?"

"No. But then again, he might have had it in the trunk of his car or in his bedroom, and I never saw it. Yet, he wouldn't have known he was going anywhere with Douglas, so he might have planned to rent it and not brought any with him. Can you ask your pack leaders to see if anyone in the pack is a diver?"

"Yeah, already on it."

They both pulled out their phones and made the calls. When Miles answered his phone, Jillian asked, "Have you been treasure hunting with Douglas?"

The silence on the other end of the phone spoke volumes.

"Why didn't you tell me?"

Vaughn looked at her while he was talking with his pack leaders.

When Miles still didn't say anything, she said, "Okay, listen, I think it's great. Tell me about it."

"Don't you dare tell Dad."

"What has Dad got to do with anything?"

Vaughn ended his call, and she put her phone on speaker. "Vaughn's here. Now talk."

"You know how Dad is. Unless you're doing something worthwhile, he thinks you're a slacker. Treasure hunting?" Miles snorted.

"Don't tell me your secrecy has to do with that one time in Pompano Beach, Florida?" She couldn't believe it. Then again, she remembered how irritated their dad had been. She'd wished her brother had found a treasure chest full of gold bullion. Instead he found a lot of trash. Which confirmed what her dad had said. Just once, she'd like her brother to prove their dad wrong.

"Yeah, and countless other times. Even though he badgered me about wasting my time—when I reminded him we were on vacation, and wasting time was part of the vacation experience—he micromanaged how I was searching for the treasure."

"So how long have you been doing this?"

"Forever. I mean, Dad was right. Locating treasure can be a pie-in-the-sky adventure, but when I have a chance, I go with Douglas. That was one of the common interests Douglas and I had."

"How? You don't dive."

"I'm technical dive-certified. And don't tell Dad that either. He thinks anything you do should be job-related. Probably because I don't have a regular job all the time. He'd just think I was some beach bum."

Jillian closed her gaping mouth. Maybe she didn't

know her baby brother all that well. "So you were planning to look for treasure off the Oregon coast? Why didn't you tell me?"

"I was afraid you'd let it slip when you were talking to Dad. I'd get the lecture all over again."

"Vaughn said Douglas had been in Fort Pierce before. Were you going to Fort Pierce with Douglas to hunt for treasure?"

"Later, probably. He always checks things out first. Then we get together, rent a boat, rent some equipment, and go out. We usually take a week. Then I'm back to looking for a job and he's back at his job. I was just here on vacation, like I said, wanted to get together with you when Douglas couldn't get away, and all of a sudden he said he was going to be here too. Maybe we could check out the Oregon treasure again."

"How were you going to hide the fact you were doing it from me this time?" Jillian sagged against the couch, not believing he had kept it secret from her all this time.

"I thought I might have to tell you. But then Douglas was injured, and I knew we weren't going anywhere."

"Would the jaguar who injured him have known you were treasure hunting?"

"How did you learn of it?"

"We saw the book on treasures, and then I did a web search."

"So see? The guy who did it might have too. I've been thinking back on all that has happened the last few months. Wondering if our treasure hunting was connected to the guy who injured Douglas. Well, and damn it, you too. I mean, if you can look up and find what Douglas has discovered, what if they did also?"

"Exactly. Did you ever have other divers with you on dives?"

"In Belize that one time. It was a group thing, and the two of us went there to check things out. We weren't really with them. There were six of us total, and the dive guide."

"So it wasn't just a boating trip!" Jillian said, totally exasperated with her brother.

"No."

"Did any of the other divers smell like cats?" Vaughn asked.

"Well, on the boat and with everyone wearing wet suits, it was impossible to tell. All I could smell was the rubber, the salt air, and suntan lotion. Afterward, we met them at a dive bar later in the evening. So yeah, they smelled like cats. Now that I know better, I'd say like jaguars."

"Did they meet up with you at the dive bar on purpose or by accident?" Vaughn asked.

"Kira invited us to join them."

"Did you talk to them about other treasure hunts you went on?" Jillian asked.

"Yeah. Everyone did. That was the fun of getting together on a group tour for a change. We all shared our various experiences, finds, and the locations."

"So Douglas dives?" Vaughn sounded surprised.

"No, he doesn't dive. Don't tell him I said so, but he doesn't like getting in the water at all. I swear he's more like a house cat than a wolf. So he's grateful I do the diving. He's the one who plans everything out; pays for the accommodations, boat, and equipment; provides medical assistance if I need it; and stays topside while I go diving."

Vaughn pulled Jillian close and wrapped his arm around her, as if he worried she was feeling poorly. She snuggled next to him and suddenly felt really tired. She guessed she'd been so wired about learning something new with the case that she had forgotten they needed to lie down.

"Hey, your sister needs to rest. Anything else you can think of that might help with the case?" Vaughn asked.

"No. Not offhand. If I think of anything, I'll let you know. Oh, and, Sis? No telling Dad about my treasure hunting."

"I won't. You have my word."

They ended the call, and then Vaughn stood and helped her to her feet. "I called Bella, and she said she'll ask the pack if anyone had been diving with Douglas. She said she knew nothing about it. But she gave me a list of places he's vacationed over the years: Belize, Fort Pierce, St. Augustine, here, the Caribbean. I'd say they all have sunken treasure."

"So it's like you suspected. He goes on vacations where he can enjoy his favorite hobby…treasure hunting."

"Right."

Vaughn was about to lift Jillian in his arms, but she said, "No way. If you don't rest your injured shoulder, I'll have to tie you down to the bed and—"

"Have your wicked way with me? Sounds good to me." He lifted her in his arms and carried her to the bedroom.

"You're just afraid I'll change my mind about napping with you."

"You're tired. I didn't want you to have to walk all the way to your bedroom." He set her on the queen-size bed and pulled off her boots. Then he went to the other side and yanked off his own.

They stood and pulled back the covers.

"We don't tell anyone about this." Jillian groaned a little as she lay down on the bed.

Vaughn groaned just as much and joined her. "I thought I was doing my job."

"Yeah, but only the doctor needs to know about it."

Vaughn closed his eyes. "How's your head?"

"Pounding. How's your shoulder?"

"Same."

"We sound like two achy old wolves."

He chuckled. "Yeah. But by tomorrow, we'll be as good as new."

She sure hoped so. She hated feeling so out of commission, and she really wanted to get back to the investigation. She wondered how the jaguars would feel once they learned one of their own kind had injured a wolf. Closing her eyes, she tried to shut her mind down about everything, then envisioned the peacock she'd been working on, some of the feathers colored, most still white, and smiled.

Then they fell asleep, and it wasn't until hours later that Jillian heard someone at her bedroom door and turned to look. They hadn't closed it, not thinking they would take more than an hour nap or so, though Vaughn had set his alarm to check on her after three hours, and they'd snuggled and fallen back to sleep. What time was it anyway? It was already dark out. She was lying against Vaughn, her head on his chest, his good arm around her, his hand gently rubbing her back, so he was awake too.

She turned her head further to see who was in the doorway. All three jaguar agents were standing there checking them out. She wanted to groan out loud.

Chapter 12

"IT'S BEEN HOURS SINCE WE RETURNED. WE WERE JUST checking to make sure you both were still alive." Demetria smiled at Jillian and Vaughn as they didn't make a move to get out of bed right away.

Vaughn sighed. "Don't tell me the cat is out of the bag now."

Howard said, "I told you they have a really strange way of taking on a mission."

"Doesn't look strange to me at all. Looks quite natural. Is the coloring book for all of us? I want the jaguar, but I might have to fight Howard for it." Demetria patted Howard's arm.

Jillian laughed, glad the jaguars enjoyed working with them as they all moved to the kitchen. "Now that's something the three of you will have to figure out. How are you feeling, Vaughn?"

"Like I'll be good as new—*tomorrow*."

"We're making spaghetti for dinner. The two of you can come in and just relax while we're fixing it," Demetria said.

"We have news." Jillian hadn't known what it would be like working with jaguar shifters. She normally got along with most people just fine, but she hadn't been sure if working with jaguars would change the dynamics a lot. Luckily, it didn't seem to. They appeared amused to see the changing attitudes between the two wolves. "And dessert's on me."

Vaughn frowned at her.

"You said the ice-cream bars are mine. So I'm sharing them."

He snorted. "You didn't seem happy to share with *me* last night."

"That's because it was my last one, and *you* didn't ask."

The jaguars chuckled.

"So what's your news?" Demetria asked, stirring the spaghetti sauce.

They told them about the treasure-hunting expeditions while Jillian pulled up the articles on Douglas to show to them.

Demetria wiped her hands on a kitchen towel, then pointed to the screen. "Says here he was in Belize this past year looking for treasure."

"Do you know something about it?" Jillian asked.

"Only that a lot of us go down there because jaguars still roam free there for now," Everett said. "That's where Demetria and I are going for our belated honeymoon this summer. We still need to have our wedding too."

"You're both invited to the wedding," Demetria said.

"Wow, congratulations to both of you. I'd love to come."

Vaughn echoed Jillian's comments.

Jillian began to set the table and explained about Douglas and Miles's group excursion in Belize this past year.

"Did the other treasure hunters smell like jaguars?" Demetria asked.

"They did, and Miles has been seeing one of them

intimately. Kira Wells." Jillian told them her brother and Douglas had been friends for ten years, and they'd even met at the Kitty Cat Club six months ago and talked about another expedition.

"I danced with Kira," Vaughn said, "if she's the same woman. And she danced with Douglas after me. But she didn't dance with Miles. He said he hadn't remembered seeing any of them there."

"So the jaguar shifters who were at the club were probably the same ones who have now been in this area. Probably one of them overheard Miles and Douglas talking about their next expedition," Demetria said.

"That was in Belize. And if it's the same people, they just happened to sign up for the same tour as Douglas and Miles did," Jillian said.

Everett pulled out his phone. "I'm going to update our boss on the situation." He called Martin Sullivan and then put the call on speaker.

"Wait, let me pull up the articles on treasure hunting you found." Martin didn't say anything, then whistled. "I'm in the wrong line of business."

They all told him where they were on the case and that this might be the first real lead they'd had.

"I suggest Demetria and Everett check out the Kitty Cat Club. Learn what you can. If Miles shows up before you leave, take him with you in case he recognizes anyone from the boat he was on in Belize. My agents may have a better chance talking with other jaguars about who might be involved. I want Jillian and Vaughn to stay here for when Douglas comes out of his coma. Howard can help track down any leads, in case you have to stay with Douglas."

"Sounds good," Everett said.

Everyone else agreed, and then they ended the call with the boss.

Vaughn served glasses of water for everyone to have with their dinner.

"We didn't do a thorough search of Douglas's cabin because I'd hurt my head," Jillian said. "If you're going to travel to San Diego tomorrow, maybe we can all do that after we eat."

"Sounds good to me," Demetria said.

"It's about an eighteen-hour drive," Vaughn said, looking it up on his phone. "Are you going to drive, or fly and get a rental car?"

Jillian looked up the information on her phone. "It's only two hours' flight time."

"I vote for the flight," Demetria said. "The JAG branch will pick up the tab, and we need to check into this sooner rather than later."

"Okay, so we go to Douglas's cabin tonight, in case there is something there. We wouldn't want the jaguar to grab the evidence and run," Everett said.

"Are the two of you okay to go?" Howard brought over a platter piled high with garlic toast. "We can run by there and let you get some more *rest*." He winked at them.

Vaughn glanced at Jillian, letting her make the call.

"No. If all of us go, we have more of a chance of finding something crucial to the case. And if he comes back, maybe this time we can catch him," Jillian said.

"We got Doc's lab results, if you haven't learned about them yet," Demetria said while serving the spaghetti. "We were shocked to learn a jaguar injured

Douglas after it appeared a wolf had. We will find the shifter who did this."

Everyone took seats at the table.

"So when is Miles coming here?" Demetria asked.

That was the million-dollar question. "I'm afraid he's going to confront Kira with some of these concerns," Jillian said.

No one said anything, and Jillian knew just what they were thinking. Miles was playing with fire. If they were forewarned, the big cats might clear out of the area, and the team wouldn't be able to locate them.

After they finished eating, they took off in two cars for the cabin. Howard stayed with the wolves and drove this time.

When they reached the cabin, Jillian warned, "A couple of the windows are open again."

"We might have left them open," Vaughn said.

Everyone was armed and ready for action as the jaguars went to the back and the side of the house. Howard and Jillian climbed the porch to open the door.

As soon as Jillian and Vaughn stepped on the front deck, it creaked. Though she suspected whoever was in the house had already heard the vehicles pull up, she still hated to let anyone who might be in the cabin know exactly where they were. Then again, whoever had opened the windows might have left already.

She tried the door and found it locked. Vaughn pulled out his lock pick, something most *lupus garous* kept on them. The lock clicked open. Then he pushed the door open and they waited, listening for any sign anyone was moving about in the cabin.

Vaughn shoved the door further aside and flipped

on the light switch. No one was in the living room that Jillian could see, but she immediately smelled her brother's scent, and it was fresh. From the way Vaughn glanced at her, she knew he did too. She nodded.

Then they moved in unison. Vaughn walked quickly around the couch, while she headed toward the kitchen. No one was in either location.

"All right, all right," Miles called out. "You caught me. I'm coming out with my hands up. Don't shoot! I was just getting ready to call you."

Jillian couldn't believe it! "Are you alone?" She was highly annoyed with her brother for coming back here. Now he really did appear to have been involved in all of this.

"Yes." Her sandy-haired brother moved toward them, walking slowly down the hall, his hands up, his phone in his right hand, his blue-eyed gaze shifting from her to Vaughn.

Vaughn had lowered his weapon but was still holding it like he planned to shoot her brother if he made a false move. Jillian hadn't holstered her weapon either, not because she didn't trust her brother completely, but she didn't trust that the cabin was clear.

"Are you all right staying with him?" Vaughn asked.

"Yeah, sure."

"I'll check out the rest of the rooms." Vaughn stalked off to search the bedrooms and bathroom.

"Do you have any weapons on you?" Jillian asked her brother.

"Just a hunting knife."

"What if the person who had injured Douglas had been here?"

"I would have taken care of him," Miles said.

Right. And her brother would have gotten himself killed. "What are you doing back here?" Jillian was so annoyed that she could have arrested him just for being stupid about this.

"I really like Douglas. He doesn't judge me like Dad does. I want to do something to help catch the guy who hurt him. I kept thinking about what you and Vaughn said about the jaguar coming back here for stuff and hurting you. So I thought maybe he left something else behind. *Something* that would prove he did it. Why are *you* here?"

"I'm investigating the attack." Jillian couldn't believe she was having this conversation with her brother.

"No, I *know* that. What I meant was what are you hoping to find…specifically?"

"Anything related to Douglas being injured."

"I found something. Probably not related to the crime, unless someone else knew it was here and wanted it, so I thought I'd better see if it was here and turn it over to you for safekeeping in case whoever injured him was after it. That's what I was getting ready to call you about when I heard the cars. I checked and saw it was you, so I didn't panic. But, well, you might want to come in here and see."

"What is it?" Jillian asked.

"Remember when we used to go camping with Dad at the old cabin, and he'd hide his gun while we went for a run as wolves?"

"Yeah, sure. Under the wooden floor planks. And he told us never to touch the gun unless he was with us."

"Yeah. Beneath the wooden floor. Under the bed,

not just in the middle of the floor, covered with a floor rug."

"You're a genius." Jillian was proud of her brother, though she still didn't know what he'd found.

"No, not quite. I told Douglas the story last year when we were swapping stories. He always had large sums of cash when he'd book a boat for us to search for sunken treasure. I wondered if he would have created the same kind of secret place to hide a lot of money. If Douglas truly meant for us to do a treasure hunt, he would have brought the money with him."

Jillian stared at him. "The cash. Ohmigod. We found it."

"You did? I'm so glad to hear it. I thought the jaguar who tore into him got it. I thought I'd find it in the cubbyhole. I flashed my penlight in there, but the bags of money weren't there. The scent was though. So I figured Douglas had hidden the money there, then got it out to pay the boat rental guy. But when I checked with the boat rental management, they said Douglas wasn't coming until today, so he hadn't paid the money yet. I told them we had to cancel. So you really got the money. How much?"

"Yeah, yeah, we've got it. Vaughn gave it to Leidolf, who put it in his safe. Ten thousand dollars."

"Yeah, that's how much he spends on a boat, fully equipped for salvage. We spend a week out on a job, sometimes returning for provisions and then heading out again."

"This is why you don't get a long-term regular job?"

"See? That's just how Dad would react."

"It's like gold fever." She studied Miles for a moment. "That's why you go off sometimes, and when you return to see me, you look like you've been sunburned on a beach. I thought you had taken up surfing or something."

"You should see how scratched up we get, between the sand on our skin and our knees on the coral. Did you know that gold always retains its gold appearance? But iron and other artifacts are encrusted in centuries of marine life and look like rocks. Orange rust could be oxidized iron of some sort. Blackened items, oxidized silver. You have to know what you're looking for. But we take metal detectors with us, and that helps to find some of it. It's down there, just waiting to be found."

"So what did you find hidden away?"

"Douglas's treasure journal. I was just about to reach my hand in to grab it when I heard the cars pull up. I worried it was the jaguar that had injured you and maybe Douglas, so I closed it back up. I hurried to look and saw it was you." Miles paused in the hall. "I thought the journal would prove Douglas was here so we could go diving. So did someone else know about the money? Maybe about his notes on treasure hunts? Had the person tried to intimidate him into telling where it was? I was going to call you," he repeated.

Vaughn got on his phone and put it on speaker. "Hey, Everett, it's all clear in the cabin. Got the phone on speaker. Miles is here. He said he found Douglas's journal outlining treasure hunts that he had hidden. That would most likely confirm he was going to schedule a boat trip to search for treasure. We're just about to get it. What are you all doing?"

"I'm glad to hear Miles is there and safe. Tell him he can go with us to the Kitty Cat Club tomorrow in San Diego. We were worried he might have gotten himself into trouble. He needs to come back to the ranch with us not only for his own protection, but so we can use his assistance to help solve the case."

Jillian was certain Everett said that because he wanted her brother to feel important in resolving the case, and she could have given him a hug for it.

"On the trip to San Diego, absolutely. I'll do whatever you need me to do," Miles said agreeably.

"Good. We're retracing the tracks that everyone has left in the area...the jaguars' and Miles's. We smelled his scent as he walked from his cabin to this one. No jaguar scents, but we've found other evidence: jaguars' hairs caught on underbrush and pugmarks in the wet soil. We'll be at this for a while," Demetria said.

"Sounds good. We'll keep searching the cabin for other clues," Vaughn said.

"Okay, out here."

"The journal was in Douglas's bedroom, right?" Jillian asked her brother.

Miles shook his head and motioned to another. "It wasn't in Douglas's room. It was in one of the other rooms."

"Douglas might have hidden it there and purposefully stayed in another room, figuring if the other rooms were empty, no one would think he would have anything in them." Though if Jillian had wanted to hide a large sum of money and an important journal, she would have put it somewhere near her so she could safeguard it better. Otherwise, she could imagine constantly worrying that someone else would find it, and she'd never get any sleep. She stared at the bed. It looked like it hadn't been moved.

"I crawled underneath to look. So yeah, you'll smell my scent underneath the bed, and on the boards where I pulled one up, but I didn't touch the journal. I had to know it was there before I could call you, then I didn't know who had arrived so closed it back up. No jaguar scent is under the bed, so they didn't find it. I smelled the money, but I hadn't been able to feel inside to see if it was there. Wait. Is your head all right?" Miles asked Jillian. "Vaughn and I can move the bed."

"Vaughn's shoulder is probably worse off than my head," Jillian said.

"I can do it by myself." Miles sounded proud that he was completely fit.

They all helped him move the bed anyway.

All three crouched over the spot and smelled for scents. Miles was right. All Jillian smelled were Douglas's and Miles's scents.

"Go ahead," Vaughn said to Miles, giving him the honor of lifting the boards.

Miles smiled at him and looked to Jillian. She nodded. She decided right then and there that Vaughn was an all-right alpha wolf. Hot too.

Vaughn put his hand on her brother's arm before he lifted the first board to stop him. "Wait. I heard something." Vaughn checked around the boards. "Let me do it." But he again paused. "What kind of a shot are you, Jillian?"

"Sharpshooter. What are you thinking?"

"I swore I heard the faintest sound of a rattle."

"Hell, I'm glad you drove up when you did, or I would have just stuck my hand in there and seized the journal. I guess moving the bed disturbed the snake. I got this."

Miles grabbed a pillow from the bed and pulled off the pillowcase. Then he readied the pillowcase and nodded at Vaughn.

"Are you sure?" Vaughn asked.

"Yeah. I used to help with rattlesnake roundups. We milked the venom to create antivenom. Douglas has done those too. I'm not surprised he might have used a snake to deter would-be thieves."

Jillian let out her breath and shook her head.

Vaughn just smiled at the two of them. She didn't. She wondered what else her brother had been doing that was that dangerous that she hadn't known about.

Vaughn began to lift a board. Jillian readied her gun. If the snake struck at them, she was taking it out. She just hoped her brother didn't get in the way.

Nothing happened. No snake coiling up and striking out. But she heard the faint rattle this time.

Vaughn gingerly moved the board aside and started on another.

Jillian's heart was pounding, and she could hear her brother's accelerated heartbeat too. But Vaughn's was nice and steady.

He moved the next board and set it aside. They had a clear view of the rattlesnake right before it lunged at Jillian. Miles jerked the pillowcase over its head and grabbed the body. Vaughn helped him shove the rest of the snake inside the pillowcase, then Miles knotted it.

Jillian was shaking from the effort. She could handle about anything. But she hated rattlesnakes and copperheads. She was glad her brother could take care of it. She wasn't sure she could have. Now she could smell the snake.

"Thanks for not shooting me, Sis." Miles set the bag aside.

"It's a good thing you reacted so quickly. I don't think I would have had a chance to shoot it. So thanks."

Vaughn shook his hand. "Good work. You'd come in real handy on a wilderness survival mission."

Grinning, Miles looked perfectly pleased with himself, but waited to see what Vaughn told them to do next.

"Why in the world would he have put a rattlesnake down there? I mean, I suppose to protect the money and the journal, but how would he have done so without getting bitten? And how would he have gotten the money and journal back out again without risking the rattlesnake biting him that time either?" Jillian asked.

"I told you. He knew how to handle snakes," Miles said. "We found a den of them in a bunch of rocks near here. He must have gotten one that was hibernating and slipped it in there."

"Now you tell me!"

Vaughn and Jillian leaned down to smell the hole, but the only one who had left a scent was Douglas. And they could smell the ink on the journal and the money that had been there. "Just Douglas has been in here," Vaughn confirmed. "Okay, go ahead, take out the journal."

Miles showed them the old journal. "Thankfully, they didn't find this. He keeps all his notes and hand-drawn maps. So he has several journals. I was afraid whoever attacked him might have found this one somewhere else in the cabin if Douglas had it out at the time. He doesn't always bring one with him, so I wasn't sure he would this time. We've had to go out and pick up a note-book before when he's forgotten to bring one. He's too meticulous not to journal about all of it." Miles gently removed the journal as if it would break and handed it to Jillian.

Jillian was busy looking through the journal, admiring the well-drawn maps, many of them even colored with colored pencils—which made her think of the coloring book she and Vaughn were playing with. Beautiful.

Everett called Vaughn, who put the cell on speaker. "Yeah, Everett? I have you on speaker."

"We're coming in. Only two jaguars were in the area recently."

"We found a journal Douglas used to document their treasure hunts," Vaughn said.

"Okay, be at the cabin in a couple of minutes."

"All right."

They heard someone coming in the front door, but before he and Jillian could check it out, Everett called, "Just us!"

Chapter 13

Miles grabbed the rattlesnake in the pillowcase and headed out of the bedroom.

Vaughn called his pack leaders to confirm the situation about the money. When he ended the call, Jillian said, "Thank you."

Vaughn shrugged. "Miles was a great help. I couldn't have done a better job."

"Miles took off to return the rattlesnake to its den. I'm glad they're in hibernation when we come here. We'll find out who injured Douglas and why this happened," Jillian said.

"You think you know someone, and then something like this happens. Let's head back to the ranch."

"Okay." She looked up at him. "Vaughn?"

"Yeah?"

"Thanks for the way you handled things with my brother."

"He was good with the snake. I'll give him that. He was a real help with locating the journal and helping us to secure it until Douglas recovers." But Vaughn couldn't say with a clear conscience that he totally trusted her brother. It seemed too convenient that Miles had known where to look. Who was to say that Miles had really planned to call his sister? He could just as easily have pulled his phone out and had it in his hand when they entered the cabin to give a cover story. He probably assumed he had to come up with a really good reason to be here, if he wasn't trying to hide evidence of his own complicity or take the money for his own personal use. He hadn't known the money wasn't where he smelled it. At that point, maybe Miles felt it was just better to give up the money.

"I want to check something out first." Vaughn headed into Douglas's room.

"What are you looking for?" Jillian asked.

"What if Douglas hid something else, only this time under *his* bed? It would be bad if he had hidden more money and someone else came along and stole it. Better to keep it safe for him until he recovers." Vaughn wasn't really looking under the bed for that reason, because he didn't think Douglas had had secret hidey-holes all over the cabin. Vaughn wanted to see if Miles had searched under all the beds, or just the one because he already knew Douglas hadn't been hiding anything under his own bed or anywhere else.

"Do you want to get the cats' help to move the bed?" she asked.

"No. This will only take a second." Vaughn began to slide the bed over with Jillian's aid, but Howard and Everett quickly joined them and helped.

No secret hideaway here.

"Looking for more cash hidden away here?" Howard sounded surprised.

Vaughn smelled Miles's scent, indicating he'd been checking under the bed. "Yeah, just in case."

"Good idea."

Miles joined them, stood in the doorway, and folded

his arms across his chest. "That was the first place I looked."

Or had he left his scent there on purpose to throw them off? Then again, if Miles had known where the money was, why wouldn't he have just grabbed it and run? It would have taken time to leave his scent under the other beds.

"You can check the bed in the last bedroom too. I didn't find any hidden compartment there either. You know how it always goes. Last place you look, there it is."

"Since we're here, we might as well check it out too just in case you missed anything," Vaughn said while Howard and Everett moved the other bed back.

"We'll move the bed this time," Howard said, his voice stern. "If you don't give your shoulder a break, you'll never heal."

They moved the bed in the spare room, and while Vaughn crouched low and felt for loose boards, he breathed in the scents again. Miles's scent was there too. Now Vaughn was satisfied.

They moved the bed back, then headed into the living room.

"Now that we have the DNA sample for the bite wound," Vaughn said, "all we need is a swab of the cats' mouths. That could confirm whether one of them is innocent or guilty."

"Yeah. We already took a bunch of jaguar hairs to the doctor to see if he could get a match. Problem was that some of them were ours," Everett said. "And without an actual hair root, he can't make a positive match either."

"You don't happen to have a glass that Kira used that hasn't been washed, have you, Miles?" Jillian asked.

"No. We weren't doing any eating or drinking," Miles said.

"I turned her panties over to the doc," Howard said, "in case he could get anything from them. But he said no. You were asleep when we returned to the guest house, and it slipped my mind."

"I'll see if Leidolf can put me up at another house so Miles can stay at the one we are at for now," Howard said.

"I can do that. No sense in having you move," Miles said.

"We'll decide when we get there then," Howard said.

Then Vaughn and Jillian headed to the guest house, where they met up with the rest of the gang. They all had ice-cream bars, and Jillian downloaded the pictures from Douglas's phone to her laptop so they could be brightened and seen in a larger view.

While she did that, Miles flipped through the coloring book. "So this is what Howard was talking about. Who would have thought a bunch of combat-trained jaguars and wolves would be coloring pages in their spare time."

"Pick a page," Everett said. "This is how we de-stress."

Miles smiled and found a giraffe.

"Okay, I've downloaded all the pictures. While I'm brightening the dark ones, why don't you look at the pictures on Douglas's phone, Miles, and see what you think of them. See if there's anyone you suspect could have hurt Douglas."

"Will do." Miles took the phone and began to go through them.

Howard watched over his shoulder. Vaughn sat next to Jillian and watched her lighten the ones at the Kitty Cat Club and others that were too dark to see well. That meant they were grainier, the color not as true, but at least they could make out the people in the photo.

"Okay, so that's you and your date," Jillian said to Vaughn.

"Yeah. And that's Douglas's with Brock and his date. We all went out the one time, and that was it."

"Did you return to the club the next day or any other?" Jillian asked.

"We did for about an hour. I'd ditched my date."

She looked up at Vaughn. "Really?"

"Hell yeah."

"You...were alone?"

"Just in case I got damn lucky."

She smiled, thinking he meant he would have liked to have danced with her. But maybe he hadn't meant that at all. "I wasn't able to go the next day. Had an important case that came up."

"That's why I was only there for an hour. Nobody who interested me was there the next night."

"You mean me?" Jillian asked.

"Hell yeah, you."

Howard laughed and shook his head.

"Okay, here's a photo of...?" Jillian asked.

"Douglas's date, my brother, and his date."

"Okay, here's the one of me with Kira when we were in Belize," Miles said, bringing the phone over to show them.

Vaughn frowned. "She's the one who danced with me at the club. No last name, just Kira. She smelled of cat... Well, all the women I danced with did. Once I saved the dancer, I swear every woman in the club wanted to dance with me to show their appreciation."

"Because the dancer was a jaguar and so were they. Probably friends of hers," Jillian said. "Here is Kira's picture. Douglas took one with you up close and personal with her on the dance floor."

"And she danced with Douglas too," Vaughn said.

Jillian continued to brighten up the photos, sharpening them.

Miles started to look over her shoulder. "Wait! Increase the size of that photo Douglas took of me with my date at the club."

Jillian did.

"Crop us out, and focus on the two men and the woman slightly behind us."

Jillian cropped the three people so they took center stage.

They all looked them over. "That's Kira in the red dress," Demetria said.

"And the two guys with her?" Miles showed them the picture of him in Belize with the others on the scuba-diving trip on the phone. "That one with the blond hair is her brother, Brutus, and the one with black hair is their friend Wayne."

"They were all at the club at the same time," Everett said. "And you and Douglas mentioned going to Belize while you were there."

"Yeah. We were talking about the trip. I didn't want Jillian to know about it, so Douglas and I were off by ourselves. It was noisy in there. We had to practically shout about our trip plans."

"So there was a good chance Kira, her brother, and their friend scheduled to be there at the same time because they'd overheard you talking. Or at least one of them," Vaughn said.

"Yeah, but why?" Miles asked.

"Like you said, all they had to do was do a search for your names. They could have easily found Douglas's and information about his treasure-hunting experience and successes. They figured on cashing in on his success by stealing his secrets. The money for the expedition would have been a boon too. But they had to get rid of Douglas," Howard said.

"Could be," Jillian said, "but what if there's more to this? That they'd hoped to hook up with the guys like they did in Belize. If Douglas is the golden goose, wouldn't it be more prudent to solicit his friendship like they seem to have done and help him and Miles find treasure, sharing in it even?"

"So you think something changed? Maybe that's why Douglas was upset about something and wanted to talk to me about it," Miles asked.

"Maybe he learned you were seeing Kira, and he was concerned she was a gold digger," Howard said. "Excuse the pun."

"Or maybe one of them approached Douglas about having a partnership with the two of you and he said no, and the one jaguar nearly killed him." Jillian continued to lighten up the club photos while Demetria straightened up the kitchen.

"Wait," Miles said, looking at another picture Jillian had just brightened up. "Well, hell."

Everyone came over to look at the photo. They all gaped at the shot. "Is that who I think it is doing what I think they're doing?" Howard said.

"Kira kissing Brutus in a totally sexual way while he's got his hand firmly planted on her butt," Miles said. "Yeah."

In that instant, Jillian felt sorry for her brother. Nothing worse than being lied to by a person he'd been intimate with.

"You don't think they have an incestuous relationship, do you?" Miles asked, sounding revolted.

"I suspect they're lovers, and he's no relation to her whatsoever," Jillian said. "They don't look alike at all, if they're jaguars and twins. Not that all twins look alike, but after seeing them in this pose, I'd say they're not brother and sister or anything else that makes them relations." Jillian turned to her brother. "So tell us more about the treasure hunts you've been on."

"I've gone on treasure hunts with Douglas a number of times. Once, I was supposed to find a lost treasure in a lake. He gave me the coordinates, and I located it. We split the profits fifty-fifty because he needed a dive-certified wolf."

"I dive, and I'm in his pack," Vaughn said.

"Yeah, I know, because you're a SEAL. He said a SEAL was in his pack, but you were out of the country on a mission."

"What was the treasure that time?" Jillian asked.

"Gold Confederate coins. He'd found the whereabouts of the ship, and he knew I was a diver. So he contacted me. He was excited about it, and I was out of work at the moment, so it sounded like a great deal to me. Even if we didn't find any gold on board, I still loved the idea of searching for it. The ship had sunk in Lake Michigan and the temperature was thirty-seven degrees when I went diving. I found a safe, and we hauled it up. Three hundred and fifty thousand in gold coins were in the safe. I got half."

"You never told me about that," Jillian said. "I thought you were always broke."

"I spent most of it when I first got it. Replaced my old car. Got more high-tech dive equipment. Before long, I was broke again. When Douglas said he'd located a shipwreck off the Florida Keys, I flew out to help him with that one too. We made only about twenty thousand in salvage that time, but I loved it. We work really well together. He did all the research about sunken ships carrying treasure and located the area where he thought they'd be. Sometimes they were. Sometimes they weren't. When he said he had a job that would be worth ten thousand, I said sure. We'd had other jobs that didn't pan out, of course, but I didn't have anything to lose. I trusted him completely, both with the money and the jobs. Why wouldn't I have?"

"Why didn't you tell me any of this?" Jillian asked.

"You are so good at saving practically every penny you earn. If you learned how much money I blew through after a job, I knew you'd be even more disappointed in me than you already were."

"You can verify all of this?" Vaughn asked.

"Yeah. Ask Fred Greyton. He's in your pack. He's the one who used to go with Douglas on treasure hunts. I'm certain newspapers published articles about the treasure finds Douglas and I made. I didn't hang around for fame, just the fortune. You can probably find the stories online even."

"We did, but no mention of you. Douglas didn't seem to have a lot of extra money on hand. My pack leaders checked his accounts," Vaughn said.

"He was like me. Big windfalls, paid taxes on them,

spent the rest. With our current longevity issues, we figured life was too short now. We might as well enjoy it while we could. Once, he said something about keeping some of his money hidden away for a rainy day. I didn't know how much, but I figured he was just better at saving money than I was. If I had money in the house like that, I would have spent it. We haven't had another successful treasure hunt like that in two years. You can check his accounts further back and see some more activity, I'm certain."

"I probably would have saved every dime of it," Demetria said. "Maybe we can learn something about these jaguars in San Diego tomorrow. Who they really are. If Kira even has a brother, and who this guy might be. Maybe someone knows where they are now. Good work on finding the treasure journal." Demetria took Everett's hand. "Everett made a super-early flight for us. We're off to bed. Get some rest. We'll see you in the morning." They headed for the master bedroom on the other side of the house.

"Hey, why don't you and I stay at the other house," Howard said to Miles. "We can talk some more. Leidolf's arranged for us to have another couple of rooms."

"Yeah, sure." Miles frowned at his sister, but then said good night to her and Vaughn, and then he and Howard left.

Vaughn placed his arm over Jillian's shoulders and walked her down the hall to her bedroom. "I still have a mission."

"Keep me safe?"

"Yeah, that too." He pulled her into her room and shut the door. "Doctor's orders. I have to wake you every two to three hours. If I'm in the other room, I'm going to sleep right through it."

"Somehow, I don't see you as someone who would forget to do his duty. And knowing you, you'll set your alarm again." She sat down on the bed, but before she could, he removed her boots.

Then he sat down on the other side and removed his. *Déjà vu.* "You're right, if I hadn't been injured too. How are you feeling?"

"Actually? Much better." She pulled off her socks, then grabbed some things from a drawer. "I'm taking a shower. I'll be right back."

Vaughn removed everything but his boxer briefs, lay back on the bedcovers, and stared up at the ceiling. He'd never worked with this many people on an assignment before, except with his SEAL team. When he worked as a PI, he always went off to do his own investigations. He thought he preferred it that way. But Jillian had changed his mind about that. Not only did he want to protect her while she helped him investigate this case and was on his side, watching his back, but he valued her opinion concerning what was going on. Two heads were definitely better than one.

While he listened to her taking a shower again, he wondered what she had in mind after this mission was through. He was thinking how much he'd like to take a vacation for the first time in eons—only this time with one savvy and sexy she-wolf.

Chapter 14

JILLIAN TOOK A QUICK SHOWER SO VAUGHN COULD also get one and they could sleep. She was exhausted. She imagined he was too. As soon as she entered the bedroom, she saw he was lying on his back, his eyes closed, and he was wearing just a pair of navy boxer briefs.

Even in sleep, he looked like he could tackle the world. One sexy package lying there for her viewing pleasure.

"Bathroom's free." She spoke softly, not wanting to wake him in the event he was already sound asleep.

He didn't stir. She grabbed a blanket from the bedroom closet and spread it over him. Then she climbed into bed, pulled the covers up, and closed her eyes. A while later, she felt the bed move. Vaughn got up and left the room. The shower ran after that. She thought of him soaping down all those hard muscles, remembering the way he'd looked when he'd walked toward his cabin, naked, all sculpted and delicious, and she smiled. Then she thought of him and her showering together, and she felt she needed to take another shower.

She must have fallen asleep after that, because the next thing she knew, he was joining her under the covers. This time, he reached for her and pulled her close. She didn't know how she'd ended up snuggling next to him last time. Unless she'd gotten cold. He hadn't seemed to mind. As long as she didn't hurt his shoulder, she really loved resting against the warm-bodied hunk on the chilly night.

"Are you checking to see if I'm still alive?" She felt dreamy and comfortable. "Oh, oh, do I need to reapply the bandage?"

"No. It's beginning to heal up fine." He kissed her neck and held her back against his chest. "I intend to do my duty…to the max. This way, I can listen to your light breathing and your heartbeat better."

"I can make sure you're not getting feverish from your wounds. You know truly, I had thought to scare you off. I was aiming at your legs, but you were moving so fast that I really didn't think I'd hit you. Any sane wolf would have run away after I shot at him the first time."

"I'm a SEAL. We're tougher and more determined than that. My mission was still straight in front of me."

"Well, I didn't know you were a SEAL at the time, but it sure explains why I had to shoot at you so many times."

"Did you really try to miss me the last time? You came awfully close to my head."

"Yeah. If I'd wanted to, I would have taken you out. On the first shot."

"Good thing you hadn't wanted to."

"Yeah, my thoughts too." She never thought she'd be feeling this way about the wolf now.

She sighed in his arms, loving his wolfish masculine scent mixed with a sweet vanilla one. She was a little surprised he'd used that body wash instead of the more masculine one Howard must have left behind. She pulled Vaughn's arm tighter around her, settled her back closer against his chest, and wondered if there was any chance a former Army intelligence officer and a Navy SEAL could see eye to eye on future investigations. Especially ones her brother wasn't involved in.

Maybe even work with the jaguar agents on future missions.

Maybe even more.

―∽∽―

Vaughn was glad Jillian had wanted him to sleep with her—even if she said it was because of the doctor's concern about her health. Any excuse worked for him, as long as the results were the same. When she turned around and curled up next to him, he was even more pleased. He hadn't expected her to begin stroking his chest, or run her fingers over his nipple in a seductive caress. Already, from the way their pheromones were kicking in, and the way she was touching him, his cock was stirring to life, eager to take this further. Though he knew he couldn't. Not yet.

He leaned down and kissed her head, her hand now sweeping down his belly toward the band of his boxer briefs. *Hell, woman.* He was going to come with barely any enticement, just from listening to her heartbeat, smelling her sexiness, and feeling her light breath whisper across his skin and her soft body pressed against his chest and leg.

Not sure what she had in mind, he swept his hand down her back until he reached the bottom edge of her pajama top, then slid his hand underneath it to caress her silky, warm skin.

"Tell me if I hurt you." On her knees, she swung her leg over his, then straddled him.

Smiling, he ran his hands up her thighs, wondering

where the wolf was going with this. She tugged her pajama top off, exposing her beautiful breasts, her nipples dusky pink and erect, mouthwatering. He really hadn't expected her to get half naked. He just stared at them. But then she scooted downward and began to slide her mound against his burgeoning erection. Then he was able to cup her breasts, to massage them and stroke her nipples with his thumbs.

He groaned as the sexual tension built between them, the friction arousing him further as she continued to rub her sweet body against him. He pulled her down to suckle a breast while she kept stroking his cock with her body.

"Is your shoulder all right?" she whispered against his mouth.

"Hell yeah." Even if it was killing him, he wouldn't have stopped this between them for the world.

She smiled against his mouth, right before she tongued his, demanding entrance.

He slid his hand down her pajama pants, caressing her soft, smooth ass, knowing they couldn't take it all the way. Not unless they agreed to a mating. But he sure as hell wished they could just enjoy the pure sex between them.

She continued to kiss his mouth, her hand sliding down his belly again. Only this time she moved aside and ran her fingers over his erection in a teasing caress, the boxer briefs still covering his flesh. Then she molded her hand around his cock and began to stroke.

"Jillian," he groaned out, his hand now pressing her buttocks so she was tighter against his leg as she continued to stroke him. He figured she thought it was safe to

stroke him if she was still wearing her pajama pants and
he was wearing his boxer briefs—until she pulled his
down and his cock sprang free. Before she could make
him come, he gently pushed her back against the mattress, untied her pants and pulled them off, then yanked
his own off, right before he moved in beside her.

Now they were both perfectly bare to each other. He
couldn't resist her touching him anymore without being
able to pleasure her too.

He turned his body so he could kiss her, then he
began to rub her clit while she stroked him. She was
so hot and desirable, smelling like sex and vanilla soap
and she-wolf, her mouth pressing against his, her fingers
firmly grasping him.

All he could think about was encouraging her climax,
while trying his damnedest to hold on to his own, when
she cried out and he muffled her cry with a deepened
kiss. Her free hand moved over his buttocks then, and he
broke. With a growl, he came…and swore, not having
planned to make such a mess of things. She was wet
with arousal and the fact he was even thinking about
how ready she was for penetration and how much he
wanted her body to surround him meant he was considering much more than being her work partner.

"Sorry," he apologized, looking down into her darkened eyes.

"For what?" She was still running her hands over his
side and hip in a gentle caress, as if she didn't want to
stop touching him.

He ran his hand over her belly where he'd spilled
his seed.

"I'll take care of it."

What he didn't expect was for her to take his hand as he stood next to the bed and lead him to the bathroom down the hall. He was damn glad Howard and Miles had stayed at the other house, suspecting the jaguar had this in mind when he made the arrangements. And Demetria and Everett had their own wing on the other side of the place. Vaughn and Jillian washed each other in the shower and returned to the bedroom wrapped only in towels.

—⁕—

Sometime in the night, Jillian had slung a leg between Vaughn's, an arm over his shoulder, and planted her cheek against his chest. Talk about claiming the wolf for her own. After she had initiated unconsummated sex with him, everything felt right with him.

He must have felt her stir or tense, because he began sliding his hand down her back in a gentle caress. "You must have felt me shivering and decided to warm me up."

She chuckled. "I just wanted you to know I was okay."

He laughed. "Hell, you're a lot more than okay. You're hot."

"I hope you still respect me this morning." She could feel his arousal beginning to take shape beneath her.

"About last night…"

"I was just making sure you didn't go after my brother again."

He smiled at her, rubbing her arm. Then he finally said, "I was just making sure you didn't shoot me again."

She laughed.

"I was thinking… I know I might be getting way ahead of myself on this, but if you have another job to do and you

wouldn't mind another investigator helping you out—"
he said.

She smiled. "Yeah, you're getting ahead of yourself.
I don't know what I'm going to do after this. I agreed
to help the jaguars out because Leidolf asked me. I like
what I do. I like working with the jaguars too. Would
working for all our shifter kind be for the greater good?
Or should I continue to work on my own? Chasing down
deadbeat husbands or cheating wives? I'd like to think I
was doing something for the shifter kind too."

He sighed dramatically. "There are a lot of terrific PIs
out there. Only three jaguar shifters are signed up to take
care of both our kind and theirs."

"True."

He caressed her back lightly. "We're the first of our
kind to even be asked to join the team. No one's offi-
cially trained us for this kind of work, so if we had some
training, we might even be better at it."

"I'm not sure the jaguars have even had time to set
up training for their own kind for dealing with mixed
shifter cases. The three of them have only had one case
to solve so far. I imagine every one of the cases will be
completely different from one another, not something
we—I mean, they—can plan for."

"Now that's something I wouldn't mind. Something
really different. I don't know. Even though I'm used to
working my own cases for the most part, I like the idea,"
Vaughn said. "I like getting in on the ground floor in an
organization like this. Then if it doesn't pan out, I can
always go back to my PI business."

"While you're with the USF, you can pair up with
Howard when you have to split up to do investigations."

Vaughn smiled at her and rubbed her arm. "I'd rather pair up with you. He can tag along, make sure we get the jaguar part of the equation right. Just think about it… delving into a whole new world of trouble."

"Are you going to tell them you want to do that?" She couldn't believe he was ready to make a commitment to the jaguar shifters.

"Yeah, I will. This morning at breakfast. You know they'll be wondering if you'll join us too."

Us. He really was jumping in with both feet. She liked that about him. "What if they don't have enough work for us?"

"Then we can do some investigating on the side. Just to keep in shape."

She ran her hand over his abs. "Keeping in shape is really important." Then she smelled bacon cooking in the kitchen and hurried to get off Vaughn. "It's time to eat, but I planned to help Demetria cook before they go to the airport this morning."

"How's your head? The rest of you looks fine."

She tugged on some panties and a bra. "Feels great. Are you coming?"

He stayed put, and she glanced at the erection tenting his boxer briefs.

"Meet you in the kitchen." She hurried to tug on a sweater and pants, then stuck her feet in a pair of slipper boots and hurried out of the room as she heard him finally getting out of bed.

"You're not afraid of the big, bad wolf, are you?"

After last night? Ha! She was more worried about herself around him. She laughed from down the hall and continued to the kitchen.

"How are you feeling?" Demetria turned the bacon in a frying pan when Jillian joined her.

"Great."

Everett was working on the eggs. Jillian thought Everett and Demetria made a really cute couple and that they worked so well together on missions.

"What can I do?" Jillian asked.

Demetria motioned to the bread. "Toast, juice."

"Got it."

"Where's sleeping beauty?" Everett asked. "Is he okay?"

Better than okay, if the way his erection had been swelling was any indication. Well, about his shoulder, Jillian wasn't certain. Why hadn't she asked? She had been thinking way too much about the way she'd aroused him, that's why.

"Shoulder's good." Vaughn joined them and winked at Jillian.

She swore her face had to be flaming beet red, as hot as it felt.

Demetria served a platter of bacon.

"I guess it's just you, Howard, and me then, Jillian." Vaughn set the table.

Jillian nodded. "Sure hope you learn something today."

"Us too. What are you going to do?" Demetria asked.

"We're going to see Douglas first. But I thought you should know. Vaughn has news for everyone," Jillian said, unable to wait any longer for Vaughn to tell them the good news. "Wait, got to get Howard in on this." She called him, and he said they were headed over for breakfast so Miles could ride with Demetria and Everett to the airport.

When they arrived and sat down to breakfast, Jillian

motioned to Vaughn. "He has something he wants to tell everyone."

Vaughn smiled at her, then opened his mouth to speak, but she did the talking for him. "We're both joining the USF. Hopefully, you'll be glad you asked us." She couldn't imagine not taking part in such an interesting venture, but most of all, it could be a way to really help their kind when the two shifter groups were at odds. And she definitely wanted to get to know Vaughn better.

"Hot damn," Howard said with exuberance.

"Hot damn is right," Vaughn said, smiling at Jillian as if he'd just won a pot full of gold.

All smiles, Demetria gave her a hug. Everett shook Vaughn's hand. Before he could give Jillian a hug, Vaughn did, and it wasn't just a way-to-go, welcome-to-the-team hug either. She almost laughed at the wolf's actions. She wondered if that was why he hadn't said he was joining yet. He really wanted to work with her on the team.

He finally released her, and Everett, Howard, and Miles gave her a sweet hug. Vaughn gave Demetria one.

"I can't say enough about what this means to us," Everett said. "Thanks. We really needed wolves on the force, but well-qualified wolves, and ones who know how to have some fun on the mission? Even better."

"I agree," Demetria said. "When we started this force after our last mission, we weren't sure how to go about finding the right wolves to join our team. I can see you were the perfect choice."

"Hey, you can team up with me," Miles said to Howard.

Everyone laughed.

Howard said, "Welcome to the USF, agents."

Jillian hadn't figured anyone would call them agents, but that was pretty cool too.

Demetria was still smiling at them, as if she suspected more was going on between the two wolves than just joining the force. Jillian suspected so too.

After breakfast, Miles, Demetria, and Everett took off for the airport, and Vaughn, Jillian, and Howard went to see Douglas.

Vaughn glanced at her as he drove his Land Rover to the clinic. "You surprised me when you told the cats we were joining the team. I figured you needed to think about it further."

"Not me. When I decide something, I go for it. I suspect you're the same way."

"I am. I would have decided a lot faster if I'd known you were joining."

She smiled. "Like right after I shot you?"

"I like to live dangerously."

Howard shook his head.

Jillian laughed. "I probably should have asked you about cases you've worked first. Before I decided to team up with you."

"Too late now." Vaughn thought about it for a moment, then said, "Well, the most recent case was when I was trying to track down a wolf—"

"Not the case concerning my brother."

"That sounds like one of those subjects best left alone," Howard said.

Vaughn agreed. "All right. You're not the first one who shot at me during a mission, you know. I have to admit, you're the only one who actually made her mark. Sometimes the would-be shooter didn't have a chance to get off a round. In one PI case, I was serving a divorce notice to a man on behalf of his distraught wife. Before I could tell the man who answered the door who the paper was for, another man came tearing to the door with a loaded 9mm. I quickly took him down, secured his gun, and served him the papers. Only they belonged to the man who had answered the door."

Jillian laughed. "Was that guy armed too?"

"Luckily, no. He knew it was coming. The two men were twin brothers living together. The wife of the armed man had been at a conference, and he thought she'd suddenly decided to divorce him because he wouldn't get them a place of their own. Anyway, it was easily resolved once he cooled down over his 'almost' divorce."

Jillian chuckled. "Okay, so I was serving divorce papers to a man, and he wanted to know if I was available."

"I hope you shot him."

She laughed. "I only shoot perps on special cases. You were definitely a special case."

"So I wonder if we'll need to move to Texas. Since Dallas is their headquarters."

"Maybe not. We might just be on call for whenever a case arises. You could still be working your job in Colorado, and I could be in Tacoma, Washington."

"Sounds to me like it would be better if we were living in a more central location."

"Like Colorado? With your pack?"

"I'm gone a lot of the time. So I don't do a lot of things with the pack." Then he smiled at her. "Of course, that could change if I was sponsoring a new wolf to the pack."

She shook her head. "You have it all worked out, don't you? What about me being close to family?"

"It's completely up to you."

"Hmm, if I moved to Colorado, some of your pack members might get the idea we're becoming mated wolves."

"No doubt. Especially after you shot me."

She laughed. Vaughn was just too funny. "So that's the only way a she-wolf could get your attention?"

"Only you."

Howard laughed.

Chapter 15

Despite the early hour, as soon as the others left for their flight, Vaughn wanted to see Douglas. "He's an early riser." Even though Douglas wasn't out of his comatose state yet, Vaughn always treated him as though he was.

"I want to run as a wolf through the area afterward. See if we might find any other trails that would give us a clue about the jaguar who was shot," Jillian said.

"I agree. But it's been raining so much, I'm not sure we'll find anything further. Still, it never hurts to have another couple pairs of eyes check things out again. They will let us into the clinic to see Douglas, won't they?" Howard asked.

"Yeah. That's the great thing about it being wolf-run. General hospital rules don't apply here." Vaughn parked the Land Rover, and they all got out.

Inside, Sally greeted them, and they went in to see Douglas. Before they could say anything to him, Jillian said, "Ohmigod, the window's open. Why would anybody have opened the window? I'll warn Sally." She ran out of the room.

Howard and Vaughn quickly checked on Douglas's condition. He was breathing fine, and his heartbeat was still steady, thank God. "No scent left behind," Vaughn said, smelling the air for any sign that a jaguar had been there recently.

"Yeah, the bastard must have been wearing hunter's spray, but he left muddy paw prints on the floor." Howard pointed to them. "Most likely a male's because of the bigger size prints. How much do you want to bet he heard us pull up, opened the window, and leaped out?"

They both looked out the window and saw pugmarks in the wet grass.

The nurse rushed into the room with Jillian. "No, I never would have opened the window." She hurried to shut it.

"Did he have any visitors last night or before we arrived this morning?" Vaughn asked, wondering how the hell the jaguar had gotten in without anyone seeing him.

"No. Well, some of the children from the pack came and read to him last night. But you're the first visitors he's had this morning."

"When was the last time you checked on him?" Jillian took hold of Douglas's hand.

"Just ten minutes ago."

Vaughn checked the window again to make sure it was locked. "Tell Leidolf to post a guard for Douglas. Do you have a room where we can shift? We'll try to track down the *visitor*."

Sally motioned toward the north side of the clinic. "You can use exam room three."

"Thanks." Vaughn, Jillian, and Howard headed for the room and saw the muddy jaguar paw prints all the way to the wolf door that led outside. "So that's the way he came in."

"He was just lucky no one caught him," Jillian said.

Vaughn snorted. "Hopefully we'll catch the bastard this time and his luck will run out."

They entered the exam room and began stripping.

"Should Jillian follow in the Land Rover with a gun?" Howard asked.

"No," Jillian said. "If a jaguar slipped in here, he wouldn't be driving a vehicle. Sally would have heard him park. And we would have seen the vehicle. If we all do this now, maybe this time we can catch one of them."

Vaughn had to agree with her. "Let's do this."

They all shifted and raced toward the back door of the clinic that had a wolf door, also another reason they preferred a wolf clinic to a human-run one.

They all headed outside, unable to follow a scent trail. But the jaguar had left his pugmarks in the wet dirt, and the race was on.

Vaughn had to admit he would have preferred that Jillian stay behind, but only because a wolf wasn't any match for a jaguar. The sky was beginning to lighten though it was a gray day, a mist of rain falling steadily as they followed the jaguar's trail to the stream. If it was the same one who had been shot before, he'd done it again—gone into the stream to hide his trail and make his escape.

Vaughn shifted. "We split up. Howard, you go north along the stream. See if you can find any sign of where he left the water. Go up about three miles. If you don't see any pugmarks, come back along the opposite bank and check there. We'll do the same going south."

Howard inclined his head, then started looking for any trail as he moved north. Vaughn shifted back, and he and Jillian headed south.

They had traveled about three miles when Jillian ran up to Vaughn and nudged his neck. He paused and glanced at her. She looked across the stream, and he saw what she had seen: a jaguar moving through the trees on the other side. Vaughn wanted to tell her to quickly go and find Howard. He should have been returning this way by now. Vaughn knew only another cat could hope to take down a jaguar. He would follow the cat as surreptitiously as possible.

Vaughn shifted. "Go get Howard and bring him here. I'll continue to track the cat."

Jillian studied him for a second. Then she lifted her chin, and he knew she meant to howl for Howard. Well, it wasn't any worse than his plan.

She howled, Vaughn shifted, and the jaguar turned to look at them. Vaughn prayed he wouldn't attack, that Howard would run like the wind and reach them before it was too late. That Leidolf would send a pack of wolves to aid them in intercepting the cat too.

The jaguar ran off, and all Jillian and Vaughn could do was take chase. They weren't all that far from the clinic, and once Sally informed Leidolf of the jaguar's presence there, he would send wolves to investigate anyway.

Sure enough, a couple of wolves howled they were coming.

Jillian paused and howled to let them know where she and Vaughn were now. The wolves could easily smell Vaughn and Jillian's scent. So they wouldn't have any trouble following them.

Then someone began firing a weapon. Vaughn didn't mind admitting he was reminded of Jillian's shooting him, and he wasn't eager to be shot again. But he especially didn't want her to get hurt. He was torn with indecision once again. Continue after his prey, the jaguar this time, or learn who the shooter was.

Howard suddenly joined them as the jaguar raced across the stream, and the three continued to chase after him. Vaughn and Howard were way in the lead, closing in on the jaguar, when Vaughn glanced back and noticed Jillian was gone.

<center>~~~</center>

Jillian knew Leidolf's men would go after the jaguar. And Howard had a good chance of taking him down on his own, particularly when a pack of wolves was coming to back him up. Her goal was taking down the shooter before he shot anyone.

She wasn't sure if he was a random hunter shooting illegally on Leidolf's property, or one of the jaguars involved in this mess.

A round hit a tree near her, and she dove for cover. She was getting close to him. The shots fired would warn Leidolf's men they still had an active hunter on their property. Someone would come to check him out.

She saw a man moving through the trees then, wearing camo clothes, hat, and boots. But he couldn't run fast enough from her. He was nearly to the edge of the woods when she saw a gravel road. A dark-gray Humvee was parked on the shoulder, and he was headed straight for it. Damn it! She had to take him down before he got away.

He suddenly swung around to take aim and shot at her. She dove back into the shrubs as he fired a few rounds, clipping the vegetation and sending leaves and twigs flying. Then he took off running again.

Jillian howled for backup, and then she raced after him again, knowing the danger. Now she was running in an open field, the tall grasses not much protection from a shooter, but she didn't use his trail, and hopefully the grass would help to hide her somewhat.

If she could just see his license plate, Leidolf's police officers could track him down. She already knew who he was, though. Wayne Grunsky, the friend of Brutus and Kira. The black-haired man. The one Miles had said was quiet. Now he was bearded. This wasn't the blond-haired man Vaughn had seen at the cabin. Was Brutus the jaguar Vaughn and Howard were chasing?

Someone got out of the Humvee and began shooting at her, and damn if he didn't look identical to the man running for the car. Same clothes. Same hair. Wayne's twin?

Wayne reached the SUV, turned around, and blasted a volley of rounds in her direction. Both men firing in her direction forced her to lie low as she waited for a chance to follow the car.

"I told you to stay in the damn car!" Wayne shouted to the other man.

"Hell, fine, next time I'll let the damn wolf take you down."

Then Wayne yanked open his door and jumped in, and the other man jumped into the driver's seat. Jillian raced across the gully to reach the road just as they drove off. The license plate was covered in mud, but the rain was washing the mud off, and she made out the words: Cat Clubber. Then the vehicle disappeared down the road.

Panting, she stood on the road staring in the direction they'd gone, furious with herself for not being able to take Wayne down before he got away. But now she realized there were two more jaguars involved in this. Two brothers. Twin brothers, it appeared.

Ten wolves raced to join her and quickly checked her over to ensure she was okay. Now she was worried about Vaughn and hoped Leidolf had sent this many wolves to help him.

She howled to let Vaughn know she was all right, just in case he could hear her.

———※———

Vaughn had to concentrate on his and Howard's situation with the jaguar, praying Jillian was just fine. Then he heard her howl, and a chorus of Leidolf's wolves howled around her, and he knew they were watching out for her. Relieved, he continued to focus on the jaguar. Suddenly, Howard leaped farther than Vaughn had ever imagined a big cat could leap. It had to be close to twenty feet.

Howard jumped on the jaguar's back, and the big cat whipped around and snarled at him. It sounded like something from a horror flick. Vaughn imagined when he and other wolves were in a fight to the death, they sounded just as vicious.

The jaguars' claws were extended like curved daggers, their wickedly large feline teeth exposed to the max. They swiped at each other, their postures rigid, tails slashing at the air.

Vaughn stopped and lifted his chin and howled to let other wolves know where they were and that they'd stopped, if they hadn't heard all the caterwauling going on. He also thought the jaguar might give up, believing Vaughn's howl would bring a huge pack of wolves. Maybe the jaguar would stand down and listen to reason.

Both cats stopped fighting and turned to look at

Vaughn. If the jaguar attacked him, the cat could easily kill him. He just hoped the jaguar would come to his senses before he had to fight him. Yet Vaughn was already planning his next move if the cat didn't give up quietly. He would assault him from the back. A frontal assault wouldn't work for him or any other wolf.

Howard refocused on the cat, waiting, both jaguars panting from exertion, their tongues hanging out. The cat shifted his attention to Howard, but he didn't attack him. Maybe he thought better of trying to kill Howard and having to outrun a whole pack of wolves.

Both Vaughn and Howard waited for the jaguar's next action. Vaughn could see Howard was as tense as he was, his body rigid, but Vaughn knew Howard could change his posture from stiffly standing still to lunging forward in a heartbeat.

The cat finally sat down on his rump, indicating he was done. Unless he was planning to attack them as soon as they let down their guard.

Howard growled at the cat. He stared back at him, glowering, his eyes narrowed. Then the cat rose to his feet and waited for Howard to do something further. Howard motioned with his head to return the way they had come. The cat inclined his head a bit in agreement and began to walk back toward the clinic.

The manner in which the cat was moving—limping, stumbling—made Vaughn think Howard's thrashing and biting wounds were probably giving the cat grief. Both jaguars' faces and necks were bleeding, their fur glistening with fresh blood. Howard fell in beside the cat. But then the jaguar turned to attack Howard. Vaughn leaped in to bite the cat's open flank, and a shot was fired. Vaughn didn't have time to look for the shooter, too intent on keeping the cat from killing Howard.

Just as Vaughn bit the cat, it stumbled and collapsed on the ground. For a minute, he and Howard watched the cat, expecting him to get up, but then Vaughn saw the dart in the jaguar's hip.

Hell, Vaughn was glad he'd only drawn a little blood when he bit the cat and that the tranquilizer hadn't spread fast enough to affect him too. That's when Vaughn finally noticed Leidolf's wolves surrounding them, moving in closer, acting as guards. A safari-type Jeep drove up. A man held up his rifle in salute to Vaughn and Howard, and the she-wolf of Vaughn's dreams jumped down and raced to join him.

Jillian rubbed up against Vaughn in a courting way, saying she wanted a lot more with him. Just like he did with her.

She turned to greet Howard too, giving him a lick on the cheek. He purred.

One of the men muzzled the tranquilized jaguar. A couple more tied his legs. Then several men lifted him into the Jeep. Howard jumped up there as if serving as a guard, just in case the cat revived before they caged him.

Then the wolves all headed back to the ranch, the safari Jeep in the lead.

At least now they had one of the men in custody and could question him, if he shifted.

Vaughn was damn glad Jillian was at his side again and that she was unharmed. He couldn't believe she'd gone after the damn shooter. Had she taken him down? She seemed tired, not bouncy, like he'd expect her to be if she'd caught him.

He never thought he'd live to see the day when he was hunting three big cats—maybe genuine cougars, but jaguars? Never.

He considered Jillian in her wolf form. She was a pretty gray wolf with a blond saddle and tummy. Black guard hairs framed her light-gray muzzle. Suddenly, she turned her head to see what he was doing. Caught in the act: gawking at her. Okay, so he was a little embarrassed and gave a sheepish wolf's grin.

He swore she smiled at him and gave a little wolf bark and a nudge, telling him she appreciated that he liked the way she looked.

As soon as they reached the clinic, Howard came out dressed, phone to his ear. "Hey, Jillian and Vaughn just made it back. I'll call you back in a minute. As soon as they shift and dress." He ended the call and said to Jillian and Vaughn, "Hell of a team. Jillian took after the hunter and kept him from shooting any of us, and you bit the jaguar before he bit me. Martin wants me to take this one to Dallas so they can continue questioning him there. He also wants me to take Miles, ask him to join the service and get some training under his belt."

Jillian wagged her tail.

Howard smiled at her. "That way Demetria and Everett can stay here to help the two of you, and I'll have someone to help transport the jaguar and aid me in the driving."

Jillian woofed. Vaughn agreed. It sounded like a good plan.

In exam room three, Vaughn and Jillian shifted, and he shut the door so they could dress. She threw her arms around his neck before he could even move to wrap her in his arms. Naked, they held on to each other in a lovers' embrace, kissing, tongues tangling, their hearts beating out of sync, rapidly pounding, and it had nothing to do with chasing anyone. It had all to do with the hot desire that flamed between them whenever they were together.

He wanted to make love to her here, right this very minute. But he knew they had to learn what was going on with the others, and they had to question the jaguar as soon as they could.

"I know," Jillian said, looking up into Vaughn's eyes. "We have to get back to work."

"You are beautiful. You scared the pants off me when I saw you weren't behind us, but I understand why you ran the other way."

"I couldn't stand the idea that the shooter might hit you or Howard. Right or wrong, I had to try to take him out. By the way, his car tag said Cat Clubber. He looked like Wayne, Kira and Brutus's friend. But, there's something more. The driver looked like his clone."

"Hell. So there are two of them? A twin? Hopefully we can soon learn who he is too. But if Wayne was the other male jaguar shifter, then the one Leidolf's man tranquilized must be Brutus."

"I agree."

They began getting dressed, but Vaughn couldn't keep his eyes off her as he watched her put on each article of clothing. She smiled at him. Then he noticed she'd been watching him too.

"I don't want to keep using old tired excuses for sleeping together, but—"

"Then we won't. We'll just share a bed, and someone

else can use the other one if they need to." Vaughn winked and buttoned his shirt, but she started to help.

Taking off clothes was more what he had in mind.

"Come on. Let's go see what Demetria has to say."

"Are you worried about your brother?"

Jillian pulled her phone out of her pocket and looked at her messages. "Nope. Let me call Leidolf about the license tag really quick so he can have one of his officers run down who it belongs to." After she did that, they left the room, but Howard led them back to the doctor's office so they could hear what Demetria had to say in private.

Vaughn was glad to see Howard had taken a moment to get patched up and was sporting bandages on his neck and face.

Demetria said, "Congratulations on catching one of the jaguars! Miles and Everett were disappointed they hadn't been there to take him down too. We found Kira's mother. She had a lot to say about the whole situation." Demetria gave them the woman's phone number so they could hear it from the jaguar's mouth. "She did say that Kira and her boyfriend and their friend Wayne were up near Portland, Oregon.

"She says she had no idea why they would have gone up there. But she knew all about the diving. Said that they were always looking for some get-rich-quick scheme if it meant they didn't have to do a lot of work. I asked if her daughter had ever mentioned being friends with Miles or Douglas, and she said no. She said she was sorry for Miles hooking up with her. She said that Kira is always catting around, won't stick with a guy for long, and if she does, woe to the guy.

"We found their home and are going through it now. Howard told us you caught Kira's lover, sounds like, and Jillian was after the one who was trying to shoot wolves."

"Cat Clubber was the license plate, in case you learn which one of the cats owns that vehicle," Jillian said. "And it appears there are two of them. Twin brothers. Same look, same camo clothes." Her phone beeped. "Wait, got a call." She took it, thanked the caller, and said to Demetria, "Leidolf said that the car belongs to Simon Wells."

"Not the same name as Wayne Grunsky then, if the other man was Simon," Demetria said.

"Wells. Wasn't that Kira's married name?" Vaughn asked.

"Yeah, it is," Jillian said. "What would be the likelihood that another man would have her deceased husband's name and not be related? But if he's not Wayne's brother, then related in some other way. Cousins maybe? I would think they would have a family resemblance, and Kira would have been wary."

"I agree. We'll see what we can learn. That's all we have for now, unless we find something in the house. Kira's mother gave us the key. Kira had her watering her plants one year, but not any more. She just never thought to get her key back. If we don't get any more leads, we'll be coming home tonight."

"That's great. We'll let you know if we can get anything out of the jaguar."

Then they ended the call and Jillian called Kira's mother, Lydia Watson, to hear the rest of the story. "I'm Jillian Matthews, an agent with the JAG branch of the USF and trying to locate your daughter, Kira. We just brought in her brother, Brutus, for questioning concerning an attack on a wolf shifter and the shooting of another jaguar." Jillian put the call on speaker.

Lydia snorted. "Hell, she doesn't have a brother. She's had three husbands though. Serves her right if one of them learned what she was up to *before* he bit the dust. But you know no matter how far she falls, she's just like a cat and lands on her feet. You sure she didn't marry that cute agent-in-training? Miles Matthews?"

Jillian hadn't expected that kind of response. "No, I hope not. Where is she now, do you know?"

"She doesn't give me her itinerary. After her last three husbands died, I stopped keeping up with what she's doing."

"How...did they die?"

"Accidental deaths. She's either the unluckiest woman in the world, or the luckiest. Not sure which."

"Luckiest how? Were they bad news?"

"No. Hell, they were the nicest guys you'd ever want to meet. 'Course, they might have been putting on a show for the old momma so they'd win me over. But if you ask me, they didn't need my help. I adored them, and she couldn't care less. After that, I didn't even want to meet them. I changed my mind when I saw Gaston Wells, her latest late husband? Oh my, he was wearing a wet suit, and if I were a few years younger, he'd have been mine. Honor student. Successful real estate agent. He bought her diamond rings fit for a queen. I'll tell you right now, I would never get a life insurance policy and make her the beneficiary. I've already made it clear that what little I own will go to a cat charity and she's not in my will."

"Are you saying she cashed in on her prior husbands' deaths?"

"Don't know about the first. They were poor and young back then, so maybe not that one. She didn't seem any richer after he died. Which was why she came back and lived with me until she met husband number two. Then he died of an accident. Convenient accident. Fell off a cliff. Witnesses said they hadn't really seen how it had happened. Kira and her husband were taking pictures at a scenic outlook, and suddenly he fell. She said she was there, but much farther away because she saw an eagle flying overhead and was trying to capture a better picture of it. She thought he'd had a selfie accident, but it kind of makes you wonder. Especially when husband number three died.

"If someone were to hook up with her permanently, if I were him, I wouldn't take out a life insurance policy on myself, just to be on the safe side. She sure had one hell of a nice windfall. She came by here with her new Cadillac convertible, dressed to snare another husband. I think she wanted to prove she was smarter than me, while I just make it from paycheck to paycheck. But, baby, you got to be able to live with yourself. She never seemed to feel any pain about their deaths either. Poor slobs. She's clever and a master manipulator. I know because she pulled that crap on me long enough for me to finally get wise to her schemes."

"How long were she and Gaston married?"

"Don't know, don't care. Well, maybe a year. He died on a scuba-diving trip. Don't know exactly what happened. If it had been a shark attack, completely believable as far as being accidental. But he just got the bends or something. Ran out of air. I don't know. Like I said, the second one died at a scenic overlook at the Grand Canyon. First one was in a car accident. That one might have been legitimate. Unless she just got tired of being poor and knew they could never even afford a life insurance policy."

"Did Gaston have a couple of brothers? Maybe close cousins who were twins?" Vaughn asked.

"Not that I know of. From what Kira said, he was an only child and had no siblings. You know that's the best person to go after if you want to kill 'em off. No family to speak of. No one to ask questions."

So had he been estranged from his family? "Do you ever hear from her?" Vaughn asked.

"Not even for Mother's Day. So truly, if you learn where she is, I don't need to know. And if you're friends with her current target, make sure he doesn't marry her. Problem is, the guys are so moonstruck when they fall in love with her that it doesn't matter what I say. Even if they believed she was up to no good, they'd never believe she'd feel that way about them. Got to get to my day job. Good luck with your investigation. For what it's worth? I wouldn't worry about her. I'd worry about him."

"Wait, one more thing. About Brutus... Who is he really, if he's not your son?"

Lydia gave a harsh laugh. "Some con artist too? Okay, look, I don't have a son, never did. Maybe she adopted a brother." She laughed again. "She's got a picture of her and her first husband and some guy who was a close friend of theirs. So is this Brutus someone new she's been hanging around? Or someone she's known from the beginning? I'll scan it and send it to you."

After she took time to do so, Lydia said, "Sounds to me like you need to dig a little deeper. I suspect you'll find he's another of her lovers. Brother, my ass. Okay, well, call me if you have any wild new stories to tell me. I'll help you to debunk them or let you know if they're for real."

"Thanks, Lydia. That close friend is Brutus. But her first husband doesn't look like the other two men who are involved in this. It proves she's known Brutus the whole time from husband number one to the current situation. You've been invaluable."

"Glad to have helped. Got to go. Happy hunting." Lydia ended the call.

"At least as far as I know, my brother wasn't even considering marrying the cat," Jillian said, and Vaughn was glad for that.

Chapter 16

JILLIAN, VAUGHN, AND HOWARD SPENT THE REST OF the day visiting with Douglas and looking for information about Simon and Wayne, in the event they were brothers. Maybe they were cousins, and that's why Wayne had a different last name. Or half brothers and they still looked a lot alike. Or Simon and Wayne were twins, and then brothers or cousins of Gaston, and Wayne had changed his name so Kira wouldn't catch on that he was related to her dead husband.

They returned to the guest house, and Jillian began doing searches for information about Simon Wells, taking a seat on the couch. "Shifters homeschool, so no records of schooling."

Vaughn brought over cups of coffee and sat beside her. "Voter registration?"

"Appears he doesn't vote. Same with either a Wayne Grunsky or Wells. But Wayne Wells has a car." She gave the make and model to Vaughn so he could call it in to Leidolf. "How much do you want to bet he's Wayne Grunsky?"

"I'd say he is. Then just changed his name for when he met up with Kira and Brutus. Does he have any property?"

"Simon has the car and a house." She pulled up the Google map that showed the location in San Diego. "Close houses, mostly one-story. Looks like garbage day for whenever the satellite caught the shot, but no garbage at Simon's house."

"Because he's up here. I don't understand though. If this is about revenge...that Simon or Wayne want to avenge Gaston's death, why not just kill Kira and Brutus?"

Jillian looked at the floor for a moment, then turned her attention to Vaughn. "What if Gaston was the honor student, like Lydia said. The good guy. And what if his brothers or cousins, whoever they are, were the screw-ups, in trouble? Maybe they looked into Gaston's death and believe he couldn't have died the way he did."

"Because they're divers too and know he's too good at what he does. We already know Wayne's a diver."

"Right."

"So then what? They check into who he married? Befriend Kira and her lover, Brutus, and learn about the diving they plan to do with Douglas for the treasure? They figure they'll wait and cash in on the treasure?"

"Could be, and then something goes wrong with the friendship. One of the jaguars is shot."

"Then your brother is shot and Douglas is injured. But by whom?"

"One or more of the four jaguars has to be the culprit. I don't see anything else here. Want to head back over to the jailhouse and see if the incarcerated jaguar will shift and talk?"

"Might as well. With three jaguars still on the loose, we need to resolve this."

When they arrived back at the jailhouse, two police officers and Howard greeted them.

"Has he shifted?" Vaughn asked.

"Nope. We have Brutus in a cell and left prison clothes for him so he can shift and dress if he decides to cooperate. So far, he won't."

"Well, we have a few more details about the situation," Jillian said.

"Hot damn," Howard said.

"Yeah, so we're going to see if that will help us get anywhere with him," Jillian said.

Vaughn wasn't sure what she had in mind and figured they should have discussed it already, but Jillian started right in on Brutus as soon as they walked into the secure part of the jailhouse where they had six small cells, one housing Brutus.

"We know who you are, and what you've been up to. Howard is going to take you to the jaguar lock-up facilities in Dallas first thing in the morning. You might as well tell us where your partners in crime are so the JAG won't be so rough on you." Jillian folded her arms and looked crossly at the jaguar. He was lying down, either pretending to sleep or maybe really sleeping from the tranquilizer, the run he'd had, and the injuries he'd suffered. "Had you figured on killing Douglas at the clinic before he could ID you?" Jillian didn't believe Douglas would have known the man in his jaguar form. Not when he'd been wearing hunter spray. So they wanted to know why Brutus had gone to Douglas's room.

"If you were looking for the money he used for the expedition or the journal he wrote showing where he was going to have Miles dive, you were too late. It's all secure."

The jaguar didn't move a muscle.

"Did you know that the man you killed, Gaston

Wells, has a couple of brothers? One pretended to be your friend," Vaughn said.

Jillian was surprised Vaughn would bluff about that, but then again, if Kira didn't know Gaston had any family, Brutus wouldn't have either. She didn't believe Brutus would have made friends with Wayne if he'd known the man was related to Gaston.

Brutus lifted his jaguar head and looked at Vaughn, his golden eyes round. Surprised to hear the news? Looking to see if they were lying or telling the truth?

"Simon Wells is the other. He looks identical to Gaston. He drives a Humvee. Owns a house in San Diego about a half hour from the club. And when Wayne was shooting at you earlier, Simon was driving the getaway vehicle. That's how we know about it. My partner Jillian caught sight of the license plate. Cat Clubber. Clever, huh?"

Vaughn was really good at interrogation, a great job of misinforming. Simon looked identical to Wayne, not Gaston. Brutus kept watching Vaughn, studying his expression, listening to his voice, probably processing the new information.

"So you think he's one of you, but something goes wrong, and you have a falling-out. Someone shoots someone. But you didn't know that Wayne was Gaston's brother and he was seeking revenge all along."

Jillian figured if Wayne had wanted revenge, he would have killed Brutus and Kira outright. She assumed Simon and Wayne wanted a piece of the action—a pile of the treasure Douglas could find for them.

Jillian's stomach grumbled, and she said, "You know, it's lunchtime. How about a pizza?"

"Yeah, sounds good. Want to make one or have a couple delivered?" Vaughn said.

"Will they deliver out here?" Jillian asked.

"Yeah. One of the guys working at a pizza place off the ranch is a wolf, and he delivers all the time. Hey, maybe while we're looking into this case, I can take you to a restaurant the wolves own. And the rest of the gang. We can do it before Miles and Howard leave with Brutus," Vaughn offered.

"I'd like that," Howard said.

An hour later, and with no change in Brutus's form, they were enjoying pizzas topped with meat and veggies, feeding the police officers too, while Brutus watched them.

Would he like some too? Jillian would offer if he would talk. Then she had a brilliant idea. She just didn't want to send the wrong message to the guys she was working with, or the police officers either. But it would seem more authentic if she just dove into what she was going to do.

She pulled out her phone and quickly set it to mute, in case someone tried to send her a real call, then she pretended to answer it. "Ohmigod, good work, Demetria! Tell Everett and Miles they've done great too!" She paused while everyone in the jailhouse was listening, waiting to hear the good news. Probably wondering why she wasn't putting the call on speakerphone. "Nah, he's not talking. But as long as you've got her talking, we don't need his testimony." She avoided looking at Brutus, dying to see how he was reacting. She smiled at Vaughn and Howard as they stopped eating their pizza.

"Wow, really? Three dead husbands? How much

life insurance money did she get?" Again, a long pause, allowing Demetria enough time to pass along further information, if the conversation had been real. Jillian put her fingers up indicating three and mouthed the word *three*, like she just couldn't believe it, her eyes wide with expression.

"Wait, so she's saying Brutus is her lover…like we didn't know that. When Douglas caught the picture of them at the Kitty Cat Club with their tongues down each other's throats and his hand on her ass, we sort of concluded that. But implicating him as the mastermind? Good. They'll both go down, but at least we know he was more to blame than she was. Was he the one who killed her husbands? Staged the car accident, the killing at the overlook at the Grand Canyon, and the diving accident?"

Nice lengthy pause.

"Okay. Well, when you bring her in, Vaughn is taking us all out to dinner. Yep, he offered and he's buying. It'll be different from the cat club. Different atmosphere, I'm sure. You'll enjoy it. Anything else you want to pass along?"

She pretended to listen, nodded, and said, "Right. Miles already told me he hadn't been interested in her as a prospective mate, and once he saw her kissing her so-called brother at the club?" She smiled at Brutus. "Right. So I'm glad he's not too upset about the betrayal." But what she really wanted to know was who had shot Miles! She wanted to shoot the culprit for having done so herself. They didn't know enough to be able to pretend they knew though. "Okay, thanks, Demetria. Wonderful news! See you soon."

Then she turned her phone off mute and stuck it in

her pocket. "Can I have another slice? This calls for a real celebration."

Vaughn served another slice of pizza for her, but she could tell he was dying to learn if Demetria and the others had really caught up with Kira. She hoped he realized she was just playacting. Even so, Brutus was just watching them, not shifting, not acting like he was going to give his version of the truth. Maybe he knew Kira wouldn't sell him out. Or maybe he believed she would, and that's what he deserved for trusting her.

Jillian noticed Howard looked a little flushed, so she finished her pizza in a hurry. She didn't want to say anything about him looking feverish, not in front of Brutus. But that's what she was worried about. "Hey, Howard, while we're waiting for the others to get here, you said you'd teach me a new board game." He hadn't, but she hoped he'd play along.

"Yeah sure, but let me tell you I won't go easy on Vaughn. You can be my partner though." Then Howard smiled at her, and he, Jillian, and Vaughn left the police officers to watch over the prisoner.

The officers knew to get ahold of them if Brutus shifted.

As soon as they were in the Land Rover and headed back to the guest house, Vaughn asked, "Did they catch her?"

Jillian smiled, glad he wasn't sure and hadn't totally fallen for it.

"No. But I had the notion that if he thought she sold him out, he might come clean. Didn't work though."

"He might have to think about it," Howard said.

"Oh, don't go to the guest house," Jillian told Vaughn. "Howard looks like he's running a fever."

Vaughn glanced at him. "Hell, Howard, why didn't you say so?" He turned around and went to the clinic.

After the doctor gave him antibiotics, Howard said, "I wondered when I mentioned playing a board game with you. I figured you needed to talk to us in private. Certainly not about this."

"You and Vaughn and my brother. All peas in a pod when it comes to neglecting your health."

"Since I'm staying at the other house now, why don't you drop me off?" Howard asked. "And I'll meet up with you when the others get in."

She didn't want to say she hoped he was going to rest, but she suspected he would. After they dropped Howard off at his place, she and Vaughn returned to the guest house and sat down to color on their pages for a while.

Wanting to take a break from the subject of the jaguars, Jillian figured she and Vaughn could get to know each other a little better. She began coloring one of the peacock's feathers aqua. "If you don't mind me asking, why did you join the navy and not one of the other branches of the service?"

"I love the water. What about you? Why did you join the army?"

"My dad was a Navy SEAL."

Vaughn didn't say anything for a moment, then swore. "Don't tell me. Kelly Matthews is your dad?"

"You know him?" She couldn't have been more surprised.

"He was our training officer, and he tried to kill me several times."

Jillian laughed. "He was just trying to teach you

how to survive." But she couldn't believe they knew each other.

"Are you sure he wasn't just psychic and wanted to make sure I didn't end up dating his daughter? Then again, his daughter tried to kill me. Like father, like daughter."

"I told you. If I had wanted to kill you, I would have. You don't hold grudges do you?" She raised a brow.

He laughed, then got serious again. "I was surprised Martin would take your brother into the organization."

Jillian frowned at Vaughn.

"Only because they're a jaguar organization, and they don't even have wolves permanently on staff yet. Well, us now, but that's just a new situation."

"Martin said he takes in at-risk jaguars and puts them through the rigorous training the JAGs offer. They often make better agents than the ones who join who weren't screwups. Maybe they'll do that with select wolf shifters now too. Miles will get paid for helping us with this mission, and once they reach Dallas, he'll be scheduled for training. Sometimes, I think Miles got himself into trouble because Dad was such a strict military man. I think the training will be good for him."

"What about us, I wonder? Are they going to send us through the training too?"

"Probably." She talked about her mother, the military wife who gave up her own career as an accountant to move around with her SEAL mate. Now that they had their own climbing business, her mom did all the accounting and marketing, and her dad did everything else.

"What about your parents?" she asked.

"Gone. We had a really bad forest fire when I was

young, and several wolves were cut off from any route of escape. Some of us were able to get to a river and were swept a long way downstream. Bella, my cousin's mate, is a red wolf, and she'd lost her family too, then was taken in by the gray pack. We actually grew up together, and Devlyn had always loved Bella. The feelings she had for him were mutual."

"Wow. Is she any relation to Leidolf?"

"No. Not that we know of."

"I wonder what my dad will say when he learns we're courting."

"Hopefully, he won't want to kill me."

She laughed, then got a call from her brother. Worried they were having trouble in San Diego, she answered it, while Vaughn continued to color on his wolf.

"We're headed out on the next flight. Be in by six tonight, and Demetria said to go ahead and make reservations for seven."

"Howard is feverish. The two of you might have to delay taking Brutus back tomorrow and wait another day or so." Then she told him about her attempt to break Brutus.

Miles laughed. "I've used the fake phone call when I was out on a date and bored stiff. I would never have thought you'd do that. But great ploy. I'll tell the others what you did so we're all on the same page. Too bad we really didn't have Kira in hand. Oh, another reason why I had to talk to you... Dad's going to be calling you. Just a heads-up. Sorry. I was telling him the news about what I was doing, that I actually have an honest-to-God job, and how I had been working with you on this case, and I kind of—"

She got a signal saying she had an incoming call. "Don't tell me. You told Dad I'm courting a wolf."

"Yeah."

"He's calling now. Talk to *you* later."

Vaughn stood, pulled Jillian into his arms, and kissed her long and hard. She began to kiss him back with a quiet desperation, ignoring the way her phone was playing its tune, not wanting to take the call from her dad.

"Want to take it?" Vaughn finally asked.

She laughed. "No, but I've got to." She sighed. "Hello, Dad?"

"I hear you're courting a wolf. When do we get to meet him?" After she was mated to him? No way was she going to let her dad interfere with her social life.

"We're working a mission and—"

"Miles told me. Good work on getting him straightened out."

She ignored her dad's comment about her brother. She could argue forever with her father, and she'd never win. Best to just let it go. "We have training after this. But we're still working this case. I don't know when I'll be back to see you."

"Miles says he's a SEAL. What's his name? Maybe I know him."

Maybe he wouldn't remember Vaughn. Then again, her dad usually remembered everything—people, places, faces.

"Vaughn Greystoke."

Silence.

Vaughn glanced at her. She put her hand over her phone's mouthpiece and whispered, "He hasn't said anything. Not sure if that's good or bad." Then she put it on speaker so Vaughn knew what he was getting into.

"Hell, honey. Is that SEAL still alive and kicking?"

"Yeah. I even shot him, and you'd never know it."

Vaughn chuckled.

"I knew you had it in you. Much better choice than the guys you've been dating. What about Brock, his twin brother?"

"I have it on good authority that he's fine too."

"Good to hear. So where are you going to end up?"

"We're not sure. If Miles is in Dallas, we thought of joining Vaughn's pack in Colorado so we'd be kind of halfway in between the two of you and Miles."

This time she heard her parents talking in the background, but she couldn't make out their words.

Then her dad got back on the line. "Okay, your mom says if you end up in Colorado, they'd better need a climbing gym because she's not going to be that far away from her daughter when you start having babies."

Jillian felt her face flush with embarrassment. "We're not mated yet."

"Hell, and he's a SEAL wolf I trained?"

Vaughn smiled and rubbed her back.

"Well, we'll let you get back to your mission. Be safe. I trained Vaughn well, and I know he'll have your back."

"Congratulations," her mom said.

"Thanks, Mom, Dad. I'll call you later."

When she ended the call, she was afraid Vaughn might not like it that her parents planned to move close to them. Or that they'd decided they were mated before she and Vaughn had gotten to that point.

Before she could talk to Vaughn about her parents'

plans, he said, "I didn't figure that you telling your dad that you shot me would go over too well. I'm surprised he didn't ask if it was by accident or on purpose."

"He knew it would be on purpose. I'd never shoot anyone accidentally."

Vaughn laughed. "Hope he's mellowed out some."

"Nope, but you can handle it. They'll be moving right next door to us."

Vaughn groaned.

"That is if the courtship works out."

"It's going to work out."

"Do they have a climbing gym in your area?"

"Nope."

"Okay, well, that's what my folks will be setting up. Believe me, if you're not busy, my dad will expect you to be over there helping out. Oh, did I forget to mention? With me, you get the whole family."

Smiling, Vaughn just shook his head.

Chapter 17

"Hey, Vaughn, we intended to see Douglas earlier when we had all the problems chasing down Brutus. Why don't we run over there to see him now?" Jillian asked. "We still have about three hours before the others arrive and we go out to dinner."

"Sounds like a good plan to me. And now that we've had this discussion with your parents about us, we're going to have to decide when we're going to do this."

She smiled. "You mean a mating? Don't you think it's a little soon?"

"No way. You stole my heart at the Kitty Cat Club."

"And then shot you here. Are you sure about this?"

"Absolutely."

She loved a man who knew what he wanted and went for it. "We can discuss it tonight after dinner." Should she insist on weeks of dating? Months? She would never last that long.

As soon as they went over to the clinic and walked into the room, the nurse smiled at them. "Douglas has had company all day, which can only be good for him. Our pack has taken him in as an honorary member," Sally said to Vaughn. "Some of the children came in and read stories to him today. Everyone's rooting for him."

"That's great. Any change?" Vaughn asked.

"Not that we've seen. He's been taken off the medicine that induced the coma. As long as he didn't have any brain injury from the loss of blood initially, he should be fine now. All his vital signs are excellent. Oh, the kids were sure he moved his fingers a couple of times, and one said his eyes opened and he smiled. The boy was persistent about it. The staff hasn't seen any change. I have to tell you, that jaguar sure gave us all a real scare. Dr. Wilders ran all kinds of blood tests on Douglas to make sure the cat hadn't injected anything into his IV. He hadn't. You must have scared him off before he could do anything."

Vaughn sat down next to the bed and squeezed Douglas's hand. "Hey, Douglas, Miles said to tell you hi. And we've got some news."

"I'll leave you to speak with him and check in a little later," Sally said.

"Thanks," Jillian said, then sat next to the bed and took Douglas's other hand, wondering what news Vaughn was going to tell him. Shouldn't it be only good news?

"You know me. You probably didn't think I'd ever settle down."

She couldn't believe Vaughn was going to talk about that!

"But Jillian—she's the wolf holding your other hand—I think she just might be considering mating me. Not sure though." Vaughn winked at her.

She was glad Douglas couldn't see her blushing. "I thought it was a done deal." She wasn't being serious. "I mean, my parents are practically planning the wedding, the move to get near us, the prospect of having grandbabies even."

Vaughn laughed. "I'm all for it, Jillian. Every bit of it." And he sounded really serious.

"What about the trip to Hawaii?"

"We're going to Hawaii?"

"I was thinking I could scuba dive there without having a bunch of training." She swore Douglas squeezed her hand. "Oh, oh, Douglas, can you hear us? I'm Miles's sister. He was shot before you got here, but recovered. We captured…" She paused. She hadn't meant to tell him anything bad. She glanced at Vaughn. He was waiting for her to speak.

She swore Douglas's fingers moved again, as if prompting her to finish what she was about to say. "We took Brutus into custody. He's not Kira's brother. And she has three dead husbands, all accidental deaths, two with insurance policies that paid out. Thankfully, we learned all this before Miles got in too deep with her."

"We all were at the Kitty Cat Club. Kira, her pretend brother, and their friend. We assume they overheard you talking with Miles about your plans to treasure hunt in Belize. Then guess who shows up on your boat?" Vaughn said. "You become friends, then guess who shows up here? Kira and her brother…well, lover. Only she's pretending he's still her brother, but she's seeing Miles at his cabin when his sister isn't around. You're attacked, and a male jaguar is searching for something in your cabin and knocks Jillian down, giving her a mild concussion."

Douglas's lips parted.

"Ohmigod." Jillian rose from her seat, not letting go of Douglas's hand, and brushed his forehead with her other hand. "Can you hear us?"

Douglas's eyes fluttered open, and he stared at her with groggy eyes. "Mate," he said hoarsely.

She couldn't believe after what they'd told him, all he was interested in was the mention of her and Vaughn mating.

"She's beautiful, isn't she? Never thought I'd manage to capture such a treasure, did you?" Vaughn said smiling. "Hell, it's good to hear you speak."

Jillian got some water for him, and Vaughn called the nurse to let her know Douglas had come to.

"Mate?" Douglas asked again.

"If she'll have me. She did shoot me already."

A corner of Douglas's mouth lifted.

Vaughn laughed. "Douglas always did have a dark sense of humor."

Douglas turned his attention to Jillian. "Accept?"

She smiled. "No. He hasn't even asked!" Though she was going to say they needed more time to get to know each other. But wolves recognized how well suited they were from the beginning. The longer courtship was more for their human halves. Their wolf halves knew when they'd found their mate.

"Ask," Douglas said to Vaughn.

Vaughn folded his arms. "You know, this is something that needs to be done in private."

"Afraid of rejection?" Douglas arched a brow.

Vaughn smiled. Jillian sat next to Douglas again. "You're putting him on the spot."

Douglas let out his breath in a tired sigh and closed his eyes.

"Jillian, I love you. I could never find anyone else who rocks my world like you do. Will you be my one and only? My mate for life?"

She laughed. Then she glanced at Douglas to see if he

would open his eyes and rejoin the party. Maybe he'd gone back to sleep. She knew how to shake that up, if he was just trying to manipulate them into agreeing to a mating.

"He's gone to sleep. I'll give you my answer in a couple of weeks," she said to Vaughn.

Vaughn frowned, and at the same time he said, "Why?" Douglas echoed his question.

She smiled. "Oh, all right." She turned to Vaughn. "My parents always said they mated in record time. Four days from the time she came on base and he met her to when he asked her and she said yes. He was always proud of the fact he could convince her he loved her in that short a time and that they were truly the ones for each other, as their happy mating attests."

"We'd beat them by a day. Think your dad will mind?"

"Probably. He'll say we acted rashly, or were just trying to beat his record, knowing my dad."

"That's a yes," Douglas said.

Jillian and Vaughn laughed as he pulled her from her chair to wait for her real response. She really liked Douglas and could see why her brother and Vaughn did too.

"To be on the safe side…" she said, looking up into Vaughn's warm, brown eyes, eager to hear her say yes.

"You should agree," Vaughn said, finishing her statement.

She wrapped her arms around his neck. "I never knew shooting a potential partner would result in a mating, but you are one hot wolf. Vaughn Greystoke, I love you, and I would never give you up for anything."

They kissed to seal the deal, their bodies pressed tight together, their tongues teasing and the kiss deepening.

Two people clapped from the doorway, and Jillian and Vaughn broke free of the kiss to see Sally and Dr. Wilders standing there, smiling.

And Douglas was smiling too.

"Go," Douglas said to Vaughn and Jillian. "We'll talk later."

"We'll see to him and make sure someone stays with him," the doc said.

"Sure." Jillian was certain her cheeks were flushed, as hot as she felt getting caught. She wondered how long the doctor and nurse had been there. She returned to the bed and kissed Douglas on the forehead, squeezing his hand. "Get better. We'll be back before you know it."

"Take time. Important business."

The mating. The doctor and nurse were all smiles. Vaughn patted Douglas's shoulder. "Be back in a bit, old man."

Then he took hold of Jillian's hand and escorted her out of the clinic. "How is your head feeling?"

"Good as new. What about your shoulder?"

"Like I can do a hundred push-ups." Vaughn could do anything and everything now that Jillian had agreed to be his mate. When they reached the parking lot, he opened the car door for her. "You didn't feel pressured into making this happen too quickly, did you?"

"Would it matter?"

"Hell yeah. But you once told me when you make up your mind about something—"

"I don't hesitate. You're right." She pulled him in for another kiss, and he loved her. Really, truly, and deeply loved her.

"Back to the guest house, right?" His voice was already husky with desire.

"Unless you had something else in mind."

"My cabin or yours, but I'd rather just go someplace a lot closer."

She climbed into the car. "Let's go before you change your mind."

He laughed. "No way am I changing my mind. Douglas would never let me hear the end of it."

"That's the only reason?"

"Hell, no." Vaughn sped off to the guest house.

"You're not in any rush, are you?"

"Yeah, if you must know, I am."

Vaughn wanted to do something more. Dinner or something before they were mated so that he didn't seem desperate. But he was. Desperate.

He fully intended to carry Jillian over the threshold as soon as they reached the house, but she tugged him inside and closed the door. When they were certain they were alone, she hurried him down the hall to her bedroom.

Then, as if she couldn't wait that long, she turned and began tugging off his jacket while she continued to slowly back down the hall. As soon as she had the sleeves down to his elbows, he was pulling her jacket down her arms too. In the middle of the hallway, her hands on his arms and his on hers, they began to kiss. Tongues, lips, their breaths mingling, their heartbeats escalating, eyes darkening with desire.

"I feel like a cave woman who clubbed her mate

and dragged him into her cave, claiming him," she said between kisses.

"Oh yeah?" His voice was drenched with lust. He dragged her jacket off the rest of the way and ditched his on the hallway floor, then scooped her, hands under her buttocks, and settled her over his good shoulder before stalking toward his bedroom.

She laughed. "I love you."

He patted her behind. "The feeling I have for you is mutual."

She half expected him to toss her on the bed, caveman style, but he was careful with her, cognizant of her recent head injury, and she loved him all the more for it, even though she felt fine now.

He gently swept her off his shoulder and onto the bed. "Are you okay? I probably shouldn't have tossed you over my shoulder like that."

"I'm fine, but what about your injured shoulder?" She sat up as he straddled her lap, and she lifted the bottom edge of his shirt, pulling it upward, her hands sliding underneath against his glorious hard muscles and soft skin.

He quickly yanked his shirt off the rest of the way. "I'm good." He began kissing her again while she ran her fingers through his silky hair, kissing him back with just as much fervor.

With finesse, he massaged her breasts through the denim fabric first, but then seemed eager to bare her breasts to him. Stopping to unbutton her shirt, he pulled it off her shoulders, forgetting about the buttons on the sleeves. She laughed and he smiled in a wicked way, pushing her gently back against the mattress. He peeled

back her purple polka-dot bra until she was exposed to
him, the cool air and his touches making her nipples
erect and sensitive.

Smiling, she watched him as he found the snap in
front and unfastened it, pushing the bra aside. He kissed
her mouth again as her hands skimmed over his warm,
smooth skin. When he kissed a path down to a breast
and suckled a taut nipple, her breath suspended. She
nearly came undone when he suckled the sensitive tip,
then licked and suckled again.

So wet and ready for him, she ran her hands over his
bare back and tried to slide her fingers under his belt.

"Too many clothes," he breathed out against her
breast, and helped her sit up so he could unbutton her
shirtsleeves. Then he pulled off her shirt and her bra.

She tackled his belt, but he slipped his hand between
her legs and rubbed her jeans-covered mound in a sensual caress, making her arch against his touch.

Loving his fondling, she caressed his steel erection,
making him groan out loud. Exquisite torture? She smiled.

He unbuttoned her jeans and slid the zipper down
slowly. Then he ran his hand down between her panties
and jeans and rubbed. She was so wet, eager for ful-
fillment. Wolf and human need was all mixed into one
rampant craving. She unbuckled his belt, unbuttoned
his jeans, and unzipped his pants in the same slow way.
Then she tugged his pants down his hips, and instead of
caressing his cock like he'd caressed her clit, she pulled
his boxer briefs down and set his cock free.

Vaughn's eyes darkened with need, and he looked
as though he would burst if they didn't get on with this.
"Hell, shoes."

She laughed.

He quickly moved down to tug off her boots, then untied his own and kicked them off. He yanked off his socks, but after he pulled hers off, he massaged one of her feet. Which had her moaning in pure, unadulterated ecstasy. *This* was how she wanted to end every day.

He did the same with her other foot, before reaching up and removing her jeans.

His jeans hit the floor, and then he pulled her purple-and-white polka-dot panties off. She slid his boxer briefs down and tossed them.

Nudging her legs apart, he settled on top of her, grinding his cock against her mound as they kissed and touched and licked and rubbed.

This felt so right, the physical mating between two wolves, the emotional bonding. She breathed in his masculine, wild wolf scent and fell under his spell as he began to stroke her, still rubbing his erection against her thigh. Hot, hot wolf. She'd known from the first moment she'd seen him standing naked—all growly, muscular, and beautiful—that he'd make one hell of a lover. If she'd been in the market.

Boy, had she ever been.

He slid a finger inside her, prodding and circling her deep. She was so close to coming that she could barely hold on.

His kisses bordered on desperate, and hers matched his desperation as she clung to him, and she felt her body elevating to that higher plane of existence. The climax hit, taking her over the precipice. She cried out in exaltation, her world exploding in a million brilliant pieces. Right before he asked her if she was ready.

All her life, she'd been preparing for this. The mating with her wolf. So yes. She was beyond ready.

"Do it."

Vaughn kissed her deeply again and settled between her legs, then nudged into the center of her being, pushing until he was all the way into her slick, wet heat, just where he'd wanted to be all along.

He began to thrust, thinking of how good this felt, how lucky he was despite the way they had first met. Yet he remembered what his brother had once said to him. It would take one extraordinary wolf to make his world stand still. Jillian was that wolf.

She wrapped her legs high around his hips and he paused, pulling one of her legs over his shoulder and then the other, penetrating her to the max. He kissed her neck, her throat, and thrust between her legs, unable to slow the pace. Unable to stop the inevitable even if he'd wanted to. He moved his hips while she lifted her pelvis to match him. Deeper, surging inside her, gathering her heat, sharing his own with her. The friction made her come as she cried out with pleasure again. He felt the end coming, yet reminded himself it was only the beginning.

With a deep, guttural growl, he let loose, enjoying the intimacy only he could share with his mate from now on.

In the afterglow, he settled beside her and pulled her into his arms. "I love you." He meant it with all his heart. "From the moment I saw you on my front deck with that kitchen towel imprinted with a wine bottle, the furious look on your face, the smell of you—all she-wolf—and then your announcement that you were the one who had shot me, well, hell, I knew I was hooked."

She laughed. "I love you right back. I needed to make it up to you. I never imagined in a million years that shooting a wolf who had intended to make mincemeat of my brother would lead to this."

"Which goes to prove you really only meant to get my attention."

She smiled. "I got it, didn't I?"

"Hell yeah. Now and forever. Let's take a nap before everyone arrives so we can dance the night away at the club."

"That sounds nice."

He pulled the covers over them, turned off the light, and they snuggled together, glad for this and for Douglas finally coming to. Which reminded Vaughn that they needed to let the rest of the team know. Before he could get out of bed and retrieve his phone, Jillian began to climb off him.

"We have to let everyone on the team know Douglas is awake." She switched on the light, grabbed her phone, and climbed in bed as Vaughn pulled her back into his arms and nuzzled her neck.

"Hey, putting this on three-way call," she said. "Douglas came out of his coma. We'll update you on his condition and what he has to say when you get in."

"And not to take away from that good news, but we're mated wolves."

The cheers blasted through the phone, and all Demetria's questions began. When were they getting married? Where were they honeymooning?

Vaughn pulled Jillian snug against his body as the ladies hashed it out.

Until they heard the front door open.

"We've got company we hadn't planned on," Jillian said softly. "Got to go."

Chapter 18

VAUGHN QUICKLY LEFT THE BED AND THREW ON HIS boxer briefs. He grabbed his gun, ready to shoot whoever was sneaking into the guest house.

Naked, Jillian ran to the window and slid it open. She whispered, "Going around to the front door as a wolf."

Vaughn didn't like it. Not because he didn't believe she could handle herself, but he wanted them to stay together, safety in numbers. Yet he realized her plan had viability. She could close in on the intruder, if that's what the person was, without him knowing while Vaughn made a frontal assault.

Jillian moved a chair over to the window and climbed out, then shifted into her wolf and raced around the house. When Vaughn thought she was in place, he turned out the bedroom light and carefully moved into the dark hallway.

He had the advantage. He knew the floor plan of the house. Though the intruder would have seen the light on in the bedroom. Maybe heard the window open. Then Jillian would be more at risk. Vaughn moved faster down the hall now, determined to distract the person.

He was glad they'd called Demetria and the others and knew for sure it wasn't them.

A woman cried out in the living room, but it wasn't Jillian's voice. Jillian growled and snarled in her wolf form. His heart pounding, Vaughn flipped on the hall light and saw Kira with a dive knife in her fisted hand, but Jillian's wolf teeth had captured her wrist. She was growling to get the woman to release the knife. If Jillian had wanted to, she could have bitten down hard and crushed the bones in Kira's wrist.

"Drop the knife, Kira," Vaughn ordered, his gun readied.

"I thought Miles was here with his sister, and he wanted to see me. That he was looking for me," Kira said, her eyes tearing up. "Isn't Miles here?"

"No, he isn't here." Vaughn didn't believe her words for an instant. "Did you ever think of knocking?" He realized in their haste to mate, he and Jillian might have left the door unlocked. Not that they would have worried about it much. They were on a red wolf pack's ranch. It should have been safe.

"The door was unlocked. I heard Brutus was arrested, and Wayne was shooting at everyone. After everything that's happened, I was afraid something bad had happened inside. To Miles. I wanted to help him."

Vaughn knew she was lying.

"I had my dive knife out just in case."

"Drop the knife."

She released her hold on the knife, and it dropped to the floor with a clatter, but Jillian didn't release her hold on Kira.

"Tell her to let me go. I'm Miles and Douglas's good friend."

"Explain to us why you shot Miles." Vaughn had no idea who really had shot Miles, but he figured he could bluff his way through and maybe get the answers they needed. He had no intention of telling Jillian what to do.

As far as he was concerned, it was her call. Until he saw blood on the floor. Was it Jillian's or Kira's?

He got on his phone to Leidolf. "Got an emergency. Kira Wells, the woman your men have been trying to track down, just broke into the guest house, wielding a dive knife."

"Sending men over now. I'll be over in a minute. Is she confined?"

"Jillian's got her in hand, but someone's bleeding."

"Me, damn it. She bit into the skin," Kira said, scowling.

"Better be you and not her," Vaughn growled.

"On my way," Leidolf said. "Be there soon."

"Tell me why you shot Miles," Vaughn said again.

"I didn't shoot anyone. I have a knife. Or had one. Hey, I gave up the knife. Quit biting!"

Vaughn realized Jillian had to be biting down on Kira's wrist with enough pressure to make her talk. "We know all about your plan to befriend Douglas and Miles so you could learn about where they're diving for treasure."

"You don't know a damn thing. Brutus didn't do anything. He's innocent."

"Innocent of killing your former husbands?"

Kira closed her gaping mouth.

"Yeah, we know all about them."

"They were accidents."

"Right. Okay, who shot Miles?"

"I didn't! I was seeing him. Intimately. Why would I shoot him?"

"He was shot before you were seeing him this time. You wanted to offer your diving services to Douglas, and when killing Miles didn't work, you figured you'd become Miles's lover instead and still work with Douglas on finding the treasure. So what went wrong? Why nearly kill Douglas?" Vaughn asked.

Suddenly, cars rolled up, and doors opened and shut.

"It's me," Leidolf called out. "And my two police officers."

"She's getting ready to confess to shooting Miles," Vaughn said, whether she was or not.

"No, I'm not. I didn't even know he'd been shot!"

"Brutus did it then. Did your lover get mad about playing the brother when you're screwing around with all these other men?" Vaughn asked.

"Of course not. You're right. I was supposed to be Miles's girlfriend. It was hard for me to pretend to really care for him because I usually like the guy I'm with. Miles was such a drifter, didn't care anything about money, and it irritated me. And I think he knew that. But that was the game plan whether I liked it or not. We didn't try to shoot him. We wanted to work with him and Douglas. Sure we would have had a four-way split between us, but that would still mean a lot of money, and we could get to the treasure quicker that way if at least three of us were diving."

"Wait, what happened to Wayne in your little scheme of things?"

Her face turned a little wan.

Vaughn frowned. "He's been with you all along on this and now he's not? A falling-out among thieves?"

"We aren't thieves. We would have worked every bit as hard at finding the treasure as Miles did."

"What about Wayne?" And all her dead husbands? She wasn't as innocent as she tried to let on.

"He decided not to work with us any longer. He didn't like our plans."

Jillian growled.

"Ow, damn it. Tell her to release me!"

Leidolf smiled at Jillian. "You can release her, and we'll take it from here."

Jillian looked like she really didn't want to. One of the officers had already grabbed the dive knife. Jillian released her hold on Kira and stepped back, growling.

Kira's wrist was bleeding, but from what Vaughn could see, the puncture marks were negligible, and she would heal quickly. But when he observed blood on the knife blade, he realized Jillian had been cut.

"Are you badly cut?" Vaughn growled.

Jillian shook her head.

"We'll wait here so you can check her out," Leidolf said. "And keep Kira here so you can question her further."

Suddenly, Howard was charging into the guest house looking like he was ready to kill someone. His face still appeared flushed, but that might have been because he was angry. "If I was working my regular job as an Enforcer and not a USF agent, I'd just terminate the bastard who tore into Douglas and left him for dead and shot Miles." Howard glowered at Kira.

Jillian woofed at him in greeting, and Vaughn was glad Howard had come to their rescue.

"I didn't bite Douglas. He was a friend, and we wanted to dive for him," Kira said.

"Come on, Jillian. Let me take a look at you," Vaughn said.

She shook her head, and he knew she wanted to

hear all that needed to be said first. She thought *he* was stubborn!

One of the police officers said, "I can confirm this right away. I just need a swab of your mouth, and then the doc can determine if you had anything to do with Douglas's injury."

"Gladly." Which had to mean she hadn't bitten Douglas, or she wouldn't be so eager to give a sample.

"We've cleared Brutus of the crime of attacking Douglas too," the officer said.

"Which means Wayne had to have done it," Vaughn said. "So where the hell is he?"

Kira frowned. "How should I know? Once we told him we were through with him—"

"Why?"

Kira glared at Vaughn, then looked at the floor. "He wanted to get rid of Miles. We didn't sanction it. We were furious when he told us he had killed him so we could be the divers for Douglas instead. We told him we were through with him. I was grateful to learn Miles was okay. I wanted to make up to Miles in the worst way."

"By having sexual relations with him."

Jillian growled low.

"It seemed to lift his…spirits. It was the least I could do for him. I might not have wanted to be his mate, but I still think of him as a friend."

"Why would Wayne try to kill Douglas?"

"I figured since we cut Wayne out of the treasure, he decided he'd get rid of Douglas because he knew where it was. If Wayne eliminated Douglas, none of us would get it."

Which was a possibility. "Brutus was looking for

something in the cabin. What was that all about then? The treasure map?" Vaughn suspected he was looking for the notebook detailing the treasure hunts, but had he also known about the cash for the expedition?

"The treasure map, sure. Douglas told us he kept meticulous details on every expedition. Brutus and I knew if we didn't safeguard it for Douglas for when he recovered, Wayne would get ahold of it and either use it or destroy it."

"So you hadn't intended to use it for your own exploration."

"No. Of course not."

Vaughn didn't believe her. "Then Wayne shot Brutus because the two of you were ending the partnership with him. Brutus was the injured jaguar that Leidolf's men tried to track down."

Kira was quiet.

Surprised he had it wrong, Vaughn raised his brows. "Wayne didn't shoot Brutus. Brutus shot Wayne, attempting to kill him. But why?"

"I told you. Wayne didn't like our plan. He wanted Miles to die. Since Wayne had already tried to kill Miles, why not Douglas too? You see what happened. He did try to kill him. We didn't want anyone to die."

"Just husbands."

Kira snorted. "We didn't have anything to do with their accidental deaths."

"Then Wayne was trying to shoot Brutus after he went to the clinic to see Douglas and ran off. Payback for Brutus already having shot him before?"

"Yeah."

"Why had Brutus gone to see Douglas?"

"He wanted him to know we had nothing to do with injuring him. That it was all Wayne's fault."

"Why not tell Leidolf? Why not tell us?"

"Brutus shot Wayne first! Somehow I don't believe his attempt to kill him would have been considered justified. If he had been defending Miles, it would have been a different story. Otherwise, he would have to answer for it."

"And there's the matter of all your dead husbands."

Kira didn't say anything in response to that.

"How long did you know Brutus? From the beginning?" Though they knew she had, Vaughn wanted her to tell them firsthand.

"He was my first husband's best friend. We were all poor."

Vaughn shook his head. "You don't have to have a lot of money to be rich. What about Wayne? Was he your first husband's best friend too?"

"No. He met us in the Kitty Cat Club a couple of weeks after my last husband died. We got to talking about diving for treasure, and he wanted to go with us on the next dive we made."

"Wayne's last name is Wells. Any relation to your last late husband?"

Kira's eyes grew wide. "What? His name is Grunsky."

Vaughn could tell by the shocked expression on Kira's face that she really hadn't had a clue. "Sorry to break it to you, but Wayne's real last name is Wells. How much do you want to bet he was related to your latest deceased husband, and he wanted to know just how Gaston died? What if they were brothers? They're both divers. What if he knew his brother was too knowledgeable about diving, that he shouldn't have had a dive accident like he had?

"What if Wayne looked into your past and learned what we did? That you left a wake of dead husbands, and his brother was the last. Now you have a new treasure-hunting scheme. How long before Miles and Douglas would have died at your hands? That's saying you're even telling the truth that Wayne attempted to kill Miles. Prove Brutus didn't have anything to do with it. Tell us where the rifle is that he shot Wayne with."

"I don't have any idea where it is."

"Don't be surprised if I don't believe you." Vaughn turned to Leidolf. "I've got to check on Jillian's injury. We'll talk to Kira more later."

"I didn't do anything. You can't hold me. I didn't hurt Douglas. They can run the tests and see that I didn't. I just came here to convince Miles that Brutus is innocent of hurting Douglas or Miles and to persuade Leidolf's men to free him."

"By force? That's what you thought, didn't you? That you would force us to free Brutus, then the two of you would disappear for good. You cashed in on your husbands' deaths. No matter what else, that shouts black widow. Murder for money. We're done talking for now. I want to see to Jillian's injury."

One of the police officers hauled Kira out to the car while Leidolf said, "I'll wait to see how badly Jillian was cut."

"Yeah, me too," Howard said, his arms folded across his chest, looking all growly.

Vaughn led Jillian back to the bedroom and she shifted.

Kira had cut her on the arm. Nothing that the doctor needed to stitch up, but Vaughn was still furious. He grabbed a wad of tissues from a box sitting on the bedside table and gently clamped it on Jillian's arm.

"Thanks. I told you it wasn't bad," Jillian said.

"Kira cut her, but not deeply." He had to let Leidolf know that the woman had actually tried to slice her.

"Are you sure you don't need the doc to take a look at it?" Leidolf asked from the living room.

"No, thanks. I'll be fine. My mate can take care of it." She took Vaughn's hand and kissed it, her eyes filled with tears.

Her words and tears bowled him over. "I've got it. I'll lock the door behind you." Vaughn kissed her mouth, then gently helped her to sit down. He was certain she was shaking from the adrenaline flooding her blood, the anger she'd felt because Wayne had shot her brother, the fight instinct, and being cut. "I'll be right back."

"I'm not going to die on you." She smiled up at him.

"No, but seeing your blood on the knife nearly gave me a heart attack." He smiled back at his lovely mate, then hurried out of the bedroom and down the hall to the living room. Both Leidolf and the police officer were still waiting to hear from him. Maybe they were worried it was worse than either was letting on.

Then Leidolf grinned at him. "You're mated? Hell, man, have you told your cousin yet?"

Vaughn smiled. "Uh, no. Just our team. Not even her parents. There will be time enough for that."

"Well, I'm sure glad I teamed the two of you up together. I feel like a mating expert now."

Smiling, Vaughn shook his head.

"You sure she's going to be all right?" Leidolf asked.

"Yeah. Just a small cut. I'll bandage it, and it should fade in a couple of days."

"Okay, my men will question Kira further and deal with this."

"Thanks. Glad you've got a place to lock her up."

"Yeah. When I took over the territory, I had to do something about wolves who go rogue. Since she's a jaguar who's involved in criminal acts, the USF will have to take her in and investigate all about her former husbands to determine if they were murdered. I can't imagine losing that many husbands to accidents. They'll have to decide what to do with her after that. Same with Brutus. Wayne and Simon too, once we catch up to them. I've seen the JAG facilities for holding rogues under investigation for committing crimes. They're perfect for long-term or short-term use."

"Sounds good."

"I'm glad to hear about Douglas too. I've got a pack member sitting with him around the clock for when he begins to talk again and to keep an eye on his condition."

"Thanks, Leidolf." Vaughn shook his hand.

The police officer grinned when Vaughn shook his hand. "Congratulations!"

"Thanks, man."

"A celebration is in order once you solve the case," Leidolf said.

The two men left and Vaughn asked, "Are you okay, Howard?"

"Hell, after you called me and the rest of the team to tell us that Douglas was awake and you were mated, I was glad…until it sounded like someone was ready to kill you and I had to rush right over here."

Vaughn smiled and slapped Howard on the shoulder. "Sorry, man. Get some rest. If you're feeling up to it, we'll all go out tonight when the others get in."

"Works for me."

Howard left, and Vaughn locked up. He grabbed a first aid kit from the bathroom and headed into the bedroom where Jillian was lying against the pillows, naked, looking sexy and desirable.

She smiled at him as if she knew what he was thinking.

"You are going to take it easy." Vaughn sat next to her on the bed and washed the cut with peroxide, then dried it carefully, covered it in sterilized gauze, and taped it up.

She ran her hand over his arousal, already stirring just from the way she looked so inviting. Now with her touching him?

He was a lost cause.

She knew it as he stripped off his boxer briefs, moved in close, and began to kiss her.

Chapter 19

SO THIS WAS WHAT MATED BLISS WAS LIKE, JILLIAN thought as she snuggled against Vaughn after making love again and napping for a bit. She kept thinking they needed to get up, to ensure Douglas was doing fine, to check on Howard and see how he was feeling. That they should learn if Leidolf's men had discovered anything more. If Brutus had shifted and spilled his guts yet. For now, she only wanted to hold on to Vaughn and cherish the moment.

"Feels good, doesn't it?" Vaughn said quietly against her hair.

"Yeah," she whispered back, not wanting to fully wake from the dream. She couldn't believe she'd mated the wolf she'd wanted to meet at the club and was now in bed with that hot, sexy SEAL wolf after making love to him.

Vaughn kissed her hand. "If we get up, it means we'll have to start making calls. That will be the end of this for a while."

She slid her naked body on top of his and grabbed her phone off the bedside table, then snuggled in his arms before she called the doctor first. She wasn't giving this up for anything. Not until they absolutely had to.

Vaughn sighed and said against her ear, "I'm so glad you're my partner."

"You like working like this?"

"Hell yeah. Don't you?"

"You know I do." She sighed next. "But it's going to make leaving the bed awfully hard."

"Worth it, don't you think?"

She chuckled. "Yeah."

She called the doctor, and as soon as the nurse got him on the line, she said, "Hi, this is Jillian. I'm checking on Douglas."

"He's doing great. He's given the officers the details of what he knows. I wanted to call you with an update, but Douglas said since you were now newly mated wolves, under no circumstances was I, or anyone on my staff, to call you. I told him about what happened with Kira and the two of you; Leidolf gave us the word. But Douglas insisted that it was too important for you to have some time alone," Dr. Wilders said.

"We're on our way over," Jillian said, sliding her hand over her hunky mate's bare chest.

"I'll have a look at that knife cut when you get here."

She was about to object.

Vaughn said, "Thanks, Doc. That will ease my mind."

She shook her head, said good-bye, and ended the call. "I'm fine."

"Sorry, but when you get pregnant, I'm going to take you in for all your checkups, and maybe even a few in between for good measure."

Jillian laughed. She couldn't help but love him. He wanted the best for her, even if he went a little overboard. "Deal. But *only* if I get to do the same for you if you're injured and need medical care."

The smile in his eyes and the curve of his mouth said he really wasn't ready for that. But he inclined his head. She was certain when it came time for her to have him checked out by the doctor, he wouldn't be quite so agreeable.

They quickly showered and dressed, then headed over to the clinic. When they walked into Douglas's room, he was sitting up and smiling broadly at them, looking like he'd never been injured, except for the bandaging around his neck and on his hands.

"You look well," Jillian said, meaning it, as she took a seat next to the bed.

"You're beautiful. I thought you were when you saw me last, but recollections were a little hazy. Now that I see you more clearly, you're beautiful. And Vaughn is one lucky wolf to have you."

"He is," Jillian agreed.

"I am." Vaughn was behind her, hands on her shoulders, rubbing them. She definitely enjoyed his massages. When they had a chance, she was giving him a good massage.

"She's the best thing that ever happened to me," Vaughn said.

"How are you feeling?" Jillian asked Douglas.

"Tired. Sore. But I'm glad to be alive. From what the doc said, the jaguar could have easily killed me. We believe you arrived while he was attacking me and scared him off. So thanks for saving my life. I owe you a lifetime of gratitude."

"I was glad to have arrived when I did. So glad you made it."

"Did Doc tell you he believes Wayne did it?" Vaughn asked.

"Yeah. He said he cleared both Kira and Brutus of the

crime. He also said that Wayne was the one who shot
Miles, according to Kira."

"Do you believe it?" Jillian asked.

"Well, he was kind of a quiet guy, just watching
everyone, listening in on what was being said. I forgot
he was around sometimes. Learning for certain that
Brutus was Kira's lover and not her brother wasn't a
total surprise. I'd caught them kissing once. I don't think
they saw me. I quickly turned away. But Wayne saw
too, and he didn't act surprised. That was when we were
at the dive club in Belize. It was noisy, everyone was
drinking, and I just figured whatever floated their boat.
But I also had no intention of getting together with them
for diving or anything else in the future. I didn't know
what to think. Whether it was an incestuous relationship, or they were pretending to be brother and sister for
some other reason. That was enough for me to be wary
of them. I never mentioned it to Miles because I never
thought we'd see them again.

"When I learned Miles was seeing Kira at the cabin, I
told him I had wanted to speak to him right away about
what I'd seen. I didn't want to ruin our own friendship by telling him, but I didn't see how I could keep
it to myself. Then I never had the chance. Once Miles
learned I was awake, he called from San Diego and told
me what had happened between him and Kira. If I'd told
him what I suspected, he would never have hooked up
with her, he said."

"We learned Wayne attacked you," Jillian said.

"Yeah. Miles and I were going to get together. He
said he'd run into Kira at the gas station, and wasn't
that a surprise? Both she and her brother were there

sightseeing. I knew it couldn't be a coincidence. Not when we'd first seen them at the Kitty Cat Club, then Belize, and now here. I didn't want to tell Miles over the phone about what I'd seen because I knew he'd be unhappy about it. I didn't know he was going to get together with her at his cabin.

"Then I heard someone pull up. I was expecting the boat rental guy to come for the money. I had gotten it out of the cubbyhole earlier, not wanting to rush in to remove it with the rattlesnake coiled up in there. The money was in a couple of plastic waterproof sacks. When I saw the vehicle with no sign on it indicating it was from the rental shop, I ran back to the bathroom and hid the money in the toilet tank. Glad you found it and not Wayne or the others. Leidolf said Kira's in lockup too now."

"Yeah. Where she belongs. You didn't tell us you were a famous treasure hunter," Vaughn said.

"I could use another diver on the next mission, Vaughn." Douglas smiled at Jillian. "Unless you'd like to go diving with me."

"Maybe in Hawaii," she replied. "It's shallow enough to be perfect for first-time dives. But only if you go too. I think it would be more fun to go with someone who's not been doing it for years. Vaughn and Miles can be our guides."

Vaughn rubbed her shoulder. "I was thinking of taking you there for a honeymoon. Four seems like kind of a crowd."

"They take groups out on the boats, right? So we do the scuba diving for fun together, and the rest will be… more private."

"I…" Douglas said.

Jillian patted Douglas's hand. "Agree. He agrees. I'm going to be the newest member of your pack, and your wedding present to me will be to come along for the ride." After what had happened to Douglas, she wanted to include him. Miles could watch out for him and vice versa.

Douglas chuckled. "I hope you know what you got yourself into, Vaughn."

"I think I'll be learning as we go along."

Jillian reached up and took Vaughn's hand. He squeezed hers back.

"Doc told me you found the money and secured it in the safe. What about the rattlesnake?"

"Freed in the woods. Miles grabbed it." Vaughn shook his head. "Hell, man, a booby trap?"

"Yeah, sorry. I never thought anyone but me or Miles would be going in there to get the cash, though I forgot to mention the cubbyhole to Miles." Douglas frowned. "How did you find it?"

"Miles told you about our father hiding the gun in a cabin." Jillian smiled. "Good thing he remembered."

"Yeah, that was it. I'd always just hidden the cash under a mattress before I paid for a boat. When Miles told me about how your SEAL father hid the gun, I thought it was a great way to hide the cash."

"Did anyone else know?" Jillian asked.

"No. That's probably why no one found it. Doc told me that Brutus paid me a visit as a jaguar too."

"Yeah, according to Kira, he wanted to tell you they hadn't been involved in injuring you," Jillian said. "Do you believe it?"

"I suspect he had something else in mind. Like asking me where the treasure map was."

They told him then about Kira and all her dead husbands.

Douglas looked shocked. "I would never have believed it. She talked about Gaston a fair amount, as if she hadn't quite gotten over his death. Even got teary-eyed once. But she didn't mention the two other dead husbands. Guess it was all just a show."

Vaughn got a call from Demetria and took it. "Yeah, we're visiting with Douglas. He's looking really good."

"That's great. We're back. We'll meet you over there," Demetria said. "And then the club?"

"Yeah, sounds good."

When they ended the call, Vaughn said to Douglas, "You wouldn't happen to have known that Wayne Grunsky was Wayne Wells, would you? He and a man who looks like his clone, Simon Wells—"

Douglas swore under his breath. "Were related to Kira's deceased husband, Gaston."

"Maybe Simon was a diver too." Jillian patted Douglas's hand. "We thought maybe they were after Brutus and Kira, figuring they had murdered Gaston. But then the treasure hunting got their attention, and they put any other plans on hold for the time being. Until someone shot a jaguar."

"I should have known when I danced with Kira at the club in San Diego, then saw them at the dive shop in Belize, that it was more than coincidence."

They visited with Douglas for another half hour, and he finally said he was tired. "If you don't leave, I won't have quality time to spend with my nurse."

Everyone smiled.

He was looking much better, and he seemed cheered to know so many genuinely cared about his welfare. But Vaughn knew Douglas wouldn't rest easy until they caught Wayne—and Simon too. For now, he would have an armed guard, just in case.

The owners of the Forest Club had completely remodeled it since the last time Vaughn had visited the place. It wasn't the Clawed and Dangerous Kitty Cat Club by any means—no dancers on platforms—but it had a lot of atmosphere. Real plants decorated it like at the cat club, but they were forest rather than jungle plants: deer fern, maidenhair fern, coastal wood ferns, native Oregon flowers—yellow asters, orange poppies, blue bellflower, roses, and more—and small trees. Skylights and black-painted ceilings arched into a rounded dome covered in sparkling lights that simulated stars, and a misty night sky partially hid the full moon. The dance floor had been expanded, more eating areas were set up, and a live band was playing. Leidolf had called ahead to reserve a special table for the agents so that they'd all be able to sit together, surrounded on the back side by plants and a mirrored wall and with a view of the dance floor. Because of their help with the case, he was giving them complimentary meals and drinks.

After everyone ordered steaks—wolves and jaguars alike loved them rare and juicy—Vaughn slipped his hand around Jillian's and took her to the dance floor. "I've wanted to do this since I saw you with that muscle-bound brute at the Kitty Cat Club," Vaughn said. "Though I would have loved to dance with you there, it's really special coming here, a wolf club, for our first time."

"As mated wolves too," she said, wrapping her arms around his waist and looking up at him with such longing that he was tempted to take her back to the guest house, ravage her, and return after the meal was delivered. That was the problem with not getting well-done steaks. Not a whole lot of time to fool around.

They kissed as he moved her slowly around the floor, two mated wolves completely in love, her body sliding against his, turning his thermostat up to high. He could smell her pheromones kick-starting, the sweet vanilla scent she used to shower, and the sweet and spicy fragrance that was uniquely hers.

"Do you know how much I want to take you right back to the guest house and ravage you?"

She laughed. "Just as much as I want to take you back there. I had planned for a long night of dancing, but I think we might need to leave earlier."

He smiled down at her. "Yeah, I don't believe I can handle a whole lot of dancing like this with you without wanting to take it further."

"I can tell." She turned her head to see what was happening at the table. Miles was waving at them to join them because the food had been delivered. She sighed. "Dinner, drinks, another dance, and let's call it a night."

As soon as they sat down to eat, Miles remarked on the Kitty Cat Club, glad they didn't have any platform performers here. "I could see Vaughn giving another stellar performance as he rescued a showgirl who was just playing her part."

No way. The platform chain coming loose couldn't have been a show, could it? Vaughn glanced at Jillian to see her take on it.

She was glowering at her brother, her cheeks a little rosy. She looked like she could bite him as either a human or wolf.

The jaguars were all quiet, smiling a little. Howard was carving up his steak, his color back to normal. Demetria turned to look at the dancers. Everett took a sip of his wine and wouldn't look Vaughn in the eye. But they were all still smiling!

Jillian sighed. "Miles is just jealous because of all the attention you got from rescuing the dancer. Over half of the single she-cats must have danced with you after that. Besides, both Miles and I thought it was totally real too. And there you were, risking your neck to save the girl. Every woman in there wished she had a hero in her court just like that."

"That had to be amazing to see," Demetria said, chiming in. "If Everett had done that, I would have worshipped him."

Everett smiled. "All it took for me to win her over was playing with an Arctic wolf cub. She figured I couldn't be all that bad."

"You were great."

Miles shook his head. "I have to admit it took real balls for you to react so quickly. Must be your SEAL training. Leap first and ask questions later."

"Well, hell. And the thing of it was, there was only one woman who I was interested in dancing with. But she wouldn't come near me." Vaughn squeezed Jillian's knee.

"I was with a date. Not a very fun date, but still, I had

my priorities. Besides, I would have had to fight off all those she-cats."

"It would have been worth it."

She laughed. "Yeah, it would have been."

Vaughn had barely eaten any of his steak when he said, "This is so good, but I don't think I can eat any more of it tonight."

Jillian smiled. "More dancing then?"

"That last dance did a number on me."

"I'll dance with you," Howard said.

"Nah, that's all right. I think I'm done for the moment." Vaughn looked hopefully at Jillian. Of course, if Jillian wanted to dance more, he would twirl her around on the floor until she was ready to call it a night.

Smiling, Jillian shook her head at Vaughn. "Okay, I'll put you out of your misery. We might be back."

"When the wolves come home." Miles saluted them.

"Have a good one." Howard raised his glass to them too.

"Remember how we were like that?" Demetria asked Everett.

"Well, I'd take you back to the guest house too, but I think this time we'll let them have the place to themselves for a while."

Vaughn got takeout boxes, glad Jillian was agreeable to joining him at home. He hadn't wanted to ruin her evening, but he really wanted to have more alone time with her. They could still join the others later tonight.

As soon as they were in the Land Rover, he asked, "You were okay with this, weren't you?"

She just laughed. "Now you ask. Of course. We're like...newlyweds. Everyone understands. And we can still return later after we get some important business out of the way." She opened her phone and began tapping on it. "You know, I was thinking the news of the accidents involving Kira's husbands would probably be online. Okay, here's a statement on Gaston's death listed in a forum on diving incidents.

"They believe he died of decompression sickness, also known as the bends. The normal gases found in the body didn't have time to diffuse and caused bubbles to form inside his body. He must have come up too fast. The sheriff's department concluded it was an accident, even though he'd been diving for eleven years and had made over five hundred dives."

"Well, accidents can occur, even with veteran divers. What I'm curious about is whether Brutus was there when Gaston had his accident."

"Says Gaston was survived by his wife. No mention of any other family. I'm going to call Lydia and see if she can give me the names of Kira's other husbands." As soon as Jillian had them, she thanked Kira's mother and started doing a search for the men. "Okay, so eyewitnesses said her first husband, John, had been drinking in a bar while his new wife was working as a clerk at a store that night. He frequented the tavern and was known to drive home drunk. He was with his usual buddies, and they said they all went home without incident that night."

"One of his buddies was Brutus, right?" Vaughn pulled up to the guest house.

"Yep. John drove through the railing of a bridge and went into the lake and drowned."

"Any eyewitnesses?"

"Nope. Kira called the police when he didn't arrive home after she did. They drove the route he normally did, found the bridge railing torn up, and discovered the vehicle in the lake. Divers found he'd died from drowning."

"Even if both could be dismissed as accidents, the fact remains that Brutus was there for that incident, and who's to say he was really drinking? Maybe he was plying John with drinks."

"True. Kira and John had only been married two weeks."

"And the second case?"

"That to me is the most suspicious." She showed him a picture of a selfie Kira must have shot of herself and her husband before his untimely death. "It's kind of hard to tell from the photo, but I swear that's Brutus wearing sunglasses in the background. He sort of photobombed it."

"But also incriminated himself." Vaughn and Jillian got out of the Land Rover and headed into the guest house. "Now we know for sure that Brutus was where her husbands were before they died."

"How much do you want to bet he was one of the divers when Gaston ran into trouble?" Jillian said. "Do you mind if we head over to the jailhouse and have a talk with her to learn if Brutus was diving that day too?"

Vaughn rubbed Jillian's shoulders and smiled down at her. "You don't want to wait until after…?"

She smiled up at him and pulled him close. "Something you should know about me. I might be able to multitask, but when it comes to a job—"

"The job can wait." Vaughn swept her up in his arms and carried her down the hall to his room this time.

Vaughn's eyes had darkened, his full, sensual mouth set with determination as he carried her into the room and sat her down on the edge of the bed.

He moved in between her legs and cupped her face. All thoughts of the case vanished when the chemistry between them ignited into pheromone-fed desire. He leaned over and kissed her, tackling her jacket with his large hands. She slid her fingers up his jeans-covered thighs, making a detour to stroke his swelling arousal. She loved how hot he became when he was around her.

He growled a little, the huskiness in his voice revealing just how much she had unbalanced him. She wanted to take control, if only for a moment. The adrenaline rushed through her every vein as he tossed her jacket on the floor and jerked off his own to add it to the collection.

A frenzy of passion swirled between them as they tugged off the rest of their clothes, yet even as she yanked up her shirt, he was leaning down to lick her nipple through her silky bra, while he struggled to unfasten his belt. Once they were completely bare, the air was slightly cool in the bedroom against her naked skin. But Vaughn was hotness personified as he began kissing her mouth, leaning her back against the bed, and crawling up beside her. He began to run his hand over her breast, then down her belly.

He smelled musky, of the woods and wolf. Of sex, all male, and vanilla soap, rich and delicious, mingling with her own sexual arousal and scents. As his tongue stroked hers, she tasted the lemon and pepper steak he'd managed to have, and sweet and spicy wine.

Then he began to stroke her clit, circling over the

sensitive nub, and she forgot about anything else but him, the wolf she'd claimed for her own. The man she would love forever. She wanted to stroke him too, but his touching immobilized her as she soaked in the tantalizing sensations. His fingers slipped into her wet sheath and thrust inside, circling until she fell off the edge of the world, crying out with sheer pleasure.

He joined her, filling her, completing her, thrusting as she lifted her pelvis in response. She needed him deeper, wanting every bit of him inside her. And couldn't believe it when she felt the climax building again.

His beautiful wolf, Vaughn thought as he pushed deeper inside his mate. He had never felt this connected with any other woman, and he loved the way they were in sync. Every thrust brought him closer to the edge. Every beat of her heart, the way her breathing was so unsteady, her spicy pheromones teasing his, and the feel of her hot, silky heat wrapped around him all added to the sexual high.

He leaned down to take his fill of her mouth, stroking her tongue and kissing her, then stepping up the thrusts, unable to hold back any longer. The orgasm hit, and he couldn't have been more pleased to feel the ripples of her own climax caressing his cock as he continued to thrust to the end. He growled with the final release, rolled off her, and pulled her into his arms.

If he kept the connection, kept kissing her, touching her, listening to her heartbeat, he'd become aroused all over again.

She licked his nipple and caressed the other one with her fingertip. That would do it too.

She kissed his chest and looked up at him with bright

eyes, not looking sleepy in the least. Which was a good thing since he fully intended to make love to her again as soon as he could. "We forgot the takeout boxes of food in the car."

He didn't move a muscle. Not when he wanted to stay just like this until after they had their next bout of lovemaking.

She smiled. "What if we get hungry and want to eat it later? It needs to be refrigerated. I'll run out and get it."

"No. I will." But he still didn't make a move to leave the bed. This was just where he wanted to be.

"I want to run as a wolf tonight. Just a fun run. The moon's out. We haven't once run as wolves together just for fun."

He smiled at her, running his hand through her dark hair. He understood her need to share their love as wolves too, and he was game. Then afterward, more loving. "All right, but just around the grounds."

"Great." She moved off him.

"But I'll get the food." He threw on a pair of boxer briefs, figuring he would be able to withstand the cold better than she would, running out in the chilly night air half dressed.

She shifted, tugged his boxer briefs playfully with her wolf's teeth, then raced out of the bedroom.

He chuckled, but by the time he reached the hall, she'd already hit the wolf door and headed outside. He was ready for a run with his mate and some fun-loving wolf business too.

Chapter 20

AFTER PUTTING THE FOOD IN THE FRIDGE, VAUGHN shifted, ran outside in his wolf coat, and looked all around for Jillian, sniffing the air. Then he smelled her sexy scent and took off after her. She was exploring a way away. He should have known she'd pick up the trail Kira had left when she came to their guest house. Jillian had already run off in wolf-tracking mode. He woofed, telling her he was coming, to hold on. The other jaguars might be somewhere in the area, which was why he wanted to stay close to the buildings and not run off too far until this business was resolved.

When he reached Jillian, he nuzzled her affectionately in greeting, and she licked his muzzle. Then she nipped at him and ran off. He barked and took off after her. Her tail held out straight behind her said she was alpha all the way, ready to enjoy herself.

He loved this part of them—the wolf side that was ready to enjoy nature as they moved closer to the earth.

On natural impulse, he tackled Jillian and took her down. She rolled onto her back, legs up in the air, kicking at him, biting as he bit back, all in a playful way, growling and having fun. Wolf play was always practice for wolf fights, if they had to deal with wolves who had gone rogue. Since Vaughn had never seen her play with other wolves, she was completely unpredictable and suddenly jumped up to tackle him back. Standing on their hind legs, they clashed, teeth exposed, her legs using his to help her stay up. But she was shorter, not as heavy, and he quickly took her down. But not for long.

She slipped out from underneath him and tackled his neck before he could react. He realized she must have had a lot of experience playing with her brother, as good as she was at countering his moves, despite his larger size. He was gentler with her, knowing he could accidentally hurt her if he wasn't careful, but glad she wasn't gentle with him. He was used to his brother giving him good exercise sessions, so he was eager to accept the challenge from his mate.

She tore off again, and the chase was on.

Ohmigod, Vaughn was such a wolf. Jillian had played with her own brother tons over the years and loved the way Vaughn could be just as aggressive, but cognizant of her smaller size and lighter weight. As much as Vaughn was panting, she knew she was giving him a great workout too. She could tell she was going to keep in great wolf shape with a mate like Vaughn, and she loved the way they played and exercised. Truly compatible.

With him giving chase, her heart skittered and she felt panicked, not because she was afraid, but just because of the thrill of the chase, the knowledge she couldn't keep ahead of him because of his longer gait. Before long, he would tackle her again.

She kept smelling whiffs of Kira's scent though, and that was distracting her. While Vaughn was almost completely focused on her. *Almost*. She saw him turn his head and take a little sniff a couple of times too, so he wasn't *all* business when it came to playing with her. They were still wolves on a mission, and once they had their fill of playing—for the moment, since she could see them playing until they were old and white—she had every intention of searching for where Kira had been.

As if Vaughn thought she might be too tired to play, but he wasn't quite ready to quit having fun with her in their wolf coats, he lay down on his stomach, then rolled over, exposing his belly and throat, saying she'd won. She was in charge, if she wanted him. Come and play some more.

She took up the challenge and bounded to join him, to tackle him, and nip at his throat. All in play. Wrestling like this with him made her want to run home, shift, and wrestle some more under the covers, woman to man.

And then she straddled him, her chest against his, their hearts beating wildly, both of them panting.

She licked his muzzle in friendship and love. He licked her back, smiling with his wickedly sharp canines exposed. Woofing at him, she rose and moved off him. He stood, motioned with his head to search for Kira's scent, and Jillian nodded. They made a great team.

Now it was time to search for where Kira had come from. Had someone left her off nearby so she could walk through the woods to the guest house? Or had she left a vehicle behind? That might hold evidence they could use to their advantage.

They'd traveled maybe two miles from the ranch house and had even crossed two streams when they found a gravel road.

There, sitting on the side of the road, was a muddy gray pickup truck. With two flat tires. They sniffed around it, and Jillian smelled both Brutus's and Kira's scents. Which meant this had to be their vehicle. Too bad they couldn't just drive the vehicle to the ranch. Maybe the flat tires were the reason Kira had crossed through the woods to the ranch, and it hadn't been because she was trying to be sneaky about it. Though Jillian couldn't imagine Kira had planned to ask Miles nicely about having Brutus released. Not when she had been carrying a weapon.

Jillian shifted and tried a door handle, but the vehicle was locked. Unfortunately, they didn't have any way to unlock the vehicle. That was until she saw her now-naked mate pick up a large rock. As cold as it was, she shifted and moved away from the truck. He banged the rock against the window until it broke and he could reach in and unlock it.

Once Vaughn had the door open, he unlocked the back doors. Jillian shifted again, opened a back door, and climbed inside, then shut it. The first thing she saw on the floorboard was a rifle and ammo. Four duffel bags too. No scuba gear. Maybe at a hotel?

Or maybe they would rent it like Miles had intended to.

Inside one of the bag's pockets, Jillian found a hotel receipt. "That's about five miles from here."

"Okay, we need to get right on it. But we also need to take that rifle and ammunition back to Leidolf so the police can run ballistics on it to see if the rounds were the same as the ones fired at the jaguar. And they can compare the round that was used on your brother to see if the same weapon fired it."

"Kira said that Wayne shot Miles. This appears to be Brutus's gun, but we can have them also confirm if it's registered to him."

"Agreed. And make sure he wasn't really the shooter.

We need to take all of this back to the guest house and get dressed, but—"

"We can only do that if we carry it back with us. As much as I hate to do it, we're wolves and this is something we have to do from time to time. We'll need to borrow some of their clothes so we can carry it all back." She began searching for a sweater and pants, hoping she could find shoes to fit her.

Vaughn found camo clothes and hurried to put on the shirt and pants. He held up a shoe. "Brutus has small feet."

"Did you want to run as a wolf?"

"You couldn't carry all of that back with you. Even though we have the two jaguars incarcerated, I don't want to risk having the other jaguars locate it and take off with it, if they have a mind to do so."

"Right. I'll give you a foot massage when we get back."

He smiled, then let out his breath. "Despite the chill in the air and the roughness of the ground in areas, I'll have to go barefoot. What about you?"

She pulled on the sweater and then zipped up the pants. She frowned at the shoes, then smiled. "Right size. Thank goodness." She didn't want to have to walk all the way back to the guest house in bare feet, yet she had to help carry all this stuff. She slid her arms into a spare woman's jacket.

As soon as they stuffed the boxes of ammo into one of the bags, she checked to see if the rifle was loaded. It was. She pulled out some more rounds then and stuffed them in the jacket pocket, looking up to see what Vaughn was doing. Watching her.

"Ready to shoot someone?" He arched a brow.

She smiled. "I promise, not *you* this time. But if we run into trouble with the other two jaguars, I'll definitely be ready to shoot."

"A jaguar," he said skeptically, as if he really, truly thought she only shot wolves!

"Yes. If he's coming after *either* of us. We wouldn't stand a chance against a jaguar. Or, if he's armed with a rifle and shooting at us. I won't have any qualms taking him down in any case."

"Good to know." He pulled her into his arms and kissed her. "Ready to go?"

"Yeah." She felt bad for him when she saw him climb out of the truck barefooted. "Maybe you could wear heavy-duty socks."

"Nah, that's okay."

She realized he hadn't buttoned his shirt, and she wondered if he thought to shift into the wolf if they ran into trouble. He would be better off as a wolf than an unarmed human. Though she wondered if he was a better marksman than her.

"If we run into trouble, did you want to take the rifle?" Discussing it now was important, not waiting until they were in the middle of trouble.

"No. I'd rather you were armed with the rifle. I'll shift. I don't have any shoes on, and it would take longer for you to strip."

"Okay. Unless you think you're a better shot than me." All that mattered was their survival.

"No. I believe you when you said you could have taken me out with the first shot. The rifle's all yours."

Appreciating that he believed in her, Jillian slung the rifle over her shoulder. She glanced back at the truck before they took off, looking into the truck's bed, but there were no spare tires.

Then they headed back toward the guest house. She recalled then that both of the streams were running high because of all the winter rains. As a wolf crossing them, she hadn't given it much thought. Their fur acted as a water-repellent insulator and kept them warm. She'd also been concentrating on locating Kira's scent on the other side of the stream. As a human, it meant wading through ice-cold water that was probably about chest deep on her. It meant keeping the rifle and ammo dry, but getting soaked and having to wear cold, wet clothes on the rest of the trek back to the guest house.

As long as Vaughn didn't cut his feet on rocks or twigs, he would probably do better than she would in wet shoes. She'd worn wet army boots and wet wool socks during water hazard and leadership obstacle courses, and then had to march for miles, ending up with blisters. Which made her think of a better way of handling this: remove the boots and tie them around her neck when they reached the stream. They didn't have that option at the army officer courses.

They'd walked for maybe a quarter of a mile when they reached the first of the streams, and she began stripping. Vaughn smiled at her.

"I don't want to drag through the water and then wear the sopping-wet clothes to the next stream."

"Just throw everything in one of the bags, and I'll carry it."

He was already carrying three bags. She had the rifle and the fourth bags.

"I can do it. I'll be able to keep everything dry. You

can run as a wolf to the next stream, cross it, and then you can shake off and get dressed again," he said.

She hated making him carry all the stuff.

"I insist."

The second stream wasn't too far from this one, so she agreed. "I'm not a pansy."

He laughed. "I would never think you were. It's just easy to do it this way since I'm a lot taller, so no problem."

"This makes me wonder how Kira came to the guest house and wasn't soaking wet. She must have removed her clothes and waded across." Jillian stuffed all the clothes into the bag she'd been carrying and handed him the rifle and bag. Then she shifted and watched to see if he really could keep everything dry.

"It would take too long to strip and dress, then have to do the same thing at the next stream. There's too much distance between the two streams to walk naked to the next one." He started to wade across, the bags held up as high as he could, the rifle tied up on top. One of the bags he'd been carrying dipped into the water, which would serve to weigh him down. He slipped a little on wet rocks, and finally made it to shore. She swam after him and then loped alongside him while they headed toward the next stream. With their wolves' night vision and the cloudless sky and brilliant full moon tonight, they could still see well.

But if jaguars were about, they could see just as well as the wolves.

So far, so good. They'd need to have Leidolf's men pick up the truck too. It wouldn't be a good idea if it was left unsecured on the gravel road. Who knew if anyone might try to steal it? And they needed to check it over to see if they could gather any further evidence.

Another eighth of a mile, and they'd made it to the second stream and begun to cross. Jillian wanted to ask how Vaughn's feet were doing. Maybe she could carry the bags and rifle, and he could run as a wolf for a while. Then he could get out of the wet clothes that had to make him feel ten times colder.

As soon as they gave all of this to the team and the police, she was taking Vaughn straight back to the guest house so they could take a hot shower and she could warm him right up.

When he reached the other side, he slipped and she bumped against him with her wolf's body, as if she could keep him on his feet. Moving away from the stream, he set the bags down and fished out the clothes she'd worn already. She ran away from him, stood and shook several times, then raced back to him so she could shift and dress. The stars twinkled against the dark sky.

Cold, cold, she hurried to pull on the long sweater and then the jacket. "Go ahead," she said, not liking that he was drenched in the wet clothes and waiting on her to dress. She was already shaking, and she could see he was shivering too.

"I'll wait."

Protective mate. "You've got to be freezing. I'll catch up."

He dropped the bags and began searching through them while she pulled on the pants. Then she realized what he was doing. He pulled out a fresh set of clothes. Before he could begin to pull off the wet ones, she was helping him strip. Not only because it was faster this way, but because she liked the way he was smiling down at her for doing so as she took a soft T-shirt and rubbed his body—all of his body—vigorously to dry him off the quickest she could before he dressed.

She smiled as she witnessed his cock stir to life. "Wow," she said. "Even in this cold."

He laughed. "Only *you* could make it happen."

"Good thing." She helped him dress, then sat down to put the boots back on. She was glad they were mostly dry, with the walk they still had to make all the way back to the ranch. He crouched down and tied on one of her boots while she worked on the other.

"Hot shower when we get back?" he asked.

"Absolutely. Back rubs, well, whole body rubs."

"And more."

"Hmm," she said as he pulled her to stand and wrapped his arms around her. "The more is what I'm really looking forward to."

"What are we waiting for then?"

They were continuing on their way to the ranch when they heard a wolf howl, and then another. Three more in unison. They paused. The howls were a warning. Families stay inside. The men were gathering for trouble. What had happened now?

"What do you think? Should we try to make it back to the guest house with all this stuff?" Vaughn asked quietly.

She didn't want to leave any of the bags behind, not if some of the stuff inside them could be important to their investigation. But then she saw movement in the woods nearby. "I think it's too late." Jillian's heart was pounding as she was certain she'd seen an animal's glowing eyes in the woods. She slowly set the bag down. "Jaguar, six o'clock," she whispered. "I think. If it were a wolf, he'd let us know it. I saw his eyes…glowing about at the level a big cat's or wolf's would be when standing still."

Vaughn dropped the other bags and began to strip off his clothes.

"You can't fight him if he wants what we have."

"Which is why you have the rifle."

She was afraid everything would happen so fast that all they'd have time to do would be to react on instinct. Vaughn quickly shifted, but waited in protective mode beside her. Jillian readied the rifle and called out, "I don't know which jaguar you are, but if you don't lie down on the grass to let me know you're not a threat, I'll shoot." She couldn't just shoot the cat where it stood. Not if he or she didn't act aggressively.

The cat lay down on its belly, but Jillian was still wary that it might be just a ploy. Vaughn lifted his chin to howl, to let others know they had one of the cats in their sight, but another cat came out of the north, running to attack her. An ambush then. Jaguars were ambush predators. But not usually in pairs. She had the gun, and that could be more lethal than Vaughn as a wolf. That's why the other cat was targeting her first.

She didn't have time to consider the first cat's actions.

Vaughn tore into the cat, but with its punishing claws and swipes, she was afraid the jaguar would kill her mate. She aimed to fire a shot, her hands and breathing as steady as she could make them when she wasn't feeling calm in the least. Not when the cat and wolf were growling, trying to get the best of each other, snarling and moving with such speed that she was having trouble keeping the cat in her sights. She sure as hell didn't want to shoot her mate this time.

Just as she thought she had a good shot, she saw the other cat in her peripheral vision racing toward her. Jillian squeezed the trigger and fired a round at the jaguar fighting with her mate. It had to be a male as big as he was.

The jaguar went down, and Jillian swung around and was about ready to aim at the other cat, which was smaller—Kira? But a third jaguar had targeted the cat.

The smaller cat dodged away, and Jillian aimed at the larger one. She wasn't sure why the jaguar was after her. But then she recalled the two men shooting at Jillian and the other wolves, and at Brutus. Wayne and Simon. Had to be. She only saw the one male jaguar though. Before another could come and help him, howls farther away rent the air.

And a couple of shots were fired. She shot the larger jaguar, only wounding him before he could hurt the female. He stumbled but made another lunge, and she shot him again. Both shots were meant to disable him, not kill him. She'd had to kill the one who had attacked her mate though. She'd had to protect him at all costs.

The jaguar collapsed, and Vaughn ran to watch over him, growling and letting the cat know he'd attack if the jaguar moved from where he was lying on the grass now. Kira ran to see the one Jillian had killed. She nudged at the male, licking his muzzle, trying to get him to move. But he was no longer breathing, his heartbeat stopped.

Jillian felt bad for her, but she wouldn't have done anything differently. Not when her own mate's life was at stake. "Kira?" She smelled her scent. And Brutus's too. "How did the two of you leave the jail?" Somehow they had managed to escape.

That was probably why all the howling had occurred. She prayed neither Brutus nor Kira had killed one of the guards at the jailhouse. And she prayed her own mate wasn't injured too badly.

"Lie down, Kira," Jillian said. "I don't want to have to shoot you too." But she would—if Kira attacked either her or Vaughn.

Jillian heard wolves racing to join them, barking that they were on their way. A couple of all-terrain vehicles were coming too, and she was glad they could take the jaguars off their hands and take care of Vaughn's injuries. As soon as one of the vehicles stopped where she was watching over Kira, another parked where Vaughn was keeping the wounded jaguar in line. Three jaguars were riding on the vehicle and they leaped off. They must have been Demetria and Everett with Howard. She recognized Howard this time.

The jaguar Jillian had wounded made a move to get up, and one of the men with the other vehicle fired a shot at him. Her heart nearly quit beating. She stifled the urge to shout out *No!* They needed the cat for questioning.

The men loaded him onto the vehicle. One of the men motioned for Vaughn to come with them, but he shook his head and ran back to join her.

She loved her stubborn wolf, as much as she wanted to tell him to go with the men and get treatment for his wounds. Another vehicle arrived and pulled up to the one near her.

Leidolf and the doctor were on that one, and they

hurried to get out. Leidolf looked over Brutus, and the doc shook his head. "Dead."

"Well, he would have been anyway. One way or another," Leidolf said.

"Did he kill the guard?" Jillian asked, handing the rifle to Leidolf and crouching down to gently hug her wolf as they loaded Brutus's body onto one of the vehicles.

"No, but he's going to have one hell of a headache and he needed some stitches. The bastard pretended to be sick. Kira was calling out that she thought Brutus was dying. The guard didn't wait for backup. When he went into the cell to check on him, Brutus was lying on his stomach, making a choking sound," Doc said, taking a look at Vaughn. "Looks like you're going to need some patching up. Again."

Before they could do anything with Kira, she leaped up on the vehicle to join Brutus. One of the men said to Kira, "Pull anything, and I'll shoot you and ask questions later." Leidolf's man got on the vehicle to serve as her guard. But she didn't seem intent on doing anything but mourning the loss of her lover.

Another man threw the bags onto the other ATV.

"The rifle was Brutus's," Jillian said to Leidolf. "Maybe one of your men can tell if it was used to shoot one of the other jaguars. Maybe my brother."

"We found Simon's vehicle on one of the ranch roads. Couple of rifles in it too," Leidolf said. "After we run some ballistics tests on them, we should be able to determine who fired what at whom."

"I've got to get back to the clinic." Doc climbed onto the vehicle. "Need to take care of the jaguar you shot before we can question him."

"But one of your pack members shot and killed him."

Doc shook his head. "Tranquilized him for easier management. He was still too aggressive to take in hand like he was. Then you can question him."

"Thanks." Jillian was relieved the jaguar was alive so they could learn what was going on. "What about the other? We heard gunshots."

"Tranquilized too."

She sighed with relief, then turned her attention to her mate. "Vaughn, why don't you go with him? I'll walk back with the others."

He wouldn't budge, so Doc and Leidolf headed back to the ranch with the wounded jaguar.

"Fine." She stripped and shifted, then nuzzled his side where he didn't have a mark on him. Together they walked to the clinic, their jaguar agent friends joining them. They were truly a team.

Chapter 21

VAUGHN WAS STILL ANGRY THAT BRUTUS HAD MANaged to get in any claw and bite marks, though he had to thank his lucky stars they weren't any worse than they were, as wicked as a jaguar's claws were and as powerful as their slashing paws and bite were. He'd managed to get in some good bites of his own and had dodged some of the jaguar's more lethal moves. Still, Vaughn wanted to be questioning Kira and the other jaguars that were now incarcerated along with her in the jail cells…well, separate cells. They had three guards standing watch. All of them would return with the jaguars to Dallas when they needed to transport them to JAG headquarters. Vaughn really thought the doctor's care was unnecessary, but his mate had insisted, and so had Demetria, so he'd finally gone along with the game plan.

Demetria, her mate, and Howard were sitting in the waiting area to show moral support, which Vaughn appreciated. Though he wasn't a fallen comrade in arms this time.

"Great shooting," he said to Jillian as Doc stitched up another cut, this one a little deeper than the rest. With their faster wolf healing, the scar would disappear in a week or so.

"Only I am allowed to take a bite out of you." She smiled at him as he smiled back. "I wished I could have taken him out before he tore into you so much."

"You had to see how good a fighter I was first."

She gave a ladylike snort. "You kept getting your big head in the way."

He laughed.

Doc took a look at Vaughn's shoulder and touched the skin where the bullet had entered. "That should be working itself out in another couple of weeks. If a human had been shot like that, cell tissue would just grow around it, and it wouldn't hurt either. But for us, the tissues won't have time to surround it before the bullet pushes its way out. Just like birthing a baby. Then the skin and cell tissues will heal up completely. No scarring."

"Sounds good, Doc. Thanks."

It was close to two in the morning, when all good little wolves—and jaguars—should be in bed, he thought. Two of the jaguars were tranquilized, so the team couldn't really talk with them yet. Kira was so torn up about losing Brutus that she wasn't making any sense. Because of that, when Doc was through with him, Vaughn and Jillian joined the others in the waiting room, glad they had brought some clothes to the clinic so they could shift and dress.

"Where has Miles been?" Jillian suddenly asked.

"He's been sidelined. But Leidolf let him in to see Kira and try to talk with her, if he can," Demetria said. "As for the rest of us, we need to call it a night, and tomorrow, we'll get some answers."

Before they all had settled down in their own beds at the guest house for what was left of the night, Miles called Jillian. She and Vaughn had just come back from taking hot showers, warming each other up, and were only dressed in towels as they entered the bedroom when she got the call.

She put it on speaker.

"Brutus wasn't her lover," Miles said.

"What about the picture we saw of them kissing in the Kitty Cat Club?" Jillian looked like she didn't believe Kira any more than Vaughn did.

"Yeah, and Douglas said he saw them kissing in a sexual fashion at the dive bar in Belize." Vaughn unwrapped Jillian from her towel and set it aside, then jerked his own off and threw it next to hers. Then he took her hand and coaxed her into bed.

"She said they were drunk. She barely remembered it. Just that they had kissed, and she had moved away from him."

"But she was so broken up about him dying," Jillian said.

"She thought of him like a brother. How would you have felt if that had been me?"

"Okay. I agree."

"She said she didn't have anything to do with him breaking out of the jailhouse. She thought he was really sick. She was upset when he injured the guard. Brutus released her from her cell, but she was afraid everyone would think she was involved in the guard's injuries and the escape so she went with him."

"Okay." But Jillian still didn't sound like she believed Kira.

"She wanted me to call her mother. She's coming up first thing in the morning."

"Lydia is?" Now Jillian sounded shocked.

Maybe her mother didn't disapprove of Kira as much

as she let on. Or maybe she was so furious that she was going to lecture her about it instead. Vaughn joined Jillian in bed and pulled her against his chest.

"She didn't kill her husbands," Miles insisted.

"All right. We'll talk tomorrow. Get some sleep."

"'Night," Miles said, sounding tired and annoyed, probably because he felt his sister didn't believe Kira.

"'Night, Miles," Vaughn said, then they ended the call and he put Jillian's phone on the bedside stand. "When you were drying me earlier by the stream..." he said to Jillian.

"Ohmigod, Vaughn, you are insatiable. How could I ever get so lucky?" But then she paused. "Are you sure you're all right?"

"You have to ask?" He pulled her onto his lap, and she smiled. *Wickedly*.

It was nearly afternoon the next day when they got up and joined Demetria and Everett in the kitchen to make lunch.

"You should have gotten us up," Jillian said, tying her hair back.

"We just got up ourselves." Demetria made them all grilled ham and cheese sandwiches while Jillian told them what her brother had said.

"Do you believe her?" Everett served glasses of water.

"Now that Brutus is dead, she could be lying through her teeth about what happened at the jailhouse. And what happened at the club. Even her mother said Brutus could have been Kira's lover."

Everett got a call and said, "Thanks." And ended the call. "Okay, ballistics showed that the rifles that the Wells brothers owned both had been used to fire on Jillian. It also shows that neither was used to shoot Miles."

"Brutus's was," Jillian said.

"Correct. It was also used when the one jaguar was shot and no one could locate him, only the shell casings. The findings were given to Kira to see her reaction. She was stunned, Leidolf said. He said he didn't think anyone could appear more genuinely stunned than she did. She collapsed on the bench in her cell and just stared at the floor. Anyway, I'd say it was possible she truly didn't know Brutus had shot Miles. That all along, Brutus had led her to believe Wayne did it."

"Because she would have turned on Brutus if she had known he tried to kill Miles," Jillian said.

"But was she involved in her husbands' deaths, or was Brutus the only one who had a hand in them?" Vaughn asked as they quickly ate lunch, cleaned up, and headed over to the jailhouse in his Land Rover.

"I think we need to split into teams to question everyone," Jillian said. "And then we'll swap off and compare notes."

"I agree," Demetria said.

Miles and Howard, Demetria and Everett, and Jillian and Vaughn. Jillian wondered how many stories they were going to get from all the people.

Everett got a call from Leidolf and informed everyone Lydia had just arrived.

First, Jillian and Vaughn spoke with Simon Wells, who sat manacled to a table in one of the interrogation rooms. He was black-haired like his brother, with a beard and black-brown eyes. He seemed at ease, not worried that he was in trouble for anything.

"We know that Brutus murdered your brother Gaston," Jillian said, though they didn't know for sure if he had. She had a recorder documenting the conversation. "How did you feel about that?"

"How do you think I felt about it?"

So he did believe Brutus killed his brother. "Not very upset. Now, see, I would have killed him for it. But what did you do?"

"Tried to shoot him. He killed Gaston, and then he shot Wayne. I was in my rights to attempt to put him down before he killed anyone else. Hell, he murdered Kira's two other husbands, too. Not that she's any less to blame."

"You know that for certain?" Vaughn asked. "That your brother didn't just accidentally die?"

"You know anything about diving?" Simon asked, his chin lifted in an arrogant way.

As a SEAL, he'd better.

"A little. Enough to know that even the most experienced divers can make a mistake," Vaughn said.

"Well, he didn't. And guess who was on the tour boat that day? Not only Gaston and his lovely new wife, but Brutus."

"We checked out the stories about each of her husbands and how they'd died, read eyewitness accounts. Do you know anything that could prove he was at the scene of your brother's death?" Jillian was eager to learn if Simon had real proof.

"Gaston's waterproof camera? Wayne and I actually went diving where Gaston had his fatal accident. He'd dropped his camera before he died. It fell in some coral. Brutus must have been too busy trying to get away from the scene so he didn't look like he was involved. Gaston had taken pictures of his lovely bride underwater and of sea life. A couple of selfies that revealed Brutus coming up behind him."

"Underwater, wearing a face mask, how could you be sure?" Vaughn asked.

"Clear water, great camera. It was Brutus. Camera's in my bag. We took it everywhere with us, just in case we had a chance to confront him." Simon smiled at Jillian. "Thanks for taking care of the bastard."

Jillian frowned at him. "You're not off the hook. Even though the JAG would probably have condemned him to death, you couldn't just kill him yourself, unless it was in self-defense."

"Yeah, sure. When Brutus shot Wayne and killed Gaston, he got away with it. So the only way to take care of this was to wait until he tried again and we had a chance to fight back?" Simon shook his head.

Jillian had to agree with him there. "Gaston never told Kira he had a couple of twin brothers."

"That's because he came along way after us, and he was our parents' favorite." Simon shrugged. "Ever think the world revolves around you, then someone comes along who's younger, gets better grades, just does everything better, and your parents constantly gripe at you because you should be more like your younger brother? He was seven years younger than us! Hell. So not only had they given up on us—the twins they had adored before that—but they worshipped him. Gaston could do no wrong. We hated him. But we never wished him dead. No one had the right to kill him and claim it was an accident. And they weren't going to get away with it."

"So instead of sharing the evidence that they had murdered your brother, you got involved in the scheme to get rich on a treasure hunt. Until Brutus nearly killed your brother Wayne."

"I'm going to ask about the camera." Vaughn left the room.

Jillian leaned back in her chair. "Okay, so why did Wayne tear into Douglas?"

Simon watched her, but didn't say anything.

"He nearly killed him. If I hadn't arrived when I did, he would have. In another vein, why did Brutus try to kill Wayne? I suspect with Gaston, it was a way to obtain some of the insurance money. Brutus was Kira's lover. But why was Wayne pretending friendship with Kira and Brutus? If you knew Brutus killed Gaston, why not just turn him in or kill him?"

Simon didn't respond.

Jillian smiled at Vaughn as he returned with the camera and began going through the pictures.

"Last couple on the disk," Simon said.

"Looks like him." Vaughn handed the camera to Jillian.

"Yeah, that's him. Looks like Gaston got a shot of himself and Brutus coming up behind him in the water. And then another where the camera only took a partial picture of Brutus grabbing at him. That's it. Okay, so answer my questions."

Simon rested his arms on the table and leaned forward. "Okay, we were afraid we didn't have enough proof that Brutus had killed Kira's husbands, or that she was even responsible for their murders, except that she had the best motive in the world. Life insurance policies. We assumed she was after this Miles guy."

"My brother."

"Right."

"But Miles wasn't married to her, and she wouldn't gain anything from killing him. Why would Brutus try to kill him?"

"Did Brutus say Wayne shot him?"

Jillian frowned. "Yes."

"We weren't sure, but with three dead husbands, two that ended giving her a lot of money due to life insurance proceeds, wouldn't any more dead husbands raise eyebrows? Wayne was to befriend them and learn what they were up to next. We still thought she was after another husband, but this time Kira and Brutus overheard Douglas talking about treasure hunts, and since they were divers too, they got real interested.

"But then they got greedy. They didn't want Wayne in on it, and Brutus tried to kill him. Brutus didn't want Miles taking a cut of the pie either and tried to eliminate him. They had it in mind that only he and Kira would dive for Douglas, since he seemed to have a pretty good success rate at finding treasure."

"All right." Jillian thought all of what Simon said was plausible. Except for the part about Wayne nearly killing Douglas.

"And Douglas?" Vaughn sounded all growly.

"Wayne went to confront Kira. He'd heard she had gone to see Douglas. But when he got there, Douglas told him he knew he and Kira and Brutus were only after the treasure, and he didn't want to see them again. He said he knew Kira and Brutus were lovers, and not brother and sister. He shoved Wayne out of the cabin. You don't push my brother around. If I had to guess, I'd say he returned to scare him a bit, but he went a little too far."

"He didn't try to scare him," Jillian said, her voice shaking with anger. "He got scared because he heard me coming, and he jumped out a bedroom window to escape. That's the only reason Douglas is alive."

Simon's mouth gaped a little.

"Wait, didn't you know Douglas is alive and well? He is, and your story doesn't match his at all."

After that, Simon wouldn't speak any further with them. They left the interrogation room to speak with Wayne, but Lydia intercepted them first in the hallway.

"I have to talk to you. I know I told Miles I was coming to speak with Kira, and I am, but I wanted to say how sorry I am for her involvement in all this. She had a rotten father. Not that it gave her a reason to kill her husbands. But she never really had a good father figure. When Miles called and sounded like he believed her sob story, I wanted to come up right away. I really like him, and I don't want to see her get out and then go after him next, because she's truly a black widow. She feels no remorse for what she's done. Yet she can turn on the tears when it suits her. She just wraps guys around her little finger without any effort. And every time, they fall for it. No mother ever wants to give up their child this way, but her killing is an obsession.

"When you and Vaughn left my house, I was going through everything, trying to find anything that would tie her further to Brutus in a more intimate way. I told you I thought he might be her lover. But I didn't know for sure." She handed Jillian a picture at Kira's first wedding. "You see, he's there in the background with

Kira. They've got their heads together, and she's got her hands on his shoulders, kind of intimate for someone who just married her first husband.

"I'd never seen him before and really hadn't noticed it. The photographer, a family friend, had been taking a photo of a group of people dancing. Who would really look at people in the background? Anyway, I thought it could help show they knew each other more intimately from the beginning. While you were talking to Gaston's brother, I had a talk with your brother. I think Miles is having a hard time believing Kira was at the root of all the 'accidental deaths,' but he needs to."

"Thanks, Lydia. I think after he sees all the evidence, he'll realize the truth of the matter." Jillian wondered if Kira would still try to convince each of them how innocent she was.

But first, they went in to see Wayne. He was lying in bed, still recovering from the gunshot wounds. He had an IV but was handcuffed to the bed, looking pale but angry.

All Jillian wanted to know at this point was why he nearly killed Douglas.

"Hell," Wayne said. "I came to see Kira and tell Douglas what she and Brutus were up to. That they tried to eliminate Miles, and they tried to murder me to get rid of their competition. Douglas was sure I was involved in the shooting and was turning on *my friends*. He threatened to kill me. He tried even."

"With his bare fists?" Vaughn asked. "And then you were so scared, you took off your clothes, shifted into a jaguar, and tore into him? If you didn't know, Douglas is recovering and told us his version of the story. We were just curious what you would come up with." Turning to Jillian, Vaughn said, "Unless you have anything further to ask him, I'd rather just let the JAG take care of them. They can determine what his punishment will be for attempted murder."

Jillian nodded and slipped her arm around Vaughn's waist. She wanted to finish questioning Kira and then see Douglas. Demetria and Everett headed their way to speak with Wayne.

"Kira will only speak with Miles," Demetria warned.

"That's fine. She can talk to the JAG at headquarters and deal with the consequences." Jillian and Vaughn walked into the last interrogation room and were surprised to see Lydia sitting in there holding on to Kira's hand. Lydia was sobbing.

Kira was stony-faced, rubbing her mother's back. "I guess it's kind of humbling to know my own mom has turned against me."

Jillian could see Kira had no remorse, even when her mother did. Kira was just coldhearted. Jillian hoped Miles knew what a phony the woman was.

"Did you even really care about Brutus dying?" Jillian thought Kira might have faked caring that he had died too. Wouldn't she have been angry at Jillian for killing him? Now, Kira didn't show anything but a sort of numbness, like she didn't know what to do when her partner in crime had died and left her alone to face the jury.

They tried talking for a few more minutes with Kira, but she clammed up. They left and saw Miles waiting with one of the officers. He just shook his head. "You must think I'm foolish for believing Kira."

Jillian hadn't thought anything of the sort. "Not at

all. She had everyone fooled. Only her mother seemed to know the real Kira."

"I was talking to Douglas after I heard some of the things these jokers said." He managed a dark, humorless laugh. "He's doing much better. Martin, my new boss, wants me to go with the prisoners and the USF agents to take them to Dallas."

"We're staying here with Douglas until he's back on his feet," Jillian said, thinking afterward she should have asked Vaughn, but he squeezed her shoulders in agreement.

"And a wedding," Demetria said, joining them.

"Always the groomsman," Howard said.

Everyone smiled.

"And our wedding after that sometime. We'll talk about it after you get back from your honeymoon," Jillian said, thinking how they were all members of the USF now, mostly married. "We'll have to work to get Howard married off next."

He raised his hands in a sign that said, "Whoa, not me."

Demetria and Jillian laughed.

That afternoon, after a farewell-for-now steak dinner, they said their good-byes.

Vaughn and Jillian intended to stay at the guest house at Leidolf's ranch until Douglas was well enough to return to Colorado and Vaughn's and his pack. Jillian's too now. They'd spent time talking to Douglas, who was enjoying the nurse's care so much that Vaughn wasn't sure he'd ever want to go home.

Vaughn and Jillian finally arrived at the guest house for the night. They were ready to fix dinner, sit down, and color some more of their pictures before they retired to bed for some more loving. To their surprise, they found a bottle of chilled champagne, fresh filet mignons, and a note that was like Santa's Christmas list congratulating them, listing signatures from Douglas, Everett, Demetria, Howard, and Miles—even Martin, their new boss—as well as everyone in Leidolf's pack. Below that, all of Vaughn's pack members had signed off.

A bouquet of a dozen red roses, and airfare and a cabana rental for Hawaii, courtesy of Jillian's parents, were sitting on the table. And more: a luau and scuba diving excursions from Douglas and Miles. Vaughn's pack leaders gave them cabin rental and airfare to one of the smaller islands during their stay there for saving Douglas's life.

With tears in her eyes, Jillian kissed Vaughn. "I love your pack already."

"I love your family already."

"Even my dad?"

"I think he approves of me, and hell, any father that approves of me marrying his daughter is a first-rate father-in-law."

She laughed. "Come on, let's unwind a bit before we eat dinner."

He thought she intended to color on her pages, since that was meant to help reduce stress. Instead, she drew him toward the hallway and the bedroom. Unwinding this way? He was ready!

Vaughn swept Jillian up in his arms and carried her into her bedroom. "Who would have ever thought we could end a mission like this?"

Jillian smiled.

Then he set her down on the bed, as gently as before, because no matter how hard-charging she might be in her duty, she was his sweet mate and he had every intention of treating her like a wolf goddess.

"Wait." She stripped off his shirt and left a trail of kisses down his chest, making him groan in anticipation.

She smiled and licked his navel, then unfastened his belt.

"Okay, first things first." He wanted to take it slow and easy with her, to prolong the pleasure, but it was like taking one bite of a toffee-chocolate ice-cream bar and trying to resist another.

He quickly removed his boots and then hers. Socks next, and she said, "Agreed, better." Then she was unbuttoning his jeans and jerking down his zipper.

He was glad he wasn't the only one eager to make love. She pulled down his pants and kissed his fully aroused cock on the way down.

He growled and kicked his jeans aside, then began stripping her—shirt, jeans, leaving just a pair of black lace panties and bra. She was so sexy and all his. He hoped she never changed her habit of wearing beautiful lingerie, as much as it turned him on.

"Beautiful," he whispered against her mouth.

She smiled against his lips. "Just as you are." She pulled off his boxer briefs and led him to the bed. "Lie down."

He raised his brows. She smiled. "I'm going to give you a massage like you did my feet and my shoulders. It was wonderful."

He'd never had a massage before. He imagined that with her touching him, he would soon be in trouble.

"Be right back." She returned minutes later with a bottle of lotion and began using some on his feet. He closed his eyes as she worked the muscles, and he didn't believe he'd ever felt anything so divine.

"You next."

"Think you can last?"

He chuckled. "Maybe afterward."

"Deal."

She worked on his legs, massaging until she got to his groin and pelvis. He was already so hard, he couldn't stand it. He flipped her over and began kissing her. "I can't take it." He didn't mind admitting she had him just where she wanted him. He kissed her mouth again, long and deep and passionately. She wrapped her arms and legs around him, and he was thanking God she hadn't been hurt today, that tonight he and his mate could celebrate the end of the case and their union all over again.

He licked her mouth and kissed her again before he parted her legs and began to stroke her. His touch was gentle but insistent, all his senses on high alert as he studied the way she reacted to his touch. The way she dug her fingers into his hips and drew in shallow breaths, the way her heart beat wildly. He smelled their mutually heated arousals, a total turn-on for wolves, and knew that every bit of his fondling was sending her that much closer to the moon.

Just as she was on the verge of coming, he penetrated her and thrust as deeply as he could manage. She settled her legs around his as he pumped into her.

Vaughn loved her, couldn't get enough of her, and needed this after she took down two of the jaguars. She was a crack shot, and he couldn't have been any prouder of her. She was good at her job, but that didn't mean he'd worry less about the outcome in a volatile situation.

He slid in and out of her white-hot heat, loving how responsive she was right before she tightened her hold on him and cried out. He soon followed her into oblivion.

For a long time, she kept her body wrapped around his as if she didn't want to let go of him, and he didn't move off her because he loved being the center of her world for just a bit longer.

But then he rolled over on his back, taking her with him so he was still inside her, stroking her back in loving caresses.

"Did you want me to massage you more?" Jillian rested her chin on his chest, her hands stroking his face, loving that she still was holding on to him.

"Later. Don't move a muscle."

Vaughn began to stir inside her, and she smiled. "You are a wolf with an appetite." She knew massaging a few muscles would be the perfect scenario for a hungry wolf.

"Hell yeah, for you."

"Then let me help it along." She began licking his nipple, knowing just what her wolf mate loved the most. What a way to end a case and begin the rest of her life with that growly SEAL wolf who had intrigued her, irritated her, and made her fall in love.

Vaughn knew being with the she-wolf would alter his life forever, but in one hell of a good way as he made love to her, slept with her, grilled steaks, shared an ice-cream bar, and made love all over again.

Next up, Hawaii. Training with the JAG would have to wait.

Epilogue

JILLIAN SAT UNDER THE SHADE OF AN UMBRELLA ON the beach, drinking her Blue Hawaiian and watching Vaughn as he raced from the aqua waters across the hot sand to her lounger. His tanned muscles were glistening with water, and he was wearing just a pair of aqua board shorts. He'd insisted she get an aqua bikini to match.

They'd been in Hawaii for only the morning after the red-eye flight, and both of them couldn't wait to hit the beach. In an hour, they were going snorkeling, then to a luau tonight. Later, by moonlight with a view of the ocean and the tropical-forest-covered mountains and with the colorful parrots all tucked away for the night, Jillian and Vaughn would be running as wolves in the lush vegetation where no one would ever be the wiser.

"I'm glad Douglas and my brother are coming next week to scuba dive with us. Douglas is doing so well, Miles said, that he's really looking forward to the trip," Jillian said.

"I thought he might even be bringing Sally with him, but he said he appreciated her nursing care while he was injured, but there was nothing more to it than that." Vaughn sat down on the lounger next to Jillian's. "I'm sure Miles and Douglas will have fun. Do you need more suntan lotion?" He raised his brows.

She laughed. "I'm so slick now, I'll never be able to shower all of this off…for days."

He laughed. "You're slick all right. Hot, wet, and totally wild. And all mine." He pulled her onto his lap, and they watched windsurfers sailing across the waves. "Besides, I will love soaping you up later and washing it all off." He motioned to the windsurfers. "Want to try that?"

"Yeah, I'd love to. Sometime during our vacation. After that long trip to the islands, we might need a nap before we go to the luau. Right now though? I'm ready to be a fish." Without warning, she dashed off his lap and raced to the surf. He waited, and she was disappointed he hadn't taken chase, but as soon as she reached the water's edge, he scooped her up and spun her around.

"That makes two of us," he said and then carried her into the waters where the two wolf shifter agents played, swam, kissed, and hugged. In a couple of weeks, they would be in training, and after that, they'd have another assignment.

The case they'd just finished was now in the hands of JAG headquarters as the agency determined what to do with Kira, Simon, and his brother Wayne. Jillian suspected Simon would be incarcerated for a while, even if the JAG learned he had nothing to do with Wayne trying to kill Douglas. Simon still had fired rounds at Jillian. As to Wayne and Kira, that was another story.

For now, being wolves in love in the tropical paradise was all that mattered. The rest of their world's problems could wait until another day.

Read on for a sneak peek of Book One in
Terry Spear's new White Wolf series

DREAMING
OF A
WHITE WOLF
Christmas

Coming soon from Sourcebooks Casablanca

Prologue

Boundary Waters Canoe Area Wilderness, Minnesota
Two years ago

CLARA HART FELT LIKE SHE WAS BEING FOLLOWED. She and her four friends had trekked through the wilderness, stopping for lunch and setting up the two tents for the afternoon, then exploring a bit more before making dinner and sharing stories around the campfire. She hadn't been camping in years. Even then, she'd only gone as a Girl Scout. She didn't think her adoptive parents had ever camped out. They preferred ritzy resorts—fine dining, the best of accommodations.

Except for the eerie sensation that they were being watched, Clara was having a ball.

"Hey, see anything?" Eleanor asked, teasing her as Clara peered around at the woods again.

"Nope."

Fisher laughed. "You've been saying something's following us for miles. When was the last time you'd been camping again?"

Clara threw her camp pillow at him. He grabbed it and threw it back to her. "You know," she said, "it could be a bear or a cougar. Be sure to take something to eat in your tent tonight so the rest of us won't have any worries."

Smiling, the redheaded guy shook his head. "You're paranoid. As noisy as we've been, nothing would come near us."

Maybe she'd watched too many scary movies. Fisher was probably right. But Clara couldn't quit checking out the pines surrounding them, just in case he wasn't.

"She's just getting psyched to write her next romantic suspense novel set on a camping trip with friends," Fisher said. "And everyone dies, except a man and a woman who hate each other's guts and fall in love over the ordeal."

He was the total geek of the bunch, a computer wizard, but he'd taken up canoeing and hiking when his girlfriend said she was dumping him if he didn't immerse himself in the real world every once in a while. The twist was that she had to work and he had to come without her on this trip.

"Why don't you write real stuff?" Charles asked.

Eleanor slapped his shoulder. "I like her books. You just keep writing them. Ignore Charles. He wouldn't know a good book anyway, if he ever read any."

Later that summer night, the full moon was bright and the stars were sprinkled across the darkening sky as Clara and her friends were ready to settle down in their tents. She closed her eyes, but she couldn't sleep. She lived in the suburbs of Houston and was used to hearing doves cooing and blue jays fighting over suet in the feeders in her backyard during the day. At night, everything was quiet out where she lived.

Here in the wilderness, she listened as a wolf howled off in the distance, its song eerie and beautiful. An owl hooted nearby, and a breeze whipped the pine and fir branches around, making her feel as though Bigfoot was walking through the forest to join them.

Eleanor and Melanie appeared to be sound asleep in their tent. Clara wished she could be too. They planned a couple more canoe trips and several more hiking excursions over the next few days, so she needed to be well rested. Her exercise was usually limited to a gym, so though she was in great shape, hiking on uneven terrain made her aware that not all her muscle groups had been getting a good workout. Until now.

Unable to sleep, Clara quietly slipped on her boots, then rummaged through her bag until she found her camera and pulled it out. Camera in hand, she grabbed a flashlight and a small tripod, then headed outside. She set everything down on the ground and stretched, smelling the crisp, pine-filled air. She loved it out here.

She set up her tripod, set her camera on it, and angled it at the sky. If she couldn't sleep, she might as well take some pictures of the stars with the pines reaching up to touch them.

Then she heard the sound of a small dog whimpering. Thinking a puppy had found its way to their campsite, she grabbed her flashlight and turned it toward the woods. Maybe it had smelled the hot dogs they'd cooked over the campfire earlier. They had seen other canoeists and hikers with dogs, so maybe someone was camping nearby.

Clara didn't see anything at first, just the glow of the moon and the stars scattered across the darkness in a beautiful, sparkling array. Then she heard movement in the brush, and she shined the flashlight on the bushes. A fluffy, white puppy with huge feet stared back at her. She loved animals and knew how to interact with them so she didn't scare them off so watched him while he observed her.

"What are you doing out here?" she whispered to him. They couldn't leave a puppy in the wilderness to fend for itself. He looked about five or six months old, so not old enough to take care of himself.

He finally approached the campfire and smelled the ashes where the juices from the hot dogs had dripped into the fire.

"You look like you could use a little meat on your bones." Clara walked over to the tree where they'd secured their food up high to keep it away from bears and other wild animals. She pulled down one of the secure bags and rifled through it for a package of beef jerky, keeping an eye on the young dog the whole time. He seemed so well behaved, sitting like an obedience-trained pup, though he wore no collar. But it made her think he'd gone exploring and the smell of food had brought him here.

She held out a piece of beef jerky to him, though in retrospect, she realized she should have tossed it to him no matter how well behaved he seemed. She hadn't thought she'd have any trouble with him. She was wrong. He was so hungry that he grabbed the jerky, biting her fingers. He only cut the skin a bit, making her bleed, but he could have injured her badly. She cried out, and he stared at her for a moment. Then, as if he knew he was a bad dog, he tore off into the woods, the beef jerky firmly secured between his jaws, and was gone.

Furious with herself for not being more careful, Clara still felt bad about the puppy, knowing he was hungry. She had to put the food away and take care of her injury. Trying not to hurt her bitten hand, though any movement was painful, she tied the food bag high up in the tree again. She considered leaving more beef jerky out for him, but it might attract bears.

Then she wondered if maybe the puppy was what had been following them all along and that's why she kept feeling like they were being watched. With flashlight in hand, she tried to locate the puppy, but she couldn't find any sign of him. She didn't want to travel too far from camp either. She could just imagine losing her way on top of being bitten!

Her hand was throbbing like crazy, and she finally gave up the search. After returning to the tent, she found the first aid kit and camp lantern and carried them outside so she didn't disturb Eleanor and Melanie, who were still curled up in their bags sleeping soundly. Clara assumed the puppy would return for more beef jerky if he got hungry. They could work on locating his owners if they could coax him to come with them.

By the light of the lantern and her flashlight propped up against the log she was sitting on, she poured antiseptic on the wounds. The stinging and burning was like a million jellyfish tentacles ripping through her nerve endings, and she clenched her teeth to avoid crying out. The notion that being in the woods like this could increase her chances of the wound becoming infected made her curse her foolhardiness all over again. Then she had an awful thought... What if the puppy was carrying rabies?

Hoping she hadn't made the worst mistake of her life, Clara bandaged her fingers and turned off the lantern. She made two trips to carry everything she'd brought out back to the tent. Making sure everything was secure so no one would trip over it if someone got up before she did, she returned to her sleeping bag and zipped it up to her chin. Her injured fingers throbbed like hell. Now she *really* couldn't sleep.

A couple of hours later, she suddenly felt her muscles twitching and her whole body heating—like she was running a fever. *Damn it!* She was so hot that she wanted to yank off her clothes.

She fought the urge to strip naked, but she was burning up and feeling so weird that she finally unzipped her sleeping bag and started to strip off her sweats and socks, as if her brain was telling her she needed to cool down before the fever consumed her.

For an instant, everything seemed to blur, and she realized she could see some light in the tent, when before she couldn't without her flashlight. Was the sun already rising? Great, and she hadn't had any sleep. Yet she was no longer hot.

She meant to reach for her flashlight, but what she saw made her want to scream out in terror. But the sound wouldn't come at all. She couldn't grab her flashlight. Her arm had turned into a white dog's leg. Ohmigod, she was hallucinating!

She ran out of the tent and stood by the fire ring. Looking down at herself in the full moonlight, all she saw was one big, white dog with a fluffy white tail. *What. The. Hell.*

Yet, despite the fact that the experience felt real, she knew she had to be hallucinating. She smelled the sharpness of the fragrances: the pines and firs, the scent of the river nearby, the strong aroma of food—their food. She could smell the ashes in the fire ring, the drippings of the fish they'd cooked for lunch, and the hot dogs and marshmallows too.

The sounds were startling: the movement of the leaves and swaying pine branches; the hooting of the owl, which seemed clearer, closer; the running of the river over stones, the water dipping and rising again as if she could "see" the movement.

When she reached the river, wanting to take a drink—which, in her right mind, she would never have done without purifying the water first—she saw the most beautiful white wolf drinking at the edge on the opposite bank.

Her jaw dropped. Wolf, *not* dog.

Which immediately made her think of the white puppy. And the howl she had heard.

She frowned. How could the puppy have gotten across the river if it had been with this wolf? And what in the world were Arctic wolves doing in Minnesota? They didn't have them here, did they?

The wolf rose to its full height, and she didn't think it was a female. Not as big as he was. Beautiful, white fur all fluffed out like he'd had a shampoo and a blow-dry treatment.

She realized he was looking at her. Staring like she was staring at him. This could be a really bad thing. If this was real.

She tore off and heard him howl, the most beautiful howl she'd ever heard. More wolves howled in response from farther away, and she figured a whole pack of them would race after her next.

The next thing she remembered was climbing into her sleeping bag and she was out like the proverbial light.

When Clara woke in her sleeping bag the next morning, she recalled the most bizarre dream she'd ever experienced. Her fingers felt fine. Had she even been bitten? Had the wolf pup even come into camp last night? Or had she imagined the whole thing? Why hadn't she taken a picture of the pup? She'd never managed to take a picture of the stars either.

She glanced at her sweats lying next to the sleeping bag, realizing she really had stripped naked. Her hand was still bandaged, which proved she had been bitten. Yet her fingers didn't hurt. Not even a tiny bit.

Everyone had already gotten up and was making breakfast—oatmeal and coffee. She could smell the meal as if she was sitting fireside. She could hear the crackling of the burning firewood and her friends commenting that they'd never seen her sleep so long in the morning, although they were talking softly so they wouldn't disturb her sleep.

She pulled off the bandages, intending to show her friends what had happened to her last night, to explain why she'd been sleeping like the dead after the wild hallucinations she'd had. But her hand didn't have a mark on it. That was way too weird.

She could understand being so hot last night in the sleeping bag that she'd taken off her sweats, but bandaging her hand over an imaginary bite wound? She still recalled how painful it had been when she'd poured the antiseptic over the injuries.

If nothing more, she had one hell of a tale to tell everyone over breakfast. She tied her hair back in a ponytail like she always did before she hiked, thinking she needed to cut it shorter so it wasn't always whipping around in her face. Then she quickly dressed. When she left the tent to join her friends at the campfire, she knew they'd give her grief for being the last one up.

Mainly since she usually gave them grief because she always started the fire in the morning and always told them they waited until they smelled the coffee before they rolled out of their sleeping bags. She couldn't believe she'd slept in either.

"Here's Sleeping Beauty," Fisher said. "You always beat us out here, so what happened? I was expecting my cocoa latte, but all I woke to were cold ashes."

"Well, I had one crazy night." Clara got her coffee, sat down on a log next to the fire, and told them what had happened to her: the puppy bite, dreaming she'd shifted, seeing a white wolf across the river.

Everyone was smiling at her.

"I tripped over her sweats this morning, so she was naked in her sleeping bag last night," Eleanor said.

The guys smiled, and Clara felt her cheeks flush with heat. She hadn't meant to tell anyone she really had stripped naked.

Then Fisher very seriously said, "Hell, Clara, they were werewolves, and now you're one."

"So you shifted and it knocked the mahogany coloring out of your hair?" Eleanor asked. "I didn't even know you were a true redhead until now."

Melanie nodded. "I love your natural color."

Thinking her friends were teasing her, Clara untied her hair and looked at the silky strands in the early-morning light. The vibrant cinnamon color of her natural hair was back. Her jaw hung agape.

"I thought the coloring you used was hair dye," Eleanor said. "That it couldn't be washed out. You had to grow your hair out or color it with something else. When in the world did you change it?"

Eleanor was correct. Clara had dyed her hair a darker color—brown with a hint of red—to add drama to her hair. Were her eyebrows also the lighter red again? She couldn't believe it, yet she had the proof right between her fingers.

After a day of hiking and pitching tents for the camp before dusk, they prepared dinner, but the topic of conversation returned to the werewolf business.

"We really should post guards to watch Clara's behavior," Fisher joked.

She snorted.

"If she's running around naked at night, I volunteer for first watch," Charles said and winked at her.

"Very funny." Tonight, Clara was sleeping normally and would be the first one up, just like usual. She looked up at the moon, and it was as full and bright as last night.

Everyone was talking about their walk and canoe trip tomorrow, but Clara couldn't shake the feeling that what she had done last night—all of it—had been real.

They all finally went to bed, and thank God, she drifted off right away. Until she felt the urge to pull off her sweats. And lost the battle. She was running as a white wolf...again.

Terrified, she realized the truth. She wasn't dreaming. She wasn't hallucinating. Fisher was right, even though he'd only been joking.

The wolf puppy that had bitten her hadn't been a full-blooded wolf at all. He'd been a werewolf.

And her life was spinning out of control.

Chapter 1

Nearly Christmas, two years later

OWEN NOTTINGHAM, ARCTIC WOLF AND PRIVATE investigator, had made daily treks into the wilderness ever since he'd seen the white wolf across the river. He knew she had to be an Arctic *lupus garou* just like him. But the fact she was running with humans had to mean she had lots more control over her shifting or she couldn't be with them on a long-term hiking and canoeing trip. Maybe she'd been born as a *lupus garou*. Maybe her wolf roots went so far back that she was a royal and completely in control of her shifting at all times.

One thing was for certain—she wasn't one of the Arctic wolves who had changed him and his friends. He would never forget that day five years ago when he and his PI partner David Davis were hunting for bear in Maine, never having come close to finding one in the five years they'd been trying. They'd spotted a bear, and the hunt was on. Never in a million years would he or David have thought his good friend would end up having a heart attack.

Nor that the Arctic wolves the guide had on the hunt weren't all wolf and that they were all from the same *lupus garou* pack. Neither the guide nor Owen could do anything to save David's life way out in the woods. Owen had been willing to pay any price to save his

friend. Whatever it cost. He'd envisioned the guide calling in a helicopter and air evacuating David to a hospital.

Owen had to admit that he'd agreed to it. Anything.
Like making a pact with a devil wolf. The wolves
wouldn't have bitten them if he hadn't asked for the
guide's help. Owen hadn't known what was going on at
the time. Only that the wolves had bitten both of them—
David, to give him their enhanced healing abilities to
repair his heart, and Owen, because he couldn't witness what they were without paying the consequences.
Which meant becoming one of them or dying.

After that, the pack took them in. They had to because
David and Owen had no control over the shifting, but
they were captives just the same, until one of the pack
members had helped them to escape. So Owen knew all
of the members of that pack. Those were the only Arctic
wolves he'd ever met, beyond his own small pack.

More than anything in the world, he wanted to find
her. Wanted to get to know her. Locating her could mean
finding a mate for either him or one of his bachelor male
partners in the PI agency. He still envisioned her standing
near the river's edge—half hidden in the brush, watching him, wide-eyed—and wondered where the hell she'd
come from. He knew she'd been a she because she was
smaller than the males. She had to be a shifter. Arctic
wolves didn't live in this part of the country.

Still, he'd tried to locate her after that, to no avail.
She and her friends had taken a canoe trip after a few
days, and he never knew what had become of her. He
wasn't even sure which of the women she'd been.

He was afraid he'd be looking for her until he was old
and gray and might never see her again.

Owen opened up the new PI office that morning in White River Falls, Minnesota, the Christmas wreath jingling on the door. He was eager to make a go of a brick-and-mortar business again after seven years of working online, unable to set up a real office.

None of the other investigators believed they'd get a call first thing that morning, so they were coming in a little later. He finished hanging his sign on his door and stringing more Christmas lights on the miniature tree in his office. The whole pack—three bachelor males, and one couple and their two sons and a daughter—had decorated the seven-foot tree in the lobby so it looked cheery and welcoming sitting next to one of the front windows.

When Owen had settled down at his desk with a cup of coffee and a Christmas tree–decorated donut, he began checking his emails. He had only read one when he got the call that would be the first job they received at the office. He was enthusiastic about solving the missing person's case promptly, hoping for their first good review.

—∾∾—

Ever since that day in the woods, Clara Hart had been a very different person, her whole world turned inside out. Her friends were no longer her friends, and her adoptive parents had disowned her. She'd changed her name to her pseudonym, Candice Mayfair. She'd moved from the suburbs of Houston to the wilderness in South Dakota. It was beautiful, perfect for her to run free and be herself. Or rather—her *other* self. The wolf part of her that howled to be free, especially during the occurrence of the full moon. But at other times too, except during the new moon. She'd finally realized this by keeping a calendar of the moon phases at hand at all times to document the trouble she was having with fighting the urge to shift. She'd also purchased dozens of books about werewolves that definitely were not written by real werewolves.

She finished hanging her Christmas wreath on the door, placed a Christmas throw rug she had hooked on the kitchen floor, and added a few more nutcrackers on the mantel. She'd set up her Christmas tree the day after Thanksgiving as she'd always done. At least that was something that hadn't changed. Though last Thanksgiving, she'd had to wait until she turned back into her human form to finish decorating.

After two years, she had finally come to grips with what she was. That she wasn't going to suddenly be her normal self again. She'd sometimes dreamed she was, but then she'd get the urge to shift and that shattered the illusion.

She suspected everyone she'd known thought she'd gotten into drugs or alcohol, because she'd disappeared from their lives. At first, she'd given excuses for why she couldn't see them. But then she realized she had to isolate herself from anyone she'd known in the past. They didn't understand what was wrong with her. And she couldn't explain.

Drinking didn't stop her from shifting either. She'd learned that the hard way. Being tipsy just made it harder to remove her clothes and shift, which meant she was caught in her clothes as a wolf for several hours one night, thankfully in her own home. So, no more drinking to try to control the shift. She'd also had the uncontrollable urge to howl sometimes when she ran as a wolf, and she was certain that would be a disaster. What if a wolf pack responded? She could be in real trouble.

She'd settled into her life, such as it was, and she'd found that writing about the subject she knew best—werewolves—was a good outlet for her. Using her former talent at writing romantic suspense, she'd started writing Arctic wolf romances. Unlike in other books where werewolves were hideous monsters out to eat people, her characters were misfits like her. She'd never encountered another like the male and the pup she'd seen that night she was camping. She knew they had to be out there somewhere in the Superior National Forest in Minnesota. She'd never been back there. Why would she be?

She had no idea if werewolves ran as a pack, a family unit, or whatever. What if the beautiful male was mated?

Candice had made a niche for herself on her fifteen acres where she still could get internet, with a small town nearby for groceries and anything else she needed. She could avoid people. Except online. Which worked great.

The worst part was her parents disowning her. When her father had a stroke, the full moon had been in full swing. Candice had been so angry, furious with her inability to control the shift. She'd even driven part-way home when she'd had to pull over on a dirt road, park, strip, and shift. She knew then she just couldn't manage the trip. When her mother had gone in for a pacemaker, the moon was nearly full. Her parents' medical emergencies never came up when the new moon or waxing and waning crescents came around. And she couldn't explain how she couldn't travel anywhere as a wolf. That she was liable to turn into a wolf in the emergency room.

Her folks must have thought their adopted daughter didn't care anything about them, so she was out of their lives. It didn't matter that she'd come to see them straightaway when it was safer to do so. They believed she hadn't wanted to help them when they needed her, and she'd felt horrible about it.

She'd learned they'd both died in a car accident, and it broke her heart. She had no one to blame for being unable to be with them when they really needed her but herself. She'd hand-fed a werewolf puppy on a camping trip and had paid the price.

Acknowledgments

Thanks to Donna Fournier for being my beta reader. Thanks to Deb Werksman for helping to make the books even better. And to Amelia Narigon for the work with promotions. I'll miss you! And thanks to the cover artists who create gorgeous works of art. I can hardly wait to reveal the next cover!